Secrets of a River Swimmer

Secrets of a River Swimmer

SS Turner

THE
ST●RY
PLANT

The Story Plant
Studio Digital CT, LLC
P.O. Box 4331
Stamford, CT 06907

Copyright © 2021 by Simon Turner
The Library of Congress Cataloguing-in-Publication Data is available upon request.

Story Plant paperback ISBN-13: 978-1-61188-321-3
Fiction Studio Books E-book ISBN: 978-1-945839-59-7

Visit our website at www.TheStoryPlant.com

First Story Plant Printing: February 2022

Printed in the United States of America
0 9 8 7 6 5 4 3 2 1

You are the sun in drag.
You are God hiding from yourself.
Remove all the "mine" – that is the veil.
Why ever worry about
Anything?
Listen to what your friend Hafiz
Knows for certain:
The appearance of this world
Is a Magi's brilliant trick, though its affairs are
Nothing into nothing.
You are a divine elephant with amnesia
Trying to live in an ant
Hole.
Sweetheart, O sweetheart
You are God in
Drag!

-Hafiz

Arrival

I dip my toe in.

It's fucking freezing.

I sit and watch the majestically sinister Scottish river hurtle along below me. I'm not sure whether to be in awe or terrified, but that was always going to be the case today, my last day. The idea of jumping into the river reminds me of the feeling you experience when you arrive at the beach, and you're thinking about jumping into the sea, but you know it's going to cause you grievous bodily harm from your nether regions up. For some reason, your legs are the one part of your body which can handle intense cold without too much stress. But all body parts above your legs are a whole different story. My voice just rose an octave, and I'm not even talking.

So you sit and watch the sea while contemplating your next move, as if this thinking time will give you the required mental strength to leap into the cold blue water. However, this thinking time just gives the water an opportunity to look you in the eye with laughing menace, because the water knows the questions you are grappling with deep in your soul. The water understands it is strong and you are weak—the eternal power imbalance at play.

The waiting period only makes it worse, of course. All it does is allow you to hand more mental power over to the cold water than a short and simple jumping-in maneuver would have done. Why do we employ such counter-productive strategies in our lives?

Hesitation only makes it harder to achieve the things we want, and yet we're always hesitating. I'm always hesitating. Maybe too many parents have called out "Be careful!" to their children when all they were doing was exploring the garden. Maybe we've all listened a little too well when we should have been rolling in the mud, or jumping straight into dangerous rivers, no questions asked. Yes, mystery solved, that's it. Surely it must be my parents' fault that I'm sitting here ready to end it all at the hands of the river. Aren't parents always to blame for the unspeakable things sitting inside the closets no one wants to open? In my case, that closet has been locked for too long, and who knows where the damned key is? I can't even picture my father's face anymore.

The water gurgles at anyone who will listen. It reminds me of a scene from a nature documentary in which the presenter, most likely David Attenborough, talks about the power of the river: "The river moves millions of tons of water to places it's needed to support life. It's the source of life for a vast array of species who depend upon it for all their needs." The film then focuses on a salmon trying to swim against the powerful current—the poster-fish for the struggle of life. With sympathy in his voice, the presenter discusses life as a salmon: "It's a tough gig being a salmon since few of them survive the arduous journey they need to undertake. Swimming all the way upstream requires an extraordinary amount of effort and luck, more than most salmon can hope for." The documentary focuses on a few of the poor salmon who've attempted the swim against the current, but have stopped at the side of the river exhausted, defeated. These poor souls are now stranded and waiting to die, or to be eaten by a passing animal in search of an easy lunch. They find themselves in a retirement home for salmon who've failed in their life's mission, the dregs of the fish world. I know those guys so well—it's almost like I'm looking in the mirror. The presenter concludes the scene with a semi-empathetic tone: "Nature is a harsh mistress."

I've always believed I'd make the perfect successor to David Attenborough as the next great voice of nature documentaries. Surely I have everything a documentary presenter needs: a compassionate voice which is both deep and soft, a love of nature, an interest in learning, and a decent knowledge of nature to start with. Of course, I've never presented anything in my life, never mind a TV production, so this is just another Walter Mitty "what if" thought which I've never followed through to its conclusion. Oh well, it's too late now. It's strangely comforting to know that everything I haven't achieved will soon stop being a weight of unfulfillment around my neck.

My thoughts have wandered away from my quest to enter the river, which I'm putting in the too-hard basket. But the river's gushing brings me back to the job at hand.

Maybe a few moments of meditation will provide me with the focus I need to jump in. Most of the world's celebrities seem keen to peddle meditation as the answer to everything, although I know it's nothing but a smokescreen. They want the world to think they're mentally healthy, but this couldn't be further from the truth. They're all wearing masks which they've customized to appear as different from their real faces as possible—because the truth is most celebrities are as mad as cut snakes. I won't judge them, though. What we see and hear is never the truth, whoever's talking. We all wear masks all the time. I've worn one all my life. Not today though. I've had enough of the pain my mask has been hiding.

The river's sounds are starting to make some sort of sense to me, like a loud drunk uncle at a family function who is only comprehensible when you're also drunk. I wonder how Uncle Bob is these days. What's the river saying to me? Does it want me to jump in? Does it want an unwelcome intruder immersed in its pure waters? It doesn't look like it cares about much, apart from moving forward to where it wants to go in the shortest possible time. There's no mask here, just raw truth on display for the whole world to see.

I dip my toe in again. Once again, it feels unbelievably cold despite the fact my toe is probably the least sensitive part of my body. This is a bad idea. There must be some other way to stop the pain of living. I cross my legs and think warm thoughts.

Could there be something positive coming my way if I were to jump straight into the river, no questions asked? Maybe I'll turn into a magical fish who can fly upstream while singing acoustic Beatles songs from their drugged-out period. I'm thinking "Strawberry Fields" will hit the mark. I can relate to the lyric "No one I think is in my tree," or in this case, river, and have always believed that line was written for me, about me. Or maybe I'll float so impressively downstream that I'll have invented a new sport for the world to enjoy: freezing river flotation. The rules are simple: competitors must relax their bodies, and let the river take them where it will. Coming out alive is a bonus. Rivers all around the world would be bombarded by random, floppy-bodied drifters driven solely by a need to go with the flow no matter where the flow is going. I was made for this sport—it's lucky I almost invented it.

But back to the bad stuff, which is sitting there like the item of necessary unpleasantness it is—and the reason I'm here. Understanding a little about science makes this part easy. Firstly, I note that the river's temperature on the oh-fuck-o-meter is all the way down at maximum ball shrinkage, which is around forty degrees Fahrenheit. At that temperature, I'll become hypothermic within a matter of minutes. My body will be unable to warm itself as it will be so low on energy after unsuccessfully fighting the cold for so long. Then my internal organs will start failing. There's a high probability I'll be dead within an hour of entering the water. Oh joy! Thanks, science, for clarifying that bloody obvious unpleasantness for me. But, fair play, with my mask off today that's what I'm here for.

The bad stuff is a can of worms, and it's officially open for business. The next worm in this can is the not insignificant risk that I'm crushed to death by the water pounding me against the sharp rocks beneath as I float through the fast-flowing white-water rapids. Without a helmet, my head is particularly vulnerable to being fatally whacked on the way through. Now I think about it, being crushed to death on rocks sounds like a better way to go than freezing to death. Every cloud has a silver lining.

The river will be heard. The water gallops over the rocks like a prized racehorse attacking a racecourse, creating white water in all directions like a huge spa as it pushes forwards with ever-increasing momentum to where it needs to go. The sound of the river's gushing is getting louder and louder. It's speaking to me, shouting at me. Stay where you are, you fool.

No! A fool I may be, but I've stayed where I am all my life, and that's not working for me. I've had enough. It's time to let the bad stuff take me to a better place.

I put my foot in. Sweet mother of god, it's cold.

I wade a few steps in. With each step, the cold water inches up my body from my feet to my ankles, and is now creeping up my legs. This is by far the coldest water I've ever been in. If immersing my legs in the water feels this painful, the idea of going any deeper is terrifying. My bones are fast emerging as the weakest link as the cold is diving deep into them. I suspect they're close to shattering like glass into infinite pieces.

Can I do this, or is this the right moment to pull out the white flag? There's no one here to ridicule my lack of balls, both literal and metaphorical, apart from me. I promise not to give myself a hard time about this in the future. I'm sure we'll all look back at this moment and laugh: me, myself, and the river.

The idea of retreating from the river, white flag in hand, diverts my thoughts to a scene from my childhood, a scene which exposed my weakness. I was queuing up alongside the rest of my classmates, awaiting instructions from a teacher who'd left the classroom for a moment. I was minding my own business when I felt a sharp push from behind, as I was shoved into the person standing in front of me. The boy I'd been pushed into turned around and hit me hard in the face. I hit the ground like a sack of potatoes. I cried, which led to my attacker adding verbal abuse to his arsenal of bullying strategies—he was a true innovator. He started throwing words like "sissy" at me as I reeled in pain on the ground. Now I think about it, he reminds me of my father—the two of them would have had scintillating conversations about the latest developments in bullying techniques.

I later discovered that the boy whom I'd been pushed into had asked the boy behind me to push me into him. He'd premeditated the whole show to create the opportunity to sock me in the face. When I asked him why he wanted to hit me, all I got back was that he felt like it. This was a bully without a backstory or motive beyond his Neanderthal need to cause pain in others. What a nice fellow. I wonder what he's up to these days. He's probably the chief executive of a global technology company.

The river seems to have moved past its initial indifference towards me, and is warming up to the idea of my uninvited visit. Or maybe it's me who's warming up to the idea of fully immersing myself into the river which is making the river appear friendlier—like when you start to like someone more, and that leads to them liking you more.

I wade out further. The cold water violently gallops further up my legs, causing shoots of intense pain. The water is still below the all-important ball-immersion zone, the line that represents the boundary between a fun day out and the stuff of nightmares. The idea of crossing to the other side is one step too far for my weakened mind.

A song jumps into my head as if the river is a radio through which a DJ has a sonic pathway into my psyche. I know this song as well as I know myself: it's Frightened Rabbit's "Swim till you can't see land." The words "I salute at the threshold of the North Sea of my mind / and I nod to the boredom that drove me here to face the tide" shiver around my ears. Swim till you can't see land. That's a pretty clear message, even for me. The river isn't messing around. Was it boredom that led me here? That will require some serious thought, but I sense there may be something in it.

The thing is, this song and the band Frightened Rabbit are important to me. What were the chances this particular song popped into my head in this very moment? The lead singer of Frightened Rabbit, Scott Hutchison, seemed to be as genuine a person as you'd ever meet, the opposite of most successful singers. He loved the art of putting his heartfelt words into music, and making something fly that had started out as an inert thought. I read that Scott had suffered through a long battle with mental illness which he was fighting through his music. He believed that once he'd written lyrics comprising the destructive thoughts which he was fighting deep inside, he was free of their power. Once released, his lyrics were free to fly elsewhere to help comfort other people dealing with similar challenges, and to let others know that they're not alone in feeling desperate. In a world short on heroes, Scott was a unique type of hero because he saved others by speaking his truth.

However, I know how Scott's story ended, and it's not great news for me, given the glaring similarities in our respective situations, excluding my singing ability, of course. In a moment of desperation, Scott ended up living his lyrics in a way most songwriters never come close to. He committed suicide by drowning. Hearts broke all around the world as Scott had become a poster-boy for singing your troubles away, uplifted by his band's inspiring music. The message was clear: it can happen to the best of us—we are all vulnerable.

I'm vulnerable. That's why I'm here.

If I just lower my body a little further into the river. Oh my god! I can't help but yell out a few choice expletives as I go below the danger line. Even in my pain, I'm grateful there's no one here to judge.

Who cares anymore? I lift my legs, and let the river's current take me. Towards something better.

What Was I Thinking?

Yes, this was a terrible idea. No, terrible doesn't cut it—this was a shockingly catastrophically disastrous idea. Fucking cold as a description sounds like a beachside holiday in the Med compared to the harsh reality of how cold the water is. Where are those upsides when you need them?

But wait. I'm due to acclimatize to the cold anytime now. Isn't that what happens? You gasp a sigh of shock when you first feel the cold hit you, and then only a few moments later you are surprised at what a pussy you were. The new, harder you then laughs at the earlier version of you in both a judgmental and relieved manner. You judge yourself for your now inconceivable weakness only moments earlier, and you are relieved that your inner pussy is no longer being revealed for the world to see. Your mask is back on.

Who's that fellow who claims he can withstand the cold for longer than any other human? I remember he set a world record for swimming under ice in seawater which was below freezing at the time. That intelligent idea permanently cost him the feeling in one of his hands. Next up, he had the bright idea to run up Everest in nothing but a pair of shorts, not even a pair of shoes.

I saw an online video of that endeavor which I'll never forget. He reminded me of the yeti's smaller cousin, trying to escape humanity at all costs. Maybe his thinking wasn't all flawed, then. That little Everest project was an epic fail due to the minor issue of his almost dying halfway up the mountain. Yes, a proper nutcase this fellow is. The Icicle Man. I think that's his name—well, if you can call a made-up superhero-type name a name. I wonder what the Icicle Man would say to me if he was floating down the river with me. Probably something along the lines of: "Imagine you're sitting in front of a warm log fire, feeling warm and cozy. All you need to do is visualize those warm flames are here in the river with you." You know how I'd respond, Mr. Icicle Man? I'd tell you to go put on some fucking clothes, to stop talking crap, and to swim faster so you can sort out a real fire for me at the other end. And a cup of tea would go down well while you're at it. I'll take the real thing over this imagined bullshit any day, Mr. Icicle Man. You remember that.

The current is slow here. I survey the scene. This is the first time I've been able to focus on anything but the cold since I got in. Both sides of the river are covered by majestic willow trees which extend out a few meters above the river. Floating underneath them makes me feel like I'm flying through space and meeting strange aliens on the way through, aliens who know a lot more than they are letting on; like the meaning of life, for example. And here we are, us poor humans, trying to figure it all out and failing miserably. Those trees are smart asses.

The good news is I'm acclimatizing ever so slightly. Well, if you can call no longer feeling like you're being stabbed by daggers all over your body acclimatizing. Finally an upside, and with it I relax into the flow of the river. My body is less rigid, more floppy, and able to go with the flow.

Not that it matters anymore, but the question occurs to me: Where the hell does this river go? I was so focused on getting into the damned thing that I haven't contemplated my ultimate destination. My soon-to-be-lifeless body could end up anywhere. The story of my life. However, the idea that the flow is carrying my flesh and blood towards an unknown destination which is out of my control is somehow comforting. Mind you, everything is comforting when you're floating through freezing water, and you let your thoughts distract you from the pain.

My body temperature is dropping faster now, edging closer towards total shutdown, the end game of end games. Given how bone-shatteringly cold the water is, I'm quite impressed that I've been able to last this long with nothing more than some violent shivering. When I was sitting at my desk only a few hours earlier, I googled how long a human can survive in water this cold. Google's answer was twenty to thirty minutes, depending how much body fat you have. Isn't that Sod's law at work? In recent months, I've been working hard on my fitness to lose fat and become trimmer, and now that I'm finally trim, what I actually need is as much body fat as possible to survive the cold. I chuckle at the irony of the situation. How ridiculous life is. Laughing like a crazed madman with no one around is like flying above the earth and glimpsing the whole charade as the comedy show it is.

How long have I been in the river? It feels like I've been in for about ten minutes, although I forgot to bring a watch. What a dickhead. Some way to measure time would have been sensible given my remaining lifetime depends upon knowing that key information. I suspect Google was being overly conservative in case a nutter like me were to scientifically test their data, and that I have at least another twenty minutes before total shutdown. That's what I'll tell myself.

Besides, there was that famous case of the Icelandic fisherman who survived swimming in North Sea water much colder than this for many hours, and reset the record books for how long a human can survive in cold water. That fisherman spent something like five hours in water that was only thirty-seven degrees Fahrenheit. Then, once he made it ashore, he got out of the freezing sea and walked a few miles through heavy snow to safety. Admittedly, he was more than a little rotund, so he had immense reserves of whale-like body fat working in his favor. However, the good news for me is that this fisherman has proven that records and Google "knowledge" are meaningless. In your face, Google!

So I choose to ignore the science in favor of the story to prolong the time I have left. Yes, if you can dream it, you can do it—and I'm dreaming of just a little bit more time before the final bell. I drift onwards thinking fat thoughts.

Incognito

The current is speeding up as I round a bend in the river. I must be moving at around three miles an hour, which means I'm already half a mile down the river, half a mile away from my life as it was. What a difference a few hours make. Earlier today, I was sitting at a tidy desk in an oppressive office in Edinburgh, trying to look productive like a mouse in a wheel while slowly dying on the inside. I wonder if everyone else who sits at a desk in an office all day feels the same. Maybe I'm the strange one for questioning the way we humans do things. Yes, jumping in was an easy decision when I remember my already distant upstream life.

There's something bright red on the side of the river a few hundred meters ahead. I wipe the water out of my eyes to squint at the colorful object. Aha, it's a fisherman wearing a red jacket, and he's got someone sitting next to him, talking to him. That must be his gillie. I've always found the ancient Scottish custom of bringing a gillie, a fishing expert, along with you when you go fishing rather amusing. Where else in the world do fishermen take along fishing guidance counsellors to help them catch a fish? It was no surprise to me when my old boss told the team he always went fishing with a gillie, who he kindly referred to as his "bitch." We all knew that was how he thought about us as well.

My thoughts drift to picture what life as a gillie must be like. I imagine you start the day by carrying all the fishing equipment your fat and wealthy clients will need for a day of luxurious and fully-catered fishing. You carry everything while they take it easy, and you locate the best spot to fish for the largest possible salmon. Your local knowledge about fishing spots has to be extraordinary. You then set up the fishing rod, position your client in the right spot, and talk them through what they need to do to catch that magic fish they're all searching for. Of course, your clients are always searching for the largest catch of the season, so they can go home and brag to their friends and family about what skilled fishermen they are. It's obvious to you, if not to them, that the subtext is being able to sing to the world that they have massive willies, bigger than everyone else's.

Beyond fishing, you're forced to listen to whatever the hell it is your clients want to talk about for the eight long hours you're on the river. Your clients are all obscenely wealthy, so it's more than likely you'll hear a lot of moaning about all the small things in life they'd like changed. Many of them will complain about local wind farm developments, council plans to develop their neighborhood, and, of course, the big one: immigration. They all believe immigrants are responsible for all the problems in the world. These people are your quintessential NIMBYs, and will always complain about progress if it affects them in any way, no matter how minor.

You do whatever you can to bring the conversation back to fishing because it's an easier conversation for you, and less productive grounds for their complaining. They're slowly sucking the life out of you with their negativity, so you carefully select your words to bring the conversation onto a more positive pathway. And, of course, your ultimate back-up plan, as it is for many British people, is to pull out the ultimate conversation filler when you're at rock bottom: the weather. Yes, it's a desperate move and the equivalent of holding up a white flag, but needs must.

If your clients do finally catch that special big fish they want, of course they'll take all the credit themselves. They'll believe the catch was entirely due to their incredible fishing expertise, despite the fact they understand next to nothing about fishing. Worse than that, they know so little about fishing, they don't even know what they don't know. Your clients are living proof that ignorance is indeed bliss. However, there's a much worse case scenario for you to contend with in the event your clients don't catch that special fish they're after, or, worse, any fish at all. In this empty-handed scenario, your clients efficiently turn their well-developed moaning skills towards you as the source of their problems. The blame for the failure will be laid firmly at your door—not theirs, never theirs. It's a no-win situation. If they catch a fish, you lose. If they don't catch a fish, you lose. The story of my life.

I feel deep sorrow for the poor sod sitting next to the fisherman I'm approaching. Like him, I've had enough of abusive people being loud and crass just because they are fat and wealthy. That red-jacketed twat next to him might as well be my boss. The poor gillie should be in here with me. Anything would be better than what he's living through. I wonder what I can do to help brighten his day.

The fisherman and his gillie are only a hundred meters away now. What should I do? I don't think there's a law against swimming in Scottish rivers, and, if there is, who cares? What are they going to do, call the fun police? I relax backwards so the top of my head is almost underwater, and I let the current carry me forwards.

As I approach them, I feel elated. I'm the incognito fish they can never catch—from a watery world they'll never be part of. I lower my head into the water so only my eyes, ears and nose are above the waterline. I'm almost completely hidden as I drift silently with the current. I'm so close to them right now, and yet they remain oblivious to my presence. They're talking to one another just above me. I'm part of their private world, and they don't even know it.

"I saw old McTavish fishing up river a couple of weeks ago," explains the fisherman. "He reckoned he'd caught the biggest catch of the season only hours before I got there. Of course, he couldn't show me the damned thing because he'd put it in the freezer by then. It sounded like fiction to me, but then that's always the issue with that drunken sod."

The moment I'm about to pass by them, I completely submerge my face under the icy river water. I open my eyes to watch them like a peeping Tom from another planet. It's as if time has stopped. The river current has slowed. Everything is suspended as I watch. The water is so cold it's hurting my eyes, but I wouldn't miss this for the world. I'm only meters away from them. I watch their faces while they talk. The gillie is listening to the fisherman and is feigning interest in what he's saying. His mind wanders, and he glances down at the river for a moment. I smile at him from underwater, the strangest fish he'll ever meet. The gillie's expression changes from boredom to terror. He stands up and cries out. A chain reaction ensues. The fisherman, scared by what has shocked his gillie, loses his balance and falls into the river. He prances around hysterically as he tries to escape from whatever terror is in the river with him. Not knowing what's in the river makes the scary thing even scarier. I can almost hear the *Jaws* music playing in his mind.

I've now drifted a few meters past them, so I raise my head above the waterline to watch the show unfold. The fisherman is screaming "Get me out of here!" to his poor gillie, who's still trying to control his own fear so he can help his terrified client. I don't think the fisherman realizes I'm in the water with him. He's so focused on the slippery riverbank he's unsuccessfully trying to climb. The gillie holds his hand out to the fisherman, who grabs it as if his life depends upon it. The gillie then hauls the not-insignificantly-sized fisherman out of the river, like a beached whale being pulled further up the shoreline. As the fisherman is being hauled out of the water, he notices me out of the corner of his eye.

To my surprise, when he lays eyes on me, the fisherman screams a ghastly scream. It's a sound I shall never forget, an expression of pure terror. He'll struggle to explain that one to the grand kids. But who am I to criticize? I'm the man pretending to be a big fish to surprise two unsuspecting strangers for a laugh. No, it's worse than that. I'm the man who jumped into a freezing cold river to end my aimless life.

As the echo of the fisherman's scream subsides, I glance over my shoulder to see both the fisherman and the gillie staring at me in disbelief. Their faces say it all—I'm a nightmare they once had which has come to life. I smile and wave at them. However, this doesn't provide them with any comfort, as they both drop their fishing gear in a frenzy of fear. The fisherman calls out, "Sweet Jesus! What the hell is it? Run!" as they start legging it for their lives. I imagine the inevitable trickle of panic-induced wee running down the fisherman's leg, and can't help but laugh. Am I that scary?

I float onward, amused. What's happening to me? I've always had a perverse sense of humor, but this takes the cake. My laughter provides a welcome distraction from the cold for a few short moments. However, in short order the reality of my situation descends once more upon me. The cold is creeping deeper and deeper into my bones like an unwelcome visitor you hoped had already left the building, but who returns like Lieutenant Columbo knocking at the door with the difficult questions you thought you'd avoided. Why does this guy always come back?

Time is flying. I guesstimate I've been in the river for nearly twenty minutes now, so the initial pain of entering the river has evolved into what can only be the beginning of hypothermia. Next stop, total bodily shut-down. I've already lost all feeling in my feet and toes, and I sense things are happening inside me. Bad things. It feels like the end of a party when everyone has left, and you know it's time to start the clean-up, but you fight against the idea at all costs. Let's keep this party going for a little while longer. That's all I ask for, a little more time to say goodbye.

Is that music again? The river DJ is playing another tune for me. Sorry, river, I haven't got the energy to listen. Wait, I recognize this one. It's a Beatles song about winning the war—"A Day in the Life," that's it. I'm starting to feel sleepy. I vaguely hear the words: "And though the news was rather sad / Well, I just had to laugh." "I just had to laugh" echoes across the water like a commandment.

I drift out of the main current into a still section on the left-hand side of the river.

I lie motionless like an exhausted salmon catching its breath in the dregs section.

Out

Where am I? I appear to be covered with leaves and moss, and my clothes are half dry. I'm still cold, but I'm nowhere near as cold as I was. Everything is pitch black. It seems like I'm enclosed in a small cave, as there isn't a lot of air flow around me. I feel my way around the enclosure and discover there's a small entrance on one side. On all fours, I crawl through the hole. The familiar sound of the river gushing past dominates the darkness like a king addressing its subjects. It's a comforting sound amidst the inexplicability of the situation.

Under the light of the moon, the rough silhouette of an enormous tree stands strong and prominent above the cave I was sleeping in. It both lines the river and hangs over it, like a gatekeeper checking on the water heading downstream. I wonder what sort of questions the tree asks the water before allowing it entry downstream—maybe something along the lines of: "How do you feel about retiring at sea? If you make it that far, you'll be due some rest."

After crawling around the base of the tree, it's apparent the cave is, in fact, a hollow section at its base. My head is spinning as I attempt to piece together what happened last night. How did I end up sleeping inside this hollow? I remember seeing this tree from my hypothermic trance in the river, but I have no idea what happened next. I may have blacked out at that point. OK, so maybe Google did know what it was talking about when it recommended not staying in freezing water for more than twenty minutes. In your face anyway, Google.

I feel a lot better than I have any right to considering I jumped off the precipice yesterday. It was meant to be game over, and yet here I am, alive and well. I can't even end my life without cocking it up. However, for some reason I feel elevated to be alive against the odds. Maybe a little bit more time on Earth wouldn't be so bad. But only a little bit. I have no intention of going back to my life as it was, so this remains a one-way ticket.

I must owe someone a thank you for my fortuitous position, but, as I have no idea who helped me, the best thing to do is return to my surprisingly comfortable sleeping place for some more warm and sheltered slumber. I crawl back into the hollow and cover myself up with the leaves and moss which have been carefully positioned inside this mysterious tree by my unknown benefactor. Falling back to sleep takes no time at all thanks to my exhaustion.

The sound of bubbling awakens me from my blissful rest some time later. I'm back in the river! And I'm not only in the river, but I'm swimming deep underwater this time. "Help!" I call out, although my words emerge as nothing but bubbles making their way slowly towards the surface. Oh brilliant! I dodged a bullet earlier, only to take the same shot in the chest a few hours later. I'm right back where I started. When the universe decides you are destined to be on a certain pathway, it doesn't mess around.

Swimming was always my favorite sport at school, and I was good at it. Maybe all I have to do is swim to the surface, and all this strangeness will be over. I push my arms forward to take a swimming stroke, but then the chilling realization hits me that I haven't got any arms. In a mad panic, I glance backwards to discover nothing but a fish tail. I am legless! I scream as loud as I can, hoping to awaken from this nightmare, but to no avail. Once again nothing but mute bubbles emerge from my mouth. What the hell is going on? I start hyperventilating as I twist and turn like a wild animal caught in a trap. There must be a way out of this bizarre situation. I scout around in all directions for an exit point, but the reality sinks in that I can't move. Escape is not an option. And another shocking reality hits me like a bolt of electricity: I'm not running out of air. How is this even possible? The answer is as plain as night, even though I don't want to see it.

I'm a bloody fish.

Life certainly has a way of keeping you on your toes. I try to piece together my earlier steps to make some sort of sense out of this, but there's no sense to be made. I remember being warm and dry when I drifted off to sleep. Could I be dreaming? If I am, this is the most realistic dream I've ever lived through. I can feel the water sliding across my scales as I roll around. It feels completely different from being a human in water. The water seems to be alive as it touches me. It's almost as if it's communicating with my scales rather than just washing over them.

I stop twisting around and grind to a halt as I attempt to recalibrate. My fish body is suspended, motionless. I'm not moving forwards, backwards, up or down. How does a fish even move? One thing I do know is that trying anything is better than doing nothing, so I attempt to wag my tail like an underwater dog. It feels so unnatural. I'm moving like a fish from a special needs school who is zigging when it should be zagging. OK, so wagging doesn't work. But somehow I wiggle my way to the surface using the most inefficient and awkward fish swimming style in the history of fish. I gasp for air at the surface. Then I realize I don't need to do that, being a fish and all. Awkward.

I survey the scene from the surface. How different the world appears through fish eyes. I'm still next to the big old tree, although it appears dramatically different from my days as a land dweller. It's no longer just a tree which I happened to sleep inside last night. There's now something far more human about its posture. If I weren't in shock at being a fish I'd even say the tree is aware I'm looking up at it from within the river. Hang on, the tree is blowing in the wind, but there isn't any wind. It's as still as a tomb here.

The tree's branches are moving energetically like arms with leafy hands! I've met drunk Italians with less emphatic hand gestures. If it weren't impossible, I'd say the tree is communicating with me. And even to a human who's dreaming of being a fish and who doesn't speak tree language, the message is clear: "Talk to me."

The Tree

There are very few great listeners in the world. Most people are far happier talking about themselves and ignoring the person they're talking to, who is only there to nod and appear interested at their incredible conversation skills. And of the small group who consider themselves to be good listeners, most of them are actually thinking about what they're going to say next in the conversation when they're pretending to be listening. It's all an act to appear sociable. That leaves only a tiny minority of people who genuinely listen to what the other person is saying with no judgment, agenda or opinion. How many times in our lives have most of us been listened to like that?

And yet, the big tree is here to listen. It's willing me to talk. It has taken me more than thirty years to understand that true acceptance is almost non-existent in the human race, only to find it in a mysterious tree hanging over a river. Here goes.

"There was once a man called Freddy."

Who knows why I've started talking to it in the third person? Let's call it necessary distance, no matter how accepting this tree is.

"Freddy was a good man trying to do good things in the world, or so he thought. There was the time he arranged a music festival to raise money for farmers in need. On the big day, he handwrote a banner for the event which read 'Always look after the hand which feeds you.' Freddy found this funnier than the farmers did, which was a theme in his life. Freddy found most people were too caught up in the details of their complex lives to have a sense of humor these days. However, despite this, the farmers' event was a huge success, and Freddy received written thanks from people all around the country. He kept every single one of them. It was important to Freddy to be a part of the solution in a world which he believed had lost its way."

The tree sways as if to say, "Hear! Hear!"

"Freddy's career served to compound his belief that the world has gone astray. More by chance than plan—well, until yesterday—Freddy worked in the investment world in Edinburgh. He hadn't planned this career path or to be in Scotland. They both just happened to Freddy when he was going with the flow. The story of his life. It was his job to find investments which would make the company's clients as much money as possible. Initially, Freddy found his job fascinating because he got to meet interesting people from all around the world. However, over time the incessant greed of his colleagues and clients weighed heavy on his soul. It seemed as though the only thing they cared about was making money. During yesterday's team meeting, Freddy's boss started thumping the desk like an angry gorilla while chanting

'Let's make some fucking money!' at the top of his voice. Freddy felt like that gillie who brought his fat wealthy client to the river, the only difference being he brought his boss to a place where he would find a big pile of gold. But the more his boss hoarded gold from the pile, the more he chanted for more gold. And the angrier he became whenever he didn't get as much gold as he wanted, which was all the time. As he violently whacked the table and shouted at the heavens, Freddy's boss shook like a drug addict in need of his next fix. In that moment, Freddy was repulsed by his boss, his job and the investment world. He realized he was wasting his time. So Freddy excused himself and walked out of the office, never to return."

I pause to look up at the tree, who's nodding gently. It's listening to every word I say, while its gestures are kind and encouraging. There's a stillness and space around me which is waiting to be filled by whatever I have left to give.

"Freddy was the type of man women liked, an old school gentleman who opened doors for the opposite sex without being asked. Freddy once stood up for a lady on a London tube, but she became upset with him because she thought he was implying that she appeared either pregnant or fat. 'You're perfect as you are,' explained Freddy with a smile, which made her relax and accept the seat. She apologized and explained she was stressed because her husband had recently left her. Freddy felt sad for her, and told her everything would be alright. She cried, and then asked Freddy out for a date. You're the only one who understands, she explained. Freddy needed some time alone, so he white lied and told her he was in a relationship. Freddy found that by being empathetic for people like this lady, he carried others' pain a lot more than he'd like. It was sometimes a heavy burden for him. At times, Freddy felt he owed his time and energy to everyone and anyone who was in pain. He believed there was always something he could do to help them, even if that just meant listening to every word they said. Freddy understood that listening, truly listening, was one of the greatest gifts anyone can give another person."

The tree nods enthusiastically as I say this. I know it understands far more than any human about what listening means.

"Freddy was the type of man confident men liked. They liked the way he was secure enough in his own skin to be his authentic self. Well, until recently. When other people were pushing people out of the way to get ahead, Freddy was often the only one to stand back and help them get to where they were trying to go. On a recent charity bike ride in the Pyrenees, Freddy had been the only one to stop and help one of his fellow cyclists who'd fallen off his bike and badly hurt himself. Freddy waited with the injured man for medical help while everyone else cycled past without a second thought. Freddy watched them cycle past and wondered what it was like to not see others' pain. Confident men saw it took courage to help, to be different, and respected him for not giving a damn about what others thought about him. Freddy had long term friendships with a number of confident, high-achieving men like Matt, a friend Freddy met while sea kayaking on holiday in Turkey. Matt and Freddy bonded through their love of nature and the great outdoors. These male relationships were a source of much joy in Freddy's life.

"Freddy was the type of man insecure men disliked. By stepping forward to help others in their time of need, he made insecure men feel disempowered, less masculine, and weaker. On the Pyrenees bike ride, one of the riders, an aggressive Australian, called Freddy a 'pansy' for stopping to help the injured cyclist. 'That's women's work, mate,' he explained angrily. 'Didn't you want to win? Maybe you were too scared to.' These types of men would challenge Freddy at every opportunity to prove they were better than him. These types of men criticized and attacked Freddy at work. They plotted against him behind his back. These men channeled their negativity into fighting Freddy simply because he was their opposing force in every way.

"Freddy bruised easily. He never understood why these insecure men were attacking him, and he hurt more and more over time. And it seemed to Freddy that the general human population was fast transforming into the insecure male stereotype Freddy found difficult to deal with. Rather than being the exception to the rule, as Freddy remembered when he was younger, this insecure persona was becoming the lot of the common man and woman in a world which has changed beyond all recognition within a few short years. It seemed to

Freddy that the media was programming the human population to become anxious and depressed and angry and short-fused. Freddy felt as though he was being attacked by the new world of negativity he was witnessing all around him.

"Freddy was lonely. When he awoke on the morning he jumped into the river, he turned on the radio and heard a bunch of people being interviewed about their upcoming plans for Christmas. And something struck Freddy as he listened to their stories: they all had families they were looking forward to spending time with, every single one of them. One lady described time with her family gathering at Christmas as 'reset time with the only people in the world who didn't judge her.' She had so much to look forward to at Christmas, she explained, as her family always played a *la boule* competition which invariably ended in fits of laughter. In a stressed-out world, it was welcome respite from the storm, and she was grateful for that.

As he listened, it struck Freddy that he didn't have any family fun to look forward to at Christmas, or any other time for that matter. In fact, Freddy had nothing to look forward to. Zilch. The joy, the will to live, had been sapped out of him by energy-sucking vampires, and there was nothing left for him. They were all the same: his boss, the bully at school, his father.

"The moment Freddy walked out of his job onto the empty streets of Edinburgh on that cold wet winter's day just before Christmas, he was painfully aware that all the little bits that added up to make his life weren't what he wanted. Not one of them brought him any joy. And, by realizing this when he was cold and tired and depressed, Freddy wanted nothing more than to disappear into the river. The river had always been the one and only place where Freddy felt welcome. So Freddy decided that the river was the perfect end point to a less than adequate life.

"Freddy felt desperate. Freddy felt lost.

"Freddy is desperate. Freddy is lost."

The tree is perfectly still and lets my words sink in.

"Freddy needs your help. You're the only one who's listened. It needs to be you."

I gaze up at the dark silhouette of the tree, which has opened its arms as if to say, "I'm here for you." A feeling of total acceptance envelops me, although the tree still hasn't said a word. All it's done is remain present while I've opened up. And by doing so, the tree has accepted me for who I am: every single molecule of me, every thought, spoken and unspoken, every out of place hair, every fart which has seen the light of day in polite company, all of my long list of mistakes, all my humanness laid bare. The tree has proven why dogs make such effective listeners. In contrast, I think about how most people judge each other, and find something in other people not to accept. Once the judgment has happened, it's game over for most relationships at a subconscious level, as the judger tends to focus on what they don't like about the judged person. It's hard to ignore the glaring truth: trees are so much better than people.

I hear music. It sounds like Taylor Swift. The river DJ has only gone and lined up a Swifty classic to lighten the mood. The words circle around my head with the agility of an excitable bird with something important to say: "And the haters gonna hate, hate, hate, hate, hate / Baby, I'm just gonna shake, shake, shake, shake, shake / I shake it off."

Ah yes, solid choice, river DJ. These words resonate with me. Who cares what anyone else thinks? Since I'm still alive for now, I may as well shake off a few memories of people who weren't good for me; and there've been a few. My old boss's face hangs in the air like the portrait of an angry man. If I could remember my father's face, he'd probably be up there as well.

I take the opportunity to draft a letter in my head to all the bullies I've ever encountered.

Dear Bullies of the World, I wanted to write to say hi, and to explain that we've all had enough of your bullshit. You may think it's acceptable to pick on people who are kinder than you, but it's time to stop confusing kindness with weakness. They are not the same thing. You are the weak ones when you attempt to turn other humans into victims to boost your own non-existent self-esteem. You won't yet realize this, but the world sees through your poorly hung masks. And, let's be honest, what lies beneath ain't pretty. It's high time you took a good look at yourselves rather than the innocent people around you. Remember, everything comes out in the wash, so please understand there's a day coming when you'll need to answer for your actions, as we all will.

When that day arrives, I hope it's one of your victims who decides your fate. And I hope your victims forgive you and free you of any obligation. By doing so, they'll have saved themselves as well as providing you with the opportunity to learn from your mistakes; and there are many. Finally, I'd like you to understand that I'm building a fortress around my soul from this moment on. I'm no longer victim material for you to prey upon, so please keep moving. I'm just gonna shake, shake, shake, shake, shake you off. Yours, Freddy.

I post the letter in my mind, and it feels like I'm putting something right. It's time to rejoin the fishy world I'm now part of. I swim back underwater, feeling lighter.

Who's Messing With Me?

Daylight awakens me. I'm discombobulated as I try to piece together where I am, and how I ended up here. I feel around with my hands and touch a mix of soil, moss and leaves. As my eyes adjust to the light, I can see I'm once again inside the tree hollow. I'm well rested and dry; and, well, human. OK, so I was dreaming about my time in the river as a fish talking to an empathetic tree. I've long suspected I'm a sandwich short of a picnic.

I've often heard of the herbs South American shamans give to people to send them on life-altering trips which help them heal, but which also mess with their minds in ways they could never imagine. I wonder if someone slipped me some shaman herbs in my weakened hypothermic state. There's no other rational explanation for my strange evening. Of course, there are unlikely to be many South American shamans strolling along the rivers of Scotland, searching for random river swimmers to heal in the freezing water. And if there are any here, they're so lost and in need of a warm climate they'll no doubt need my help more than I need theirs. Yell out if you need me, lost shaman.

On all fours, I crawl through the entrance of the tree hollow. I emerge into the daylight, if you can call it that, bearing in mind this is deepest, darkest Scotland, a land where sunlight can be as elusive as kindness. I discover a large, neatly stacked pile of apples and blackberries outside the entrance. OK, this is more than a little weird. Maybe that lost shaman did pay me a visit. However, I'm famished, so these apples and blackberries are a godsend. A momentary thought occurs to me that maybe the fruit is drugged or poisoned by whoever has been playing with my mind, but a less momentary "Oh bugger it" takes precedence. My stomach has hijacked all sensible intentions.

I pick up an apple and take a gigantic bite out of its juicy flesh. It's delicious. I feel like the cat that got the cream as I devour every single part of it, including the pips, in an eating frenzy. I lick my lips, feeling moreish as I eye up the blackberries. They look plump and luscious and ready to be eaten. I pick up a blackberry and sink my teeth into it. The juices explode in my mouth and float down my throat in a scrumptious purple river of sweetness. I work my way through the pile of blackberries like an Olympic sprinter, while still savoring each one as if it were the last food I'll ever eat. I lie back like a satisfied king who has eaten a royal banquet delivered by his trusty subjects.

The idea of getting back into the river hangs heavy in the post-banquet air like a potent, fruit-induced fart. Whoops, that was indeed a fart. Lucky I'm in the great outdoors. Despite my better judgment, my feet are now making their way towards the river without asking for permission. Is this what living life instinctively is like? No more thinking, only doing what feels right in the moment. Rather than being free, I feel controlled, like a puppet living my life at the mercy of the puppet-master, whoever that may be. Come forth and introduce yourself, oh great master of human puppets. My feet deposit me unceremoniously beside the river like a pile of pebbles ready to be skimmed across the water.

The river's bubbling noises are louder this morning, although I don't recall hearing any rain last night. As I listen to the river, I relax into the moment. There isn't a single thought running through my mind.

I climb down the riverbank and wade into a slower part of the icy river as if this were a normal thing to do. The cold water forces the air out of my lungs as it did yesterday, but, rather than being terrifying, this time it's reassuring. Out with the old air, in with the new. What a difference a day makes.

Without further ado, I lift my legs and let the current take me away. As I start drifting, I catch a glimpse of the tree that was my bedroom and savior last night. As the distance between us grows, I feel like I'm leaving home for the first time. I consider turning back to the comfort and safety of the paternal tree. My mind flashes back to a memory of my mother crying when I left home to go to university for the first time. She was crying as if she would never see me again, letting her emotions create the moment. However, the tree is not crying as I drift off. Rather, it is comforting me, willing me forward towards better things, like a parent who's read every manual on how to parent effectively. Thanks, good luck and goodbye is the message I'm receiving loud and clear. Right back at you.

It's a slow start as the icy world of the river accepts me again. The sky is unusually bright blue this morning, which makes the river sparkle and dance. If I put my head underwater, I can see a couple of meters below the surface. It's like swimming in the Med, and I'm sure I'm the first person to have ever had this thought while swimming in Scotland. The sensation of floating above such clear water transforms the experience into the feeling of flying. I'm a human fish flying like a fishy bird.

Out of the corner of my eye, I see something moving nearby. The sun is reflecting off a large shiny thing which is moving faster than me downstream. It's most likely a salmon, methinks. The shiny thing glides ahead of me with clear purpose in its movement. But at the very moment it's about to disappear out of sight, it switches back and reappears only a couple of meters ahead of me. From this distance, I can see it's a salmon, and a big one at that.

Out of the blue, the salmon jumps up to a spectacular height a few meters above the river's surface. As the athletic fish turns in the air, time seems to slow, allowing it to look me in the face, *mano a mano*. Unless I'm hallucinating, the damned salmon smiles a knowing smile at me before it re-enters the river. Its face hangs in the air well after it has disappeared. Who does it remind me of? I'm sure I recognize that face from somewhere. That's it, there's no mistaking it—the salmon looks like Jimmy Carr after he's told a joke and is awaiting the audience's laughter. It's a unique facial expression which acknowledges that this whole being alive situation is totally ridiculous, and is worthy of nothing less than rollicking laughter. I wonder what the salmon's joke would have been. Explaining the joke behind its smirk may help me become more comfortable with its strangeness, its absurdity, its all-knowingness. Maybe the joke involved me. Maybe the joke is on me. Maybe the salmon has not been meeting the type of female salmon he'd like to these days. I should have told him not to worry about it, because there are plenty more fish in the sea. I chuckle. I still have it. The salmon and I still have it.

The salmon swims away to wherever it's heading. I continue on my way with a pang of regret that our moment together didn't last longer. There was something about that salmon that intrigued me. I imagine he had some interesting tales to regale me with, and some life-affirming humor to impart, to make the burdens of life a little easier to bear. However, there's no time to dwell as the river is picking up pace.

And it's immediately apparent why I've started speeding up. I'm approaching some serious white-water rapids only a few hundred meters away. This is not the right place to take your time waking up. You just need to blink and your situation can change from good to bad. The white water is quite magnificent from a distance as the river mercilessly pounds the rocks with the power of a million horses running in the same direction.

The me from yesterday would be scared and searching for the fastest way out of the situation. The me of today smiles and lies back in the water. I'm up for a little more time in this strange watery world.

Rougher Waters

As the river speeds up, the river DJ starts playing "Ride" by Lana Del Rey, another favorite. The words "I hear the birds on the summer breeze, I drive fast / I am alone in the night" are carried along by the wind, which then swiftly changes direction and keeps the song moving in a circular motion around me.

The music video for this song has always reminded me of the way I've lived my life as a seeker. Of course, that's just another way of saying being lost. How did I end up living in Scotland, for example? For someone who loves warm sunny weather, it's a hard question to answer. As Lana screams "I'm tired of feeling so fucking crazy!" in perfect pitch, she's doing a good job of making her point. The river acoustics create a haunting echo of the words "fucking crazy," which bounce from one side of the river to the other as if both sides have separate Lana Del Rays living there. Two Lanas for the price of one. One is kind and caring, while the other is upset with me about something, and she's watching from the side currents, wishing me a painful end.

I'm now only meters from where the white-water rapids come to life. It's becoming obvious that it's only possible to see the scale of these bad boys from above.

I've underestimated their size by convincing myself they'd be easier to gauge up close and personal. It's another upstream schoolboy error, and another downstream life-threatening situation to deal with as a result.

I'm moving as fast as green grass through a goose. The ups and downs of the rapids are starting to take control of my vulnerable body. How did a half-sensible human end up hurtling towards these deadly rapids out of choice? As Lana keeps saying, this is fucking crazy.

I imagine myself anywhere but here. My mind flashes back to a parent-teacher evening when I must have been around eight years old. My teacher, a Miss Tucker, is talking with my mother about my behavior in class.

"Freddy is always entertaining his classmates. He's always the first to crack wise during class, and whenever I have to leave the room for even a few minutes, he causes mayhem amongst the other children when I'm gone. The other day I returned to the classroom to discover Freddy was leading the entire class in a running race on the tops of their desks. They were all charging around and laughing wildly. I had to stop myself from laughing because the kids were having the time of their lives. But, of course, it was bad behavior, and I had to tell Freddy off for it. From now on, he'll have to wait outside the ladies' toilet whenever I need to relieve myself during the course of the day. It's about maintaining order, you see. I hope you understand, but Freddy has given me no choice. The question I have for you is: Why does Freddy need to make others laugh so much? Is there anything going on at home I should know about?"

There's no more time to pay heed to ghosts from the past as I'm about to become one with a massive wave at the top of the rapids. I hold my breath as I'm launched upwards. White water rushes at me from all directions at the peak of the wave before sending me deep underwater. A sharp rock hits me hard in the coccyx, otherwise known as the pain-in-the-ass area. Owwwww! But there's no time to compute the extent of the damage as I'm already riding high on the crest of another enormous wave. And before I have time to scratch myself, I plummet again into the unknowable abyss below. Ahhhhh! That one hurt where the sun don't shine. The water relentlessly carries me up another crest. I attempt to breathe in some much-needed air during the split second I'm atop the crest of the next wave. However, I breathe in too early, and I inadvertently suck in large quantities of the cold river water, which forces me into a choking fit. Before I have time to choke to death, I'm forced underwater again, this time with nothing inside my lungs but river water. The difference between "I can make it" and "Oh fuck it" is minuscule to non-existent. It could go either way. But if I were a betting man, I'd say the "Oh fuck it" team have the winning hand. They always have in the past.

My body starts to relax as the fight inside me prepares to leave the party. I've been inside this boxing ring for one round too many, and I sense I'm about to be knocked out by a monstrously large and aggressive opponent. I should never have been fighting this nutter in the first place. On the next watery ascent, I manage to clear my lungs and suck in a tiny breath of air. But the next drop is even harder. I'm hammered onto the sharp rocks beneath the surface without mercy. The pain is compounding with each collision, and I can only imagine how bruised and battered my body is.

As my body starts to accept my fate, so does my mind. I wonder if I have enough breath left to say "Oh fuck it" out loud. Maybe that would feel good. A picture pops into my head of one of my favorite Gary Larsson comics, one in which a dog is juggling bowling pins on a unicycle while he cycles across a tightrope above a circus audience, simultaneously balancing numerous objects on his nose. The caption underneath reads something like: "High above the hushed crowd, Rex couldn't shake a nagging thought: he was an old dog and this was a new trick." In better days, this light-hearted comic would bring me laughter on a regular basis. Something about Rex even thinking he could over achieve like that, despite the evidence to the contrary, touched on something in my own life. Now it hangs heavy in the air like a lesson I should have learnt but haven't. Why did I think I could keep going for a while longer in this deadly river?

All I want to do is slow down and get off this crazy merry-go-round. The more stressed I feel, the more relaxed my body becomes, which is counterintuitive. Although I once read that stress can be helpful if you view it as helpful. And, conversely, it only causes you problems if you view it as a problem. Bugger me, it's all in our heads. Balmy theories are all I've got left, so I start thanking the stress I'm experiencing as I'm battered against the rocks. Oh thank you, river, for pounding the bloody life out of me like this. I'm sure we'll look back on this moment and have a right old laugh about it. Once more I rise high with the water's flow, and I relax at the top of the crest in preparation for the next crushing drop. I have to fight every instinct in my body to stay relaxed when I'm aware I'm about to be dropped like a stone.

It works! I can't believe it. My impromptu survival strategy is working. The more I thank the stress and relax, the more I escape with merely grazing the tops of the protruding stones. My body is no longer being pushed as deep underwater, so I'm dodging the sharp rocks which were causing me so much pain beforehand. I'm grateful with the last ounce of energy I have left. Keep thinking relaxing thoughts is all I can tell myself amidst this most unrelaxing pain.

As with all things in life you want to end in a hurry, the rapids seem to go on forever. And as with all things in life, the moment I start to think the rapids will never end, they come to an end. I notice a small beach section alongside the river in a couple of hundred meters, and there's a protected area of slow-moving water next to the beach. I focus all my remaining energies on swimming the few strokes required to pull myself into the slow water and towards the beach. I've got nothing left.

Eventually I touch the sand. I drag myself halfway out of the water and lie motionless on the beach like a half-dead mussel which has been swept off its rock.

Found

Someone is shaking me.

"Georgie, wake up. Are you alright? Georgie?" says this unknown someone.

I open my heavy eyelids to see a middle-aged man dressed in Tweed peering down at me with a deeply concerned expression on his face.

"Friend or foe?" I ask without thinking.

"Let's get you out of here, old chap," is the response.

He helps me to my feet and supports me as we walk away from the river. Away from the river? Why?

The river's gushing is fading to become a distant sound as we climb up a long, wooded pathway towards a light at the end of a long, tree-lined tunnel. The trees which line the path appear incredibly old, and sway gently as though they've seen it all before. My companion occasionally talks to me as if I'm a child. He throws in encouraging comments like "There there," and "Whoopsy daisy" whenever I stumble. I assume he must have a small army's worth of children somewhere given his strong parental tendencies. I imagine they're all very posh and well groomed, as is his vast collection of racehorses.

As we emerge into the light at the end of the tunnel, we enter a foreign world which no longer revolves around the river. Straight ahead stands a huge manor house which towers over the scene like something out of a Jane Austen novel. If it could talk, it would talk loud and proud. My paternally inclined companion guides me towards the house saying "Nearly there" as we stride forwards with small, child-like steps. The more he talks to me like I'm a child, the more I'm inclined to behave like a child. My sentences are becoming shorter, my words simpler. Soon I'll be left with nothing but "Goo-goo gaga" in my communication arsenal.

We walk up the ornate front steps to the house and approach the dramatic front door. It's big enough for giants to enter should they be so inclined, and it's the sort of place they're likely to enjoy spending their spare time, at least on weekends. My companion rings a cacophonous bell, which reverberates like a church bell at a funeral. Rather than helping me, I think he's just deafened me. Thank you, sir. The ringing continues in my ears well after the bell stops.

The front door opens, and a round, smiley woman steps forward.

"Alice, hi. Check out what I found in the river today. Would you mind helping me take our bedraggled friend here inside?"

"Aye aye, Captain. Step forth, me matey, and let's get you warm and fed," she responds warmly without a moment's hesitation. It's as if she was expecting me, but I don't remember my companion calling ahead once he found me.

Alice and "the captain" support my exhausted body as we walk through the enormous entrance hall. There are paintings of old men and dead animals on the surrounding walls. Why were painters from previous eras so focused on dead animals, I wonder. It's all so morbid, so one-dimensional. The only point of living in those days was clearly to kill as many animals as possible. To be a vegetarian must have meant being a social outcast.

One painting in particular makes an impression on me as we walk past. It's entitled "Where the river floweth." It must be a portrait of "the captain" from a few years ago when he was a younger man. I recognize his strong chin and wavy hair, neither of which have changed much. But his demeanor is quite different these days— he's less upbeat and more serious. In the painting, "the captain" is standing next to the river, searching anxiously for something, although it's unclear what. The painter has given his body the tension of a man who is ill at ease for some reason. Join the club, buddy.

We continue along the hallway and find ourselves in a large living room centered around a blazing fire, which appears ready to be photographed for a *Country Life* magazine. The room has an old-worldly feel, and smells of old charcoal, whiskey and dogs. It's the type of place which makes you want to sit down in front of the fire and start regaling everyone with tales from simpler days when people used to talk to one another. It's not a place for mobile phones to be stared at. I like it.

"Take a seat next to the fire, old chap. Alice will fetch you some towels and warm clothes, and I'll see what we've got in the way of warming food. Back in a jiffy."

The fire's warmth wraps around me like a much-needed hug. I gaze into the blazing flames and listen to the crackling of burning wood. It smells wonderful.

For the first time since I entered the river yesterday, I'm not cold. Yesterday's me would never have guessed how life-affirming not being cold can be. Today's me understands that the cold has a way of penetrating everything all at once, and creeping into places you didn't know existed. And once you've discover they do exist, the cold makes you wish they didn't. Given the choice between being warm and cold, I'd always choose warmth, which makes my choice of jumping into a near-freezing river in the middle of winter all the more perplexing in the cold light of day.

It's time to recalibrate. Here I am sitting in the living room of a Scottish aristocrat who wants to help me. However, it's fair to say I haven't met too many helpful Scottish aristocrats before, so I'm cautious. For all the good things about Scotland, and there are many, I've found some of the locals can be grumpy in a world-is-coming-to-an-end way. I understand why. The climate is cold, dark and wet most of the time. It's the worst I've ever experienced. One winter will always remain imprinted in my memory. It rained every day for six months; every single day. That much rain gets inside your soul, no matter how hard you try to shut it out. And the more you try to shut it out, the more it drills into you like an unlicensed jackhammer.

Despite understanding this, I don't appreciate the way grumpiness spreads like a virus during the winter months here. It seeps into all aspects of social interaction, allowing life's challenges to become the most important news of the day, the only news of the day. What about all the good stuff? But those grumpy Scots would prefer to ignore all things positive when it's cold and dark outside. The upside, of course, is that many of them have a wonderful sense of humor. They're able to channel their seasonal depression into generating comic energy. It's a cunning survival strategy. OK, so maybe I can relate to that little party trick as well, and maybe this is me, the kettle, calling the pot black. Maybe that's why I can understand that when a Scot is cracking a joke, it's in truth a valiant effort to alleviate their deep-held pain. And I understand that an apparently uplifting conversation can be inundated with sub-currents bubbling beneath the surface, hidden beneath the jovial smiles and laughter. As I discovered in my river adventure, sub-currents can override the main current when you least expect it, so it's worth paying them heed. I'll no doubt need to prepare myself for multiple momentum changes this evening, as I suspect this household has its own unique brand of sub-current going on which they don't want the world to know about. Yes, there are skeletons in the closet in abundance here.

Alice returns with some towels, a blanket and a change of clothes.

"Here you go, laddy. There's a bathroom over there. Why don't you go and dry yourself off, put on these clothes, and come sit by the fire to warm your toes and everything else that needs warming."

"Thank you very much."

The clothes Alice has given me are very old-mansy. There's an ancient pair of cords, a flannel shirt which has been washed in the strongest smelling washing powder known to man, and a jumper vest straight from the eighties. The only thing that's missing to complete the "aristocrat in the country" look is a pipe and a glass of whiskey. I suspect both of these will be coming my way later this evening.

What a transformation. Dried and dressed, I emerge from the bathroom as a new man dressed as an old man who's been living alongside "the captain" for decades. Only hours earlier, I was a river monster *en route* to oblivion, and now I'm living the life of the landed gentry from a long-gone era. You never know what's around the next bend in the river.

The fire attracts me to its side with its warmth and gravity. I gaze deep into the flames, letting them dance for me. For a brief moment I feel at home.

"The captain" returns with a cup of hot soup.

"Here you go, old chap. How are you feeling?" he enquires with genuine interest.

"Much better already, thanks to you."

"I'm Willard, by the way."

"Freddy. Nice to meet you."

"And you. So, Freddy, what on earth were you doing in the river? It's not quite the Amalfi Coast in there at this time of year."

What was I doing in the river?

"Good question. I was walking alongside the river upstream earlier, but like an idiot I slipped down the riverbank and fell into the drink."

"Gosh, that must have been a shock."

"Yes, it was. When I hit those rapids things turned hairy. I thought I was a goner."

"I don't doubt that. Those rapids are famously dangerous. People have died in there before. I'd say you're one lucky fellow, old chap. So where do you live when you aren't falling into icy-cold rivers?"

"A few miles south of Edinburgh."

"Goodness, that's a long way to come for a walk along the Tweed."

Think fast. What am I doing here? What would make sense as an explanation for the current state of my life? Note to self: that's a question which I need to answer when I have some time and sense on my hands.

"Yes, I often drive out here to walk alongside the river with my dog. The fresh air and the sounds of the river help clear my head."

"Ah, yes. Clarity. I understand that. Where's your pooch, then?"

I need to change the subject pronto.

"And yourself. Have you lived here long?"

"Only forever. I was born into the family which has owned this place for centuries. The family tradition is that one of us inherits the job of protecting this little pad for future generations, and that lucky family member ended up being me. Hooray."

He chuckles, but I don't see what's funny. Maybe it's just a Scottish moment.

"So what should we do with you, old chap? Shall I order a taxi to send you somewhere? Back to Edinburgh maybe?"

"No. Thank you, though. I'll finish this soup, and then I'll be on my merry way."

"But we're in the middle of nowhere. Where could you go from here without a taxi?"

He eyes me up suspiciously all of a sudden. I want to run for cover like a fox in one of the hunts which are no doubt held in these parts on a regular basis. The hounds are closing in on me fast, and I don't have an escape plan. Think fast.

"I think there's a village up the road, isn't there? I love a good walk, so that's where I'm heading next."

"You don't mean Coldstream? That's at least twenty miles from here, for god's sake. You can't walk that far in this weather with night falling, and without appropriate clothing. At least not unless you're crazy."

He stares at me as if he's assessing how crazy I am. I turn from his gaze, as I don't want him to see the truth behind my eyes. He can't handle the truth. I can't handle the truth.

"You're probably right, old chap."

Old chap? Help, I'm already talking like him.

"OK, so why don't you stay here this evening? It's almost dark already, and we aren't short on space, as you can see. I insist."

"But I don't want to be any trouble."

"My man, you will only trouble me if you don't accept my invitation. You don't want to upset a fellow searcher, do you?"

Has he seen me for what I am after all?

"A fellow searcher?"

"That's a long story. Please say yes, and let's open some bubbly. It will be fun."

"OK. Thanks, that would be smashing."

Smashing? What's in this soup?

"Good, that's settled then. I'll tell dear old Alice you'll be joining us for dinner. She'll be delighted to have someone new to impress with her famous cooking."

The Longest Dinner

A commanding bell rings throughout the house like a warning signal. Even the flames flicker in recognition of something shifting. Willard jumps out of his chair with the edge of a man ill at ease.

"Dinner time! I could eat a horse. Let's get you to the feast, my friend. Hopefully Daphne will be joining us for the festivities."

"I can't wait. Who's Daphne?"

"Daphne is my wife. She's a quiet thing these days, but boy she loves a good laugh." He giggles like a schoolboy.

We walk along another endless, painting-lined corridor into a large room like a banquet room from Henry the Eighth's time. There's an enormous table in the center of the room, with three place settings on separate sides of the table. I can't imagine we'll be passing the salt and pepper to one another unless we're good at throwing. Willard and I take a seat at the table.

I notice a painting nearby of a pretty woman playing with a large dog in a garden.

"Ah yes, you've noticed the painting of Daph with one of the hounds. Speak of the devil."

A woman enters the room quietly and walks over to the third place setting.

"Daph, this is Freddy. Freddy, this is my wife, Daphne."

She nods in my direction, but she doesn't say a word. I glance again at the painting of the smiling woman, and then back at the real version. It's hard to believe they are one and the same person. Rather than the happy woman the painting portrays, the lady in front of me is downcast and glum as if she's just come from a funeral. With cold, reptilian eyes, she appears to be devoid of any personality and emotion.

Daphne sits down across from Willard and me. Once in position, she sits motionless, and her eyes appear to shut down like a doll who hasn't been played with for many a year. I'm immediately reminded of Aunt Sally, one of the characters in *Worzel Gummidge*, a TV series I watched as a child. I was always horrified by the way Aunt Sally's eyes became motionless whenever she turned from an animate person into an inanimate doll. She turned her life on and off like a switch, and she used this power to escape from reality whenever she needed to. Aunt Sally was downright scary, because it was unclear if she was alive or dead, or somewhere in between. I feel the same about Daphne. I wonder if she'll change heads tonight like Aunt Sally's friend Worzel Gummidge did when he wanted to escape reality. A replacement head could improve our prospects of a decent conversation with her, so I'm all for the change. I hope her next head is a version of the happy lady in the painting, or at least someone who doesn't suck the life out of the room.

"Nice to meet you, Daphne, and thank you for your hospitality."

Another slight nod in my direction is all she has to give. This is going to be a very long evening.

"What a beautiful home you have. I think it's the biggest house I've ever visited."

Is there anyone home, Daphne? I suspect the answer is a resounding no. She's clearly more interested in throwing back some champagne than in talking. But I'm the one who needs numbing. Poor Daphne, poor Willard, poor me.

"So, Freddy, did you notice many salmon when you were in the river? We're always trying to count the buggers at this time of year so those damned gillies have the information they need to use in their marketing. More fish in the river means more pounds in their pockets, and, after all, that's why they're here." Willard swiftly takes the spotlight off his mute wife.

This clearly isn't the right moment to mention Jimmy Carr the salmon as it may increase his chances of being caught.

"No, I'm afraid I didn't see any salmon at all."

"Oh? That's a shame. Mind you, when you've fallen into a freezing river and are trying to survive the white-water rapids, your observation skills wouldn't have been at their sharpest, would they? You'd hardly have been a reliable salmon observer."

"I'm sure you're right, old chap."

Alice arrives carrying plates piled high with generous dinner servings. She places our meals down with a smile and leaves. It's clear Alice was my best chance of a decent conversation this evening, so I immediately regret her absence from the dinner table. Willard and Daphne are now all I have to work with. It reminds me of the time I tried to cut an orange in half with a spoon. Rather than eating a juicy orange, I ended up with juice on my face. Daphne is the spoon, Willard is the orange, and I'm the monkey who should have known better. However, the good news is this is a roast dinner like no other. The carved chicken is dripping with thick luscious gravy, and is surrounded by roasted sweet potatoes, beans dripping with butter, which smells freshly made, and a perfect Yorkshire pudding. This cloud has a very tasty silver lining.

"Wow, what a delicious dinner. Thank you for inviting me. Interesting fact: Did you know that Yorkshire pudding was originally served alone as a starter with the sole objective of filling people up ahead of the main course? Its purpose back in the day was to reduce the amount of meat eaten in an attempt to make modest food supplies stretch that little bit further."

Willard pauses to reflect.

"What a curious story, old chap. Why on earth would those olden-dayers fill up on pastry instead of the good stuff. They must have been a bit thick back in the day."

Why are stereotypes alive and well everywhere you turn? Willard shoves a particularly large fork load of chicken dripping with gravy into his mouth. He reminds me of Veronica in *Charlie and the Chocolate Factory* when she insists upon eating blueberry chewing gum because she should be allowed to have whatever she wants, and then promptly explodes into a living blueberry. The two of them share a similar level of ignorance of the common man's condition. I imagine Willard turning into a giant chicken and walking around the table squawking while pecking at crumbs on the table. It's a good look for him.

"Oh, you know. Those were hard times, so I guess it would have been a case of needs must."

Without a word, Daphne puts down her napkin and walks out of the room. It's the most sensible thing she's done since I met her. We can all live in hope that she's off to change her head into something a little more sociable.

"Night, dear," shouts Willard at her fast-retreating back, but she doesn't respond.

"She's had a very busy day, if you know what I mean, old chap," he says to me with an awkward wink.

What a strange time to wink. Unless he's got a nervous tick, he must be winking at me to signal that we men communally understand all challenges relating to the opposite sex. From one man to another, you know what I'm going through, old chap, and by god they are a pain in the ass. That's the message I'm receiving. However, I don't know what he's going through. His wife appears mentally ill to me. As some famous Russian philosopher once said, "All happy families are happy in the same way, while all unhappy families are unhappy in their own unique ways." Willard and Daphne are clearly showcasing what uniquely unhappy looks like. But I'm not the right person to help them deal with their long and no doubt disturbing list of problems. They need a good shrink with a lot of time and a love of expensive whiskey. I'm just the guy who jumped into the river and ended up in their home against his will and better judgment.

"Do you fancy retiring to the sitting room for scotch and games, old chap?"

Fuck no.

"Sure, why not."

Singalong

Willard pours me a large neat Scotch, and then pours himself an even larger one.

"Thanks for a lovely dinner," I say as I take a large swig of whiskey. It sets the back of my throat on fire for a moment before it evolves into a soothing and warming sensation.

"Absolute pleasure, old chap. Alice knows a thing or two about cooking. We're lucky to have her."

"Indeed, she does. Has she been with you long?"

"Yes, forever. She worked for my father when I was a youngster, and has stayed with us ever since. She's as much a member of this family as Daph and I are. In fact, probably more so in some ways."

"I could certainly get used to being cooked for like that on a regular basis."

"Remember, old chap, nothing is perfect. Not everything is as it appears."

"Indeed."

"I think we deserve a little fun after eating, don't you?"

Willard is adept at changing the subject when it's heading in a direction he doesn't want. I recognize the skillset straightaway, as it's also one of my specialties.

"Sure, why not."

"You much of a singer, old chap?"

"I can't say that I am, although I do love music. Why?"

"I have a surprise for you."

"Aha?"

I sound so Edinburgh these days.

Willard pulls out a small machine attached to a microphone.

"What's that?"

"A miniature karaoke machine. Can you believe it? We can perform karaoke without having to fly to Japan."

"What were the chances?"

The freezing cold river is shaping up as a better place to be than here.

"I ordered it in to brighten up our evenings in this quiet part of the country. Sometimes it's hard to figure out who's alive and who's dead around here, if you know what I mean."

"I can imagine."

"You're up first, old chap. I've set the song selector to random to keep us on our toes."

Is this really happening? Is this strange aristocrat who pulled me out of the river only hours earlier really asking me to perform karaoke with him in his big manor house? The lunatics have taken over the asylum. Willard presses play on the karaoke machine and gives me a thumbs up along with a smile of encouragement.

"You're up first, old chap. You are singing 'Ride' by Lana Del Rey. You know this one?"

Do I know it?

"Yes, a little."

As someone who doesn't believe in coincidences, this is scary. I expect a director to walk out and yell "Cut!" at any moment.

The song starts playing on the low quality karaoke machine, which sounds like an old fuzzy AM radio. My heart sinks. Get me out of here.

Oh well, when in Rome. Reluctantly, I stand up and start singly along as quietly as I can, so quietly that I'm hoping no one can hear a single out-of-tune word coming from my mouth. However, the more I sing, the less aware I am of my singing, and the less quietly I sing. Goddamn it, Lana, why did you have to make this song so singable? By the end of the song, I'm at full volume despite my better judgment. I'm sure I'm amongst the worst singers Willard has ever invited to perform karaoke with him. Confirming my suspicions, his face suggests he's in physical pain from listening to my performance. Like me, he can't hide the truth very well.

"Well done, old chap. It's remarkable the way your mouth appears too big when you're singing. Like a fish gulping for air."

You twat.

"Thanks, I think."

He jumps up like an excitable child, and I sit down like a tired adult.

"Righty-o, my turn. And the spinning wheel says 'Shake It Off' by Taylor Swift. I'll take that. It's one of my favorites."

This is beyond any conceivable coincidence. How's it possible that the two songs the river DJ last played for me have been selected randomly? I shift nervously in my seat and glance around the room, looking for an eye in the wall. I suspect I'm being watched, and this entire scene is rigged.

Willard starts singing. It's the worst singing I've ever heard; even worse than mine. I'm certain there are dead people with better voices. By the time he finally finishes the song I need a cold shower. I clap loudly, and try to appear suitably impressed. However, I'm sure my face is betraying my underlying feelings of horror. Note to self: never agree to karaoke evenings with random strangers ever again.

Willard steps forward for a high five, and then brings his hand back for a backward high five. Sweet mother of god.

Who the Fuck is Alice?

"Your turn again, old chap."

Oh great, the joyous fun continues.

"I thought we were done."

I hoped we were done.

"No way. One more song. Come on, you'll enjoy it."

Willard presses the random song-selector button once more, and the roulette wheel starts spinning towards the next source of embarrassment for the evening. The wheel makes its decision with clinical efficiency.

"Alice! What a classic. Let's hope it's the clean version eh?" Willard giggles as he presses play.

After drinking all this whiskey, I no longer care what I'm singing or to whom. I pick up the microphone and start singing along to the lyrics popping up on the screen. Alice is about as fun a song as I could hope for, so I allow myself to get into the moment. As I approach the chorus, I raise my voice as high as it will go without scaring children: "Cause for twenty-four years I've been living next door to Alice."

I hold my breath. Is this the old version or the new version? The next lyric will reveal the answer. The words pop up on the screen like the solution to a riddle. It's the new version. I need to make a quick decision. Do I sing the line, or be an adult and let it go?

"Alice, Alice, who the fuck is Alice?" I sing with far too much gusto. Being an adult always was overrated. And besides, there's something about these words which inspire turning the volume up to eleven. It's as though they exert magic powers over the singer which force them to override their better judgment. I've barely made it through this lyric when the door opens. Alice storms in. I stop singing like a naughty school child who's been caught by the teacher.

Alice picks up the used glasses and marches towards the door without engaging with us. Phew! Maybe she didn't hear my singing after all.

But Alice turns around abruptly, looking mighty angry. There's something on her mind, and, based on the way her nostrils are flaring, I hope it stays there. Please don't look at me.

Alice glances at the empty glasses in her hands while contemplating whatever is going on inside her head. I shift position uncomfortably on my feet as the mood has turned decidedly dark all of a sudden. Without warning, Alice throws the empty glasses at the nearest wall, shattering the no doubt old and expensive glasses into tiny shards of nothingness. I wouldn't say it to her face in her present mood, but she's gone and lost her kindly older lady vibe. I'm petrified. Willard freezes like a frightened rabbit in headlights. So much for his position as the big boss of this household. Reluctant passenger is a more accurate description. There's only one person in control right now, and I wish she'd back off.

"Anything but that. Bring it down to third gear, you bastard! I would do almost anything for this family, Captain. But I will not be made a fool of by anyone, you hear me? Not even for you, or him. You owe me that much respect for all I've done for you," Alice hisses at Willard with an expression of pure anger on her face.

Willard squirms in his seat like he has ants in his pants, but I don't think the attack is over. Alice remains in an explosive posture, like a volcano which has a significant backlog of lava left to erupt; possibly enough of a backlog to change life as we know it. All we can do is stand back and hope for the best. She turns her furious gaze on me. I wish I was somewhere else, anywhere else.

"And you, who are you?"

Not knowing the answer to this question myself, I assume she doesn't want an actual answer. I remain as silent as a human can, hoping she'll forget I exist.

"I'd appreciate it, Captain, if you'd let this wet scallywag of a drifter know that he's emptied the whiskey bottle, and it's time you two drunks fucked off to bed."

Ouch. That one hurt.

Alice marches off, slams the door, and exits as abruptly as she entered. She leaves a whirlwind of angry energy behind to continue her dirty work for her. It's trapped in the room, searching for an open door to escape through. Quick, someone open a window before it lands on us.

Willard and I glance at one another. The initial feeling exchanged is one of pure shock. Willard is squirming as though he's just been kicked hard in his nether regions with a pair of steel-capped boots. However, I sense Willard is feeling more than shock. Earlier, during Alice's tirade, I saw him smirk ever so slightly, but luckily not enough for Alice to notice. I recognize the symptoms of laughing-in-unfortunate-moment-itis as I am a fellow sufferer, and have been throughout my life. It's a cruel disease for everyone involved. Beneath his controlled exterior, I'm certain Willard was holding back his laughter from the moment Alice let rip.

Amidst all this tension, just the thought of holding back laughter is all it takes to bring my inner giggle bubbling towards the surface. I giggle out loud. Bugger, that was inappropriate. Willard appears as surprised as if something long and sharp has just been inserted where it wasn't welcome, which makes the moment even funnier to me. Here it comes again. My giggle morphs into a chuckle, which evolves into a laugh, and before I know it I'm in the middle of an uncontrollable belly laugh. The longer Willard looks shocked, the funnier it is. But, as suspected, Willard can no longer hold back the tide. His face breaks into a laughter of necessity as he joins me for the hysterics. He's still trying to stop himself, but he's failing miserably. And the more he laughs, the harder it becomes for him to control it.

"Shhhhhhh," Willard whispers, "Alice will hear us!"

"Who the fuck is Alice?" I respond, realizing it's so wrong but also so right.

It's too much for either of us. We laugh and laugh until our bellies are sore, and our eyes are dry.

"Have you met Alice?" Willard asks.

We're off again. The laughter is becoming painful now.

"I'm stuck in fourth gear I'm afraid, old chap." Willard smirks while pretending to change a manual gear stick in a car.

Ultimate Loss

We're left exhausted from the laughing. The good news is the energy in the room has shifted from Alice's fury towards something better. It's hard to share hysterical belly laughter for that long with another human without feeling connected to them. In my post-laughter buzz, I realize I'm having fun with Willard. More than that, I'm comfortable with him. Now is my best chance to learn more about this mysterious household I find myself in.

"Tell me about Daphne," I say as casually as possible.

"What would you like to know?" Willard responds, evading the real question.

"Why doesn't she talk?"

Willard moves awkwardly in his seat. I suspect he's contemplating whether to deliver the truth or a bucket-load of shite.

"Like a lot of married folk, she's run out of things to say, old chap. That's all there is to it."

So a bucket-load of shite it is. I know he can do better than this.

"Did something happen to her?"

"Perceptive river rat aren't you?"

"I'm much better at listening than I am at singing."

Willard is silent for a moment, as if he's contemplating whether to open up or not.

"Yes, something happened, just over a year ago."

I try to channel the tree's accepting energy towards Willard.

"Go on."

Willard takes a deep breath and closes his eyes. He's quiet for a moment as if to summon up the energy to go somewhere he's shut off, probably for a long time. I know the truth is coming this time.

"Alright. We married five years ago. Daph was the most stunning and vivacious woman I'd ever met. I was blessed to have met her, and to have her in my life. When we married we had plans to travel the world, to experience the world, to conquer the world. We believed we were walking on air, and anything was possible."

"Then Daph fell pregnant on our honeymoon in India, so our grandiose travel plans were cut short, at least for a while until the baby arrived. Our son Georgie was born healthy, happy and wise after we returned home. He was all we wanted in a son—a beautiful happy baby—and we were so grateful to be a family together."

Were? His use of the past tense hangs tragically in the air.

"But then one day everything changed when Georgie was three years old. While I was working on the other side of the estate one morning, Daph lost sight of Georgie when she was baking cookies in the kitchen. As soon as she realized he wasn't with her, she searched everywhere and became stressed when she couldn't find him. Daph called me to tell me Georgie was missing, so I rushed home across the estate to help with the search."

Willard is fighting back the tears.

"When I arrived home, Daph explained she'd searched everywhere in the house without finding Georgie, so he must be somewhere outside. I'll never forget the chill that ran down my spine as I recalled how fascinated Georgie had been by the river when I'd taken him fishing with one of the gillies. He once told me it was his favorite place in the whole wide world because it made him feel like a superhero who could swim like a fish. I ran to the river faster than I've ever run anywhere in my godforsaken life."

Willard pauses with the look of a man who doesn't want to go on, a man who can't go on.

"Once I arrived at the river, I was relieved when I couldn't find any sign of Georgie in the river or beside it. So I started walking alongside the river, calling out his name at the top of my voice. I was desperate, but I kept telling myself that everything would be alright, it had to be alright. Georgie would be safe and sound playing somewhere, and we'd look back on this moment and laugh at how over-the-top our reaction had been. But there was no response, of course."

The ticking clock on the wall suddenly sounds loud and intrusive. Each second moves slowly as Willard regathers himself for the rest of his ordeal.

"Then I remembered that little beach area where I found you today as a place Georgie had enjoyed skimming stones. I ran down to the beach to check. Time stopped. Little Georgie was lying motionless where you were lying on the beach. I ran over to him and tried to resuscitate him. He didn't respond, but I kept trying. I pleaded with him to come back to us because we loved him more than any river could. I desperately pushed his little chest, and I breathed air into his little mouth for ages, but it was far too late. Georgie had been stone cold dead for a long while before I found him."

Willard slumps in his chair, exhausted.

"I'm so sorry to hear that, Willard. What a heart-breaking thing to go through."

"Indeed. It was a nightmare. Every single aspect of our lives changed that day. And that brings me to my poor lovely wife. She never forgave herself for losing sight of Georgie that morning. And she never forgave me for not being at home, or for introducing Georgie to our danger-ous foe, the river. It was me who took him fishing on all those precious moments we shared down there, and Daph has replayed each of those outings many times over in her mind. Her initial anger lasted for a few painful months, and then what was left was pure bitterness towards herself and me. She just stopped seeing either of us as worthy of love anymore. You may have noticed it at dinner—there's an undercurrent of sadness in every interaction between us. The reality is we've been dying a slow death since the day we lost our son."

"What an incredibly difficult situation for both of you."

"It's certainly been a tough time for us. But many people have their cross to bear."

"Please let me know if I can do anything to help lighten the load."

"Thanks, old chap. If you can turn back time, I'll take you up on your kind offer. But apart from that there's not much that can be done about it. On that note, all this talking has tired me out, so I'm going to hit the hay. I think dear old Alice has prepared the Riverview room for you. Let's hope she hasn't unprepared it since your singing performance. Go up the stairs, and it's the third room on the left. Till tomorrow. Night night, old chap."

"Night."

Strange Turn

Willard stands shakily and wobbles off into the silence of the enormous empty house. His footsteps echo around the room like suppressed voices from the past. I hope he makes it all the way to his bed in the state he's in. I wonder if he snuck in a few more scotches before dinner. It wouldn't surprise me.

My glass isn't quite empty, so I decide to reflect for a moment. I'm sure this room has met many interesting characters in its time, but I doubt it's ever met any "scallywag drifters" quite like me. Alice was right.

What a day. Just when I thought my time was coming to an end, the river saved me, then Willard saved me. Despite not achieving my morbid goal for the day, I'm not upset about it—not being a corpse is working for me right now. I'm even glad I met Willard and his tragic household. He's shown me it's possible to keep on going even when life seems unbearable. And his life does look unbearable. If I was offered to exchange my life for his, I'd stick with what I've got. Note to self: others are in just as much, if not more, pain than me. I'd have struggled to believe that earlier today when I jumped into the river.

As I gaze into the glowing embers in the fireplace, I suddenly wonder if anyone is missing me. I think through all the people in my life. There are my friends Matt, Peter, John and Steve. However, they won't notice I'm not around as we generally catch up every couple of months. My now ex-colleagues certainly won't notice my absence, as they'll have no doubt black-listed me after my abrupt exit. My mother struggles to remember she has a son these days, so that's a no. My grandmother would have missed me, but she passed away a few years ago. And my father, wherever he is ... Well, let's just say he wouldn't have noticed even if little Georgie's fate had befallen me as a youngster. So the answer is a resounding no one.

That's enough. I'm tired, and it's time for me to turn in after a most unusual day. I make my way up the long staircase covered with faded pink carpet. The red wine stains which are not quite hidden in the carpet tell a million drunken tales from times old and new. I imagine the stories from different generations in this household chime with similar themes, many of which revolve around the bottle. History has a way of repeating, even though we all think we are living terribly original lives.

Around halfway up the stairs is a striking painting of a little boy. It must be Willard and Daphne's son Georgie. In the painting, he's rosy-cheeked, with a mischievous expression on his young face. It's hard not to like the look of him. I experience a moment of intense sadness for what this household must have gone through since that fateful day. Losing a young child must wreak unspeakable damage on the parents.

After a couple of failed attempts of stumbling into large and empty bedrooms, I locate my bedroom for the night. Luckily, Alice has left the bedclothes in place despite her anger towards me. I collapse into bed and fall seamlessly into a deep sleep, aided by the whiskey, the laughter, and my state of total exhaustion. It's blissful.

Some hours later I'm abruptly awoken by a strange voice nearby. I've forgotten where I am, who I am, what I am. It takes me a moment to gather my bearings in the darkness. Last night's events come rushing back. I remember I'm upstairs in bed at Willard's ludicrously large mansion.

But who is talking to me? I peer around the room and notice the dark silhouette of a person sitting in a chair next to the bed. It's a woman. And she's talking softly but urgently, as if she's telling an important secret to someone who will be able to use the information she's sharing to save the world. Is this information meant for me?

"How many fish are there in the ocean?

Big ones, little ones, fast ones, slow ones,

All players in a watery game only they understand,

The water is the source of their wisdom,

And it's infinite,

Us foolish humans can't comprehend,

How infinite wisdom dresses itself,

Addresses us,

Because it would dress us as the smallest fish of them all,

If only we could hear,

If only we would open our eyes,

It would teach us,

That living is the greatest success,

So watch the little fish swimming hard against the current,

Towards something better,

And when it jumps out of the water,

Revealing its face to the world,

Showing the world what joy looks like,

It's a sight to behold."

As she says the last line, her head turns abruptly so she can look me in the eye. Help! Even though I can't see her eyes, they are piercing through the darkness to penetrate deep inside my soul. She's asking me questions I don't want asked, pushing me in a direction I don't want to be pushed.

When I was a kid I discovered that playing dead was the safest strategy when you found yourself in a situation you didn't want to be in. Don't oppose forces which aren't aligning with your future, my grandmother always used to advise in her wisdom. By opposing the force, you are giving it power to influence your own direction. So I close my eyes and pretend to be fast asleep, as though this nightmarish mirage wasn't sitting there staring intensely at me. I breathe deeply like a sleeping person to complete my academy-award-winning performance as someone not to be talked to. It's working. The mysterious woman stops talking and stands up. She pauses for a moment before walking over to me and stroking my forehead. She whispers "Sweet dreams, Georgie" into my ear.

I want to scream! Georgie!?

Finally, the woman walks towards the door, hopefully never to return. Before she departs, she turns back to give me one final intense stare. For the first time, I can see her face glowing in the light of the moon coming through the window.

It's Daphne.

I can't stomach whatever this is for one second longer. These people make me seem normal. I need to be somewhere else, somewhere I feel less dried out, somewhere I can breathe. Anywhere but here.

Escape

Sneaking out has been a specialty of mine ever since I was a kid and in need of sanctuary, so I don't need to think twice about my exit plan.

I open the bedroom door and tiptoe towards the stairs with the light-footedness of a cat burglar. Despite my best efforts, there's a loud and unhelpful creak at the top of the stairs, but it doesn't appear to wake anyone up.

Down the stairs I go. As I pass the painting of Georgie looking carefree, a cool breeze tickles my neck. After the night I've had I'm not in the mood for any more weirdness, so I speed up. I walk past the bottom of the stairs through the entrance corridor, and towards the front door. It's a long walk considering I have to feel my way along the corridor in the pitch black. Finally, I reach the end of the hallway. Freedom is near.

Expecting to have to deal with the world's most complex door lock, I reach out for the door handle, only to discover the front door is already open. These aristocratic types are crazy cats. The cool breeze of the morning caresses my face like a caring lover. I step through the front door into the great outdoors. The urge to celebrate is strong, but I must keep moving back to what I was doing before I became embroiled in this side current. As I stride forward, it strikes me that I haven't got a fucking clue what I'm doing. I'm running away from the person who saved me from certain death to return to my life of escaping from my life. I'm a real genius at work here.

The one thing I'm sure about is my need to be moving forwards rather than backwards, even if I don't know which way forwards is. Momentum may not be a direction, but it must be better than stagnating in Willard's family's cesspool of problems. There be monsters. And besides, the river's motion, power, and definiteness of purpose must count for something. Being a part of the river's world is a lot more than I had going for me yesterday. And maybe that's what this is all about: more than yesterday.

Navigating has never been a strength of mine. It's one of those skills that most women expect men to be good at, but, sadly, my brain doesn't work that way. I'm wired to be lost as my default position. I'll never forget my experience of being a scout when I was teaching a bunch of younger scouts how to navigate. They ignorantly assumed I knew what I was talking about since I was older and had been trained by the best. However, they were so wrong.

The receding tide exposed my navigational ineptitude when one of the senior scouts came up with the brilliant idea of the older and younger scouts all competing against one another in an orienteering event. Great idea, buddy. We all headed out into a large forest together, and I returned alone at the back of the pack, and behind the younger scouts I was supposedly teaching. I was more naked than the emperor without his new clothes, and I experienced intense embarrassment when all the young scouts laughed as I finally crossed the line. The senior scout looked me severely in the eye and said, "Until you learn to navigate the unknown, you'll be forever lost." He delivered this uplifting message as an annoyed command, rather than as a piece of life advice to be treasured and put away in a bedside drawer. In hindsight, that's what it was. Note to younger self: learn to navigate the unknown. Note to current self: welcome home, this is the unknown.

Think hard. How did I get here? I remember there's a tree-lined pathway somewhere behind the house which leads back down to the river. I make my way to the back of the house, and there it is, the yellow brick road glowing under the light of the moon. It's a small win, but it's a win.

Something inspires me to glance back at the house before I leave. To my surprise, someone is standing at one of the windows. They're watching me. The white light of the moon transforms the person's face into a ghostly mask which appears supernatural from where I'm standing. See you later, Daphne.

Reuniting With An Old Friend

The pathway back to the river is lined by trees which sway in all directions at once, like a buoyant welcoming committee. I'm bounding along light on my feet, relieved to be free of the house and its heavy baggage. As I emerge from the forest, the sound of the river roars a welcome my way like an old friend joyfully greeting another after too long between drinks. "Hey, where the hell have you been? It's fantastic to see you," the river gushes at me. I can't help but smile to be back where I'm meant to be. It's astounding how I can feel these emotions when seeing an inanimate body of water, while I struggle to feel anything when seeing the vast majority of humans I encounter. I can even think of so-called friends whom I've felt less for when spending time together.

A friend of mine, Tom, comes to mind. He's a pilot, and obsessively collects old cars which he refurbishes because he has an obsession with fixing broken things. It's the only part of his life which makes any sense to him. At last count, I think he owned ten cars, two motorbikes, two mopeds, and a small airplane. It became apparent at some point in our friendship that Tom had no other friends apart from me, and it also became clear why. In the brief moments his mask wobbled, I discovered he judges humans in the same way he judges each car he's refurbishing. He searches for what he needs to tinker with. But once he identifies the part which needs replacing, the realization hits home that there's no hotline to order it from, so he gives up and returns to his more predictable vehicles. So he's a giver-upper extraordinaire when it comes to humans because none of us come with the instruction book he needs. And, like most men, he prefers to look outwards rather than inwards. So he habitually judges, and then lets down the people who enter his life. Potential new friends, myself included, walk away thinking Tom is uncaring, unloving and inhuman. However, having talked with the big tree, I now realize I was wrong. The truth is he's scared of having to accept flaws in others, because that means accepting his own flaws, or, worse, seeing the flaws in himself for the first time. We were all forced into not accepting Tom in our lives for the simple reason he refused to accept himself.

I've always been surprised by how hopeless most men are at building friendships, and here's the river explaining it all to me, or rather helping me see the truth for the first time. It's all so obvious when you step away from the noisiness of humans for a while. The male ego blinds us to the self-awareness we need to build relationships based on positive emotions, rather than feelings of inadequacy and insecurity. The river sounds a loud gurgling note as if to say, "Hear, hear. If only the common man would open his eyes and see."

I sit, watch and listen. The rhythmic sounds of the gushing water are hypnotic. It's hard to focus on anything else. So I lie down, and let the gushing take me away from being lost for a moment. I forget where I am, and soon drift into a deep sleep.

A short while later I feel different. I open my eyes to discover I'm once again in the river. I'm underwater, being pushed backwards by a strong current which tells me my chances of being human are on the low side. I know this drill. This is a fishy dream. Oh joy, river, how do I thank you for another opportunity to experience life as a fish?

Oh well. I make a pact with myself to make the most of my underwater freedoms this time. Remembering how I was able to propel myself forward last time I was a fish, I wiggle my bum like it's the eighties. However, nothing about this feels natural, and I'm hardly moving. I'm still a fish out of water even when I'm a fish in water. If this were a David Attenborough documentary, his next comment would be: "Watch this salmon wrestle against the overpowering tide. It's touching to watch its efforts despite its lack of progress. Let's hope the tide turns for this fellow soon." The scene would then fade out to show the salmon slowly dying after his failed efforts, followed by a sympathetic: "But alas, it appears not to be. That's the way of nature." Why don't you focus on the zebras for now, Dave?

Out of the blue, I'm aware of something, a presence, approaching me from behind. What next? I turn around to discover a little fish is swimming towards me with a big grin on its face. I do a double take, but, yes, this fish is indeed grinning. It reminds me of a movie star arriving on set for a day of filming. Who knew that fish could be so charismatic? The little fish knows how to swim like a real fish, as opposed to my fish swimming for dummies approach. It swims over to me as if we're old friends and stops when it's face to face with me. It's still grinning inanely, as if someone told it an excellent joke only a few moments earlier. Is it expecting me to communicate with it?

"Excellence is the gradual result of always striving to do better," says the little fish in a shrilly voice like a gypsy fortune teller. It winks at me as if it has kindly imparted some life-changing information in my direction. It seems to think it's just done me a big favor. Jeez, thanks buddy.

There was me thinking that expecting a fish to speak English may be a stretch, but the little fish is more fluent than I am. I'm not sure whether I should be happy or disappointed that we have a means of communication available to us. However, I'm aware my gut instinct was more positive on this fish when it was approaching from a distance, when it wasn't imparting life advice to me, one fish to another. I would have preferred a simple "Hello, how are you?" as a greeting, or even an acknowledgment of how ridiculous this whole fish-talking situation is. However, this little fish is not one for small talk.

"Pardon me?"

"You have to expect things from yourself before you can do them," continues the little fish, who seems to think it knows a lot about me.

"Oh yes? Are these motivational quotes, then?"

"A champion is someone who gets up when they can't."

I take that as a yes. Chatty little critter this one. Shame about its listening skills.

"Who may you be, then?" I enquire, more out of politeness than genuine interest.

"The real question is: Who are you? And what are you doing here?"

There appears to be an underwater echo down here.

"OK. I'll answer your questions. My name is Freddy. I'm either a fishy human or a humany fish. I don't know which. All I know is that I'm meant to be here. Why I'm meant to be here is less clear to me."

"Does the swimmer choose the river, or does the river choose the swimmer?"

OK, so it's not the sharpest tool in the shed.

"Maybe it doesn't matter, eh? As long as the swimmer and the river meet at the right time, and start moving in the right direction together."

"If you don't change direction, you may end up where you are heading," replies the little fish, before it suddenly changes direction and starts swimming down-stream with the current. How incredibly annoying. Nice meeting you, you arrogant prick of a fish, I think to myself as I swim away, propelled by anger. Where is a fisherman with a big hook and expert fishing skills when you need one? I'm sure the little fish would make a mighty tasty dinner—best served silent.

After swimming away as fast as I can for a few min-utes, I try to stop myself thinking destructive thoughts about the little fish as it's obvious they aren't helping me. I assume the little fish must have believed it was helping me with the never-ending supply of life advice it customized for me. A question bubbles up into my mind: Why would the little fish's motivational advice annoy me so much? Rarely can I remember being so annoyed. The answer suddenly hits me like a pectoral fin up the ass. I didn't like the little fish giving me life advice because it implied that I don't know what I'm doing with my life. Or, worse, it implied that the little fish knows much more than I do. But why would that bother me so much? And, on cue, two words march uninvited into my mind: male ego.

OK, I get it. The little fish's advice may be exactly what I needed to hear, but who am I if a little fish who is smaller than me, and only a fish for god's sake, is wiser than I am, cleverer than I am, and far ahead of me in the river of life? Like every other small-minded male I've ever met and felt sorry for, I reacted defensively because I'm a long way from perfect myself. Just like Tom, I've been fighting against admitting it to myself.

How many other pieces of valuable advice have I willingly ignored throughout my life? What an idiot. Me, not the little fish.

I'm ready to hear what you have to tell me, little fish. I waggle my tail harder. The current is moving hard against me. I pick up speed regardless.

Hooked

Swimming as fast as this makes me feel like a super-fish. I muscle my way through the water away from the little fish, and away from Willard and Daphne's craziness. If I could only replicate this momentum in the human world.

The river DJ starts playing a song. It's another familiar old friend, "That's What Friends Are For," an emotional ballad best sung loud and underwater. I sing along, and open up at the chorus: "For good time and bad times / I'll be on your side forever more / That's what friends are for." Even the bubbles emerge from my mouth out of tune to the music. My singing voice hasn't improved since my performance with Willard, but who cares? Everyone knows fish can't talk, never mind sing.

I know the river is once again testing me by nudging a song my way which has answers for me hidden in plain sight. That's What Friends Are For. I know friendships are important, but what do I need to learn about friendship? I've always considered myself a good friend to my friends, and in most cases vice versa. But there's something here, something about the way the big tree accepted me so unconditionally. Am I accepting my friends without judgment, and with total acceptance?

And the little fish showed me how unproductive the male ego can be. Is it holding me back from making closer friendships?

Ouch!!!

Agony arrives unannounced as something as sharp as a knife penetrates the side of my face. It hurts, it bloody hurts, as my flesh is ripped apart and my cheek is carved up like a hot knife through butter. The nerve endings in my face are being sliced into pieces.

There's no time to figure out what the hell is going on, as I'm being yanked out of the current by a powerful force attached to whatever is tearing my mouth apart so carelessly. The pain is unbearable. Sweet mother of god! This must be what it feels like to be eaten alive by a wild animal.

It strikes me that if my life is going to end, I want to be the one who ends it, not this uninvited item of unpleasantness. So it's a no, whatever you are. My life is mine, not yours. With newfound fighting spirit, I swim as hard as I can in the opposite direction, despite the intense pain, ignoring my grandmother's advice about not fighting opposing forces. Maybe things are different here, and that advice only works in the human world. Maybe in this underwater world you just get what you want for the simple reason you want it, and in this case what I want is for the pain to stop right fucking now. Besides, if I can swim upstream against a current as strong as this, surely I can swim away from whatever is pulling at me. This is my time to move beyond surviving. I wiggle my ass like two squirrels in a gunnysack to generate greater momentum. Despite not being able to see him nearby, I can hear the little fish's voice whispering in my ear: "It's the courage to continue that counts." His voice is still annoying, but fair play to him. He's right. Or is he? Holy shit, the force pulling me back is so strong. How can I be expected to outswim this, you silly little fish? I make a few meters progress away from my tormentor, but all of a sudden I'm pulled even harder out of the current. I'm losing both the battle and the war as I'm dragged into a side cove. This makes no sense. I'm listening to all the advice being thrown at me, and yet the harder I swim away, the weaker my position becomes. Little fish, you sold me up the river, you bastard of a smart ass. I can't imagine I'll be asking you for life advice again any time soon.

The pain in my mouth is now the least of my problems. I am caught.

What sort of dream is this? I preferred the simpler swimming-around-as-a-fish-in-a-river version. That version didn't involve pain and hooks and the prospect of being fried up for dinner. Those things belong in the human world.

My exhausted body has been dragged almost lifeless to the side of the river, and lies motionless like a floppy wet cloth which was used to dry the dishes.

Enough already.

But what's that awful noise? I open my eyes to discover two men nearby on the rocks. One of them is screaming loudly, and the other has fallen onto the rocks. He must have hurt himself as there's blood all over his knees. The two of them look as terrified as if they've seen a ghost. In my exhausted state, I wonder what's wrong with them. Haven't they seen an almost-dead fish before? People in this part of the world are as highly strung as they are famous for.

Hang on. Something isn't right here. I glance down at my exhausted fishy body to discover I'm no longer a fish. Where there was once a pectoral fin is now an arm, and where there was once a tail are now two rather floppy legs. I'm nothing but a wet and bedraggled human who's spent far too long in the water. OK, so this dream has taken a turn for the worse.

The two men are running for their lives away from me. One of them is talking on his radio as he runs.

"Boss, we've just caught a man swimming in the river in front of your estate. Aye, that's right. Roger to that."

That's the last I see of those two as they charge off into the forest to escape the beast in the river, otherwise known as me.

The sharp pain reverberates throughout my body. My mouth is bleeding severely where the fishhook cut through my cheek. The intense throbbing pain has spread from my cheek throughout my body, and blood oozes all over me.

What now? I hear the sound of someone approaching on foot. I turn to discover a red-faced man with a large rifle in his hands, charging towards me from within some nearby trees. His red face and rifle suggest the chances of him delivering good news aren't high, so I use the last of my energy to push myself back into the river in the hope of drifting far away. I don't want to allow this crazed madman to make this dream any worse than it is.

The problem with my escape strategy is that I'm no longer in the river's main current. Despite pushing as hard as I can, I'm moving away from the riverbank painfully slowly in a weak side current. I'm still only a few meters away from the rocky beach as the rifle-yielding madman closes in on me. Please, river, take me far away.

My thoughts drift away, as anywhere must be better than here. A Gary Larson comic pops into my head, one which has always made me laugh. A severely beaten-up man is sitting in a court witness box, listening to a lawyer who is holding a hat with two large fake eyes painted on the front. The lawyer says something along the lines of: "So you're saying that Professor Longname handed you this hat on that fateful day on the Serengeti expedition knowing full well that baboons consider eye contact threatening?" Ha! It's a classic, which even now inspires a chuckle through my pain. However, it strikes me that a more sensible man, or even fish, wouldn't be laughing so freely in my position. The hard truth is I'm no better off than the injured and slightly stupid professor in the comic. My disguise was being a fish, and yet, unwittingly, being disguised as a fish is what got me into all this trouble in the first place. The message is loud and clear: I'm in the wrong place no matter what I do, whatever species I happen to be at the time.

The man with the rifle has caught up with me. He's standing on a large rock adjacent to where I'm drifting, looking at me through the rifle lens with his finger tensely perched on the trigger. He's holding that rifle like a man who's about to shoot first and ask questions later. I wonder if it's true that if you die in your dreams, you die in real life.

That's What Friends Are For

"**W**hat the fuck are you doing in my river?" asks the red-faced militant. His nostrils are flaring like a bull in a rage.

No introduction is needed. I instantly recognize the type of man addressing me—this is your quintessential angry little man. I guesstimate from his tone that he must be around five foot four and a half in heels.

"I'm passing through towards greener pastures," I manage to blurt out.

"What? No one passes through my river," he continues, while a large vein pulsates on his forehead. "And do you know why, laddy, eh? Speak up."

"No, why don't you enlighten me?"

"Listen, son, you are in no position to talk to me with that insolent tone, you understand. I'm the Duke of Sutherland, and this is my estate, all ten thousand acres of it. It's been in my family for, oh, let me think, six hundred and seventeen years, and counting. The reason no one is allowed to swim here is because you daft river swimmers scare away all the good fish with your disgusting noises and smells. Can you imagine being a salmon and meeting you underwater? It would be bloody terrifying. And that's bad for my business. You are bad for my business, laddy. Do you know what I do to things that are bad for my business? Speak up. I fucking annihilate them."

Nice guy. I think he'd do well as a tourist guide.

I close my eyes to find some space. One thing I've learnt since entering the river is that shutting up and listening is almost always more productive than shouting back when life has something to say, even if it is dressed up as a vertically challenged nutcase. "Never oppose a force which could push you off your own track," sounds a voice in my head. Is that you, little fish, wherever you are? OK, bring it on. Whatever is going to happen in this moment is going to happen. Let this angry little man get as angry as he wants to. Let that vein on his forehead pulsate as much as it needs to. I lie back and await his no doubt violent response.

But nothing happens. Maybe this is a dream in which nothing bad can happen to me after all.

A second voice pipes in from behind us.

"That's the best looking fish I've ever seen you catch!"

I'd recognize that posh voice anywhere, but I most certainly wasn't expecting to hear it here.

"Willard, what do you want, you twat?" responds the duke.

It's hardly a friendly greeting.

"Shouldn't you be tending to a chicken or something, old chap?"

"Your humor is maturing like a fine wine turned to vinegar, a bit like your estate."

Willard turns to me and waves with a smile.

"Morning, Freddy. Off for a morning dip before breakfast are you, old chap?"

The duke's forehead vein is now throbbing like a frog in a sock.

"So you know this insolent trespasser? Why doesn't that surprise me? Cretins like other cretins. It's the way of the cretinocracy."

"Easy up, old chap. And besides, no one is trespassing. The river is public property in case you forgot."

I really hope this is a dream, as Willard is going in to bat for me, despite the fact I did a runner this morning. I feel like a proper dickhead. Aha! The river DJ played "That's What Friend Are For" as a lesson for me, not for my friends.

"That old chestnut. The land this river flows through is mine, so this wet sod is on my land. I don't care to hear anything to the contrary from you or any other idiots who don't understand the lay of the land."

"Ah yes, the red-necked imbecile's manifesto of innovative land management strategies," responds Willard with fast-witted flair.

The duke's anger is close to boiling point, and that vein on his forehead is attempting to escape his head stage left. We may need to call an ambulance soon.

The duke steps towards Willard and pushes him hard like a bully who is used to picking fights with people who don't want to be picked on. Willard falls over onto the rocky ground and grimaces in pain. This is a slow-motion car crash.

Once he recovers his senses, Willard pulls himself up and approaches the duke, putting his face right up in the duke's face. He's as angry as I can imagine Willard ever being. This is the portrait of a kind man being pushed beyond his limits in every way.

"Touch me one more time, old chap, and I promise you'll regret it."

The duke laughs like a madman who's escaped the loony bin. He looks like he's been granted a season pass to fly over the cuckoo's nest whenever he feels so inclined.

"Why don't you go round up your old lady's club of grief counsellors to join you for a wee cry about it? Oh boo-hoo-hoo."

Ouch. Willard stiffens. He's visibly upset. He steps forward and raises his arm with the expression of a possessed man ready to take vengeance. The duke stands motionless as if he's been told a bad joke which he finds both funny and ridiculous. He's willing Willard to fight him. I imagine this is what he lives for.

The duke isn't disappointed. Willard raises his arm, appearing to initiate a punch. But in a last moment change of tactics, he opens his fist up and slaps the duke across his face. The sound of the slap echoes across the river, reminding everyone present that Willard is indeed a man-slapper. The duke's face is now throbbing into a deeper and more angry red. The vein on his forehead is trying hard to keep up with events. The bad news for Willard is that the blow he inflicted doesn't appear to have caused the duke any pain whatsoever. Rather, the duke roars with laughter; not-quite-right-in-the-head laughter. His eyes are ready to pop out of his head at any moment as he stares intently at Willard, willing on more aggression. It's hard to watch his descent into madness unfold before our very eyes.

"What the fuck was that? A bitch slap? You poofter! It's time you learnt a thing or two about how to be beaten the crap out of."

The duke raises his arms into the fighting position. This doesn't look good for Willard. There's an unwritten rule that all angry little men are viscous fighters who punch well above their weight, so they are best avoided when their emotions are running riot. It has something to do with their low center of gravity and high center of aggravation. I feel so guilty lying here bleeding and useless, while Willard has put his rather ineffective body on the line to protect me. The duke throws an angry punch at Willard's face, and Willard skips out of the way just in time to avoid its destructive force. But the duke is unperturbed. His second strike is delivered with more power, and Willard skips in the other direction, once again avoiding the blow against the odds. Steam appears to be shooting from the duke's remarkably hairy ears.

The duke screams like a wild beast who has been taunted one too many times to look at himself in the mirror the same way ever again. He starts throwing punches left right and center, like a high-speed windmill which is out of control. Willard doesn't stand a chance. I can't watch, so I close my eyes for a moment. Willard is about to be obliterated, and it's all my fault for escaping like I did.

Suddenly, I hear a lady scream hysterically. Opening one eye, I see Willard Morris dancing his way around the duke's punches. He's avoiding each and every blow, like Neo in *The Matrix* when he bends backwards to avoid the bullets flying at him, but far less gracefully. It becomes shockingly clear that it's the duke who's screaming, and they're high-pitched screams of embarrassment. It sure ain't pretty to watch, but it's hard to feel anything but admiration for the spectacle unfolding in front of me. If David Attenborough was presenting this scene he'd say: "Isn't nature amazing? The weaker animal is tiring out the stronger animal by dancing a dance of desperation, and, bizarrely, it's working. Sometimes acting the clown is in fact the superior survival strategy in a world which can be far from fair."

The duke is spent. His windmill has run out of wind, and his punches slow to a grinding halt. We're all in shock, including Willard. The only thing which is still moving is the duke's dancing vein, which doesn't yet realize the party is over. The duke stands small—a broken man wallowing in disbelief.

"You know what you can do? You can take this ruffian, and you can get the fuck off my land. You're not worth any more of my time," says the duke in a last ditch attempt to get in the last word.

He turns angrily to depart. However, his exhaustion has thrown his balance off, and he falls flat on his face. Both Willard and I laugh despite it all; because of it all.

The duke's anger turns to embarrassment. He gazes at us like a lost little child who is being bullied by the big kids at school. How the tables have turned. I'd be sorry for him if he wasn't so damned mean and unlikable. Maybe there's more to the duke than red-faced little-man anger, but that's a world for him to discover one day, when he's ready. Today, the best we can all do is part ways.

"Best you bring it down to third gear, old chap—both for you and that vein pumping away on your forehead. Why don't you sod off home now, little fellow." Willard smirks, relishing his glorious victory.

The duke completes his ungracious exit without a word.

Hello Humility

Willard walks over and sits down on the river edge next to me. He's exhausted.

"We must stop meeting like this, old chap."

I laugh weakly.

"Ouch, that looks painful," he says, pointing at my bloody face.

"I'm sure it looks worse than it is."

"I hope so." Willard smiles before an awkward silence forms between us. I take a deep breath, knowing what I have to do.

"Willard, thank you for your help. I suspect you've saved my life for the second time in two days."

"Always a pleasure, old chap."

"I suppose I should explain what I'm doing in the river again, and why I didn't say goodbye."

The humble pie is sitting in front of me ready to be eaten.

"When you're ready, old chap. Let's first get you cleaned up and fixed up. I'll help get you back up to the house, if that's an agreeable plan for you."

Willard is helping me despite it all.

"Yes, I'd appreciate that, thank you."

Willard helps me out of the river, and we make our way to the pathway towards to the house. As we walk, he once again talks to me like a father talking to his child with unconditional love. He steadies me whenever I stumble. Nothing is too much trouble. The more he helps me, the more the guilt becomes overwhelming. I feel like I've betrayed one of the planet's last good guys when he offered me help, and at a time when I needed saving like never before. Worse than that, I let him down when he needed my help, or at least my company. I've never met someone so in need of a genuine friend with an open ear. And that's what friends are for. Willard should have left my bedraggled body and washed up soul attached to that fishhook by the river. That's where I deserve to be. I assume that's where I'll end up again by the end of this dream.

We reach the end of the tunneled footpath. The house sparkles in the daylight, and appears far less sinister than when I last saw it. It's hard to believe I was so scared and unsettled by something so beautiful, something which is meant to be here so much more than I am. With Willard's help, I walk up the steps to the front door. Willard rings the doorbell which once again nearly deafens me. The sense of déjà vu is overwhelming.

Alice opens the door. She welcomes me with her efficient smile once more. And, like yesterday, she rushes forward without skipping a beat to help me. She supports me as we enter the house.

"Poor laddy. What on earth happened to your face?"

"It's a long story, but let's just say I now understand what it's like to be caught."

"Now now, come on in. The good news is I have something to help fix that up in no time, but the bad news is it's going to hurt like hell."

"I'd expect nothing less. Thanks, Alice."

Alice and Willard each hold one of my hands to support me as we walk down the long corridor. They sit me next to the blazing fire in the living room, which is still burning bright. Alice rushes off to find her medical kit.

There's still an awkward silence between Willard and me. I know Willard is waiting for me to open up, to explain why I'm such a dickhead. Finding the right words is next to impossible when I don't know all the answers myself. I'm fighting hard against an inbuilt need to change the subject and pretend nothing needs to be discussed, to return to being the ostrich I've been all my life. No. Not this time. Willard deserves better than that. If I could only channel a bit of the little fish's wisdom.

"I owe you a monumental apology, Willard. I'm so sorry for leaving this morning without saying goodbye."

"Was it something I said, old chap?"

"No, not at all. The truth is I was scared."

"Scared?"

"Yes. Someone—I think it was Daphne—was sitting next to my bed in the middle of the night, reciting a poem about fish."

Willard is silent.

"She frightened me. I ran because I didn't understand what was happening or why."

"Was it a poem about a fish who jumps out of the water?"

"Yes, that's the one."

Willard looks away for a moment while he takes this in.

"I'm sorry she scared you, old chap. Daph's still dealing with her guilt and anger about Georgie's passing, and she sometimes does stuff she used to do for Georgie to help her relive some of her memories. It's hard to explain. Georgie heard Daph reading that poem out loud one evening, and he immediately believed it was about him. He thought he was the little fish jumping for joy out of the water the poem refers to."

Shoot me now.

"Right. In that case I can understand why it's important to her."

"Can I be honest with you about something which is to remain between you and me?"

"Please do, Willard."

"Daph confided in me that she feels some of Georgie's energy in you. It will no doubt sound crazy, and Daph doesn't understand how it's possible, but she feels what she feels."

"Aha. Well, that helps explain last night's events."

And that makes my escape from their problems all the more heartless.

"I understand why the whole shooting match would be so scary to you, old chap. Most people would feel the same if they were to spend time in our little circus here. But I have a question for you, if I may."

"Fire away."

"Something struck me about your story. You told me that you fell into the river in an unfortunate accident when you were out walking. However, this morning you were once again back in the drink. You'd clearly jumped in of your own accord. Well, that's a long way from normal, even in these parts. What's going on, old chap?"

Shit. The truth is circling me like a hungry wolf searching for an easy kill. Will honesty set me free, or will it become a noose around my neck? I remind myself this is all but a dream. So it's a safe place to practice opening up to another human, and right now I can't think of a better human to practice with.

"It's hard to explain, but here goes. Yesterday, I jumped into the river to escape my life. I'd had enough, and I believed the river would destroy me. More than that, I hoped it would. However, in my moment of despair the river did something for me which I wasn't expecting. It accepted me. I felt at peace for the first time in my life."

"Oh yes? How did that happen?"

"It listened to me, and made me feel at home. So, by the time you found me beside the river and saved me from freezing to death, I was a very different person to the one who'd jumped in."

"Right, understood. And today?"

"Today, I was running scared after that little incident upstairs. After I walked out the door, I didn't know where to run to. All I knew was I couldn't return to my old life and my old problems. But as I racked my brain, my list of options seemed to be non-existent. There was only one place left for me to go, so I jumped straight back into the river."

"I see."

Why isn't Willard running from me, terrified? I'm opening up in a way I've never opened up to anyone about things which must surely cast me in a crazy light. He should be the one running for the river.

"So the river treated you like an old friend who accepts absolutely everything about you?" Willard enquires.

"Exactly! How did you know that?"

"Little Georgie called the river his old friend, his best friend. He used to say it still loved him even when he was naughty."

Ignorance is not Bliss

Alice returns with a first-aid kit. She sits down next to me with her customary efficiency and starts clearing the blood from around my mouth with cotton wool.

"Right. I am going to apply the Dettol next. Get ready for the pain. Three, two one."

Before I can say anything, intense pain takes over all my bodily functions and I can't talk. All I can do is wait for the tide to turn.

"Why don't you go put the kettle on," Alice says to Willard, who obeys like a well-trained dog.

"I want to talk to you about last night," Alice says with gravity.

I nod as a tear of pain runs down my face. I suspect there will be more to follow once Alice is finished with me.

"I'm sorry for losing my heid with you, laddy. My heid was mince last night. You weren't to know it, but that song carries very very bad connotations for me."

I nod again like the helpless mute I am, and try to look forgivable.

"It all started at a karaoke night at the local pub, the Pig & Hare, around a year ago. It was just after wee

Georgie's passing. A bunch of my local mates thought I should get out for some fun, as the atmosphere in the house was so heavy and sad at that time."

I know this is important. I'm hanging on every word Alice is sharing.

"And it worked. I was having fun for the first time in donkey's years. To do something normal with friends was just what I needed after what had happened here. Anyway, our nearest neighbor, Donny the Duke of Sutherland, was also out that evening. And he was called up to the stage to sing a random song in the karaoke. The song that was selected for him to sing was that 'Who the Fuck is Alice?' song you were singing last night."

Could the guilt be any heavier to bear?

"Donny sang the words that came on the screen, very badly mind you. However, instead of singing the chorus as 'Who the Fuck is Alice?' like the original song, he changed the words to 'Where the Fuck was Alice?'"

Alice pauses with the exhaustion of a marathon runner who has hit the wall and is unsure if they can finish the race.

"It didn't take a genius to figure out what that creep Donny was saying through that bloody song. He was questioning where I'd been when little Georgie walked off that day. He was suggesting to the whole community that I was to blame for Georgie's death, which was the horrible thought I'd been fighting hard against myself. The guilt was strangling me, and I ran out of there heartbroken."

I feel Alice's pain.

"So ever since that evening, that song is like a living nightmare for me. I can't stand to hear it."

A tear runs down my cheek for my part in compounding Alice's pain. I'll never forgive myself for laughing at Alice's reaction to the song. Note to self: ignorance is not bliss when you find out later what a twat you've been. If the little fish were here, he'd no doubt explain to me that the people we are most scared of are usually more scared than we are. There must have been so many other situations in my life I've misread simply because others' fear scared me.

"Willard has a heart of gold. He would never have knowingly been a part of something which caused me pain like this. So I understand no one is to blame for last night's unfortunate singing incident, including you. You weren't to know what that song means to me. And besides, you've got bucket-loads of your own stuff to deal with. One fall into the river may be an accident, but falling into the river twice in two days is no accident. It's obvious you're in your own world of trouble."

I walk over to Alice and put my arms around her, giving her a proper hug. She reciprocates with warmth.

"I'm so sorry, Alice."

It feels good. I'm getting better at this apologizing gig. Alice starts crying. I join her.

Willard Has an Idea

Willard returns with two cups of tea. I don't fancy my chances of drinking anything hot for a while given the sensitive state my mouth is in. Alice and I wipe the tears from our eyes, and she excuses herself to get on with some work, leaving Willard and me alone.

Willard doesn't ask why Alice and I were crying, which shows remarkable restraint. Like a stereotypical aristocrat from a bygone era, this strange fish has inhuman control of his emotions on occasion. He sips his tea slowly in deep thought.

"Old chap, the most wondrous idea occurred to me while I was making tea. Are you in the mood to dream big?"

I nod and smile, knowing this is all but a dream.

"Piecing puzzles together has always been a passion of mine. There's something enchanting about putting the final piece of the puzzle in place, and allowing it to make sense of all the other pieces. So I've been pondering a few random and unrelated pieces of our respective puzzles, to see if they may fit together in some way."

"Go on."

"Righty-o. Well, firstly, we have your strange connection with the river which brought you to us. We know you weren't in a good place when you jumped into the river—well, twice—and that the river is somehow helping you through your challenges. Secondly, there's Daph's belief that there's a connection between you and our little Georgie, wherever he is now. It's another inexplicable one, but let's accept it as a given for now. And, finally, we have Daph and my need to say goodbye to Georgie, which we've not been able to achieve by ourselves after all this time. Bear with me. It may appear there's no logical way to connect all our stories together. However, I then realized there's in fact a simple connection when you delve deeper," Willard says with excitement building in his voice.

"Oh yes?"

This seems important.

"You want to move on with your life in a more positive way. And Daph and I want to move on from Georgie's passing so we can live better lives again. So the common denominator in our stories is that we all want to live our lives in a more positive way."

"There's no arguing with that. We're all ready for a better tomorrow."

"Yes. And the common character connecting us together is the river. It brought you to us, it played its role in little Georgie's journey, and Daph feels this connection between Georgie, you, and the river."

"When you put it like that, yes, the river is at the heart of everything."

"So what if we were to allow the river to give us all what we want?"

"Allow it to?"

"Yes, stop fighting it, and start believing in it."

I need to take a deep breath. Willard seems to have inexplicable insight into what I've been through to be here.

"That does sound like a magical idea. How?"

"OK. So my idea is we bring the river into our lives in a bigger way."

"Aha. Please explain."

"An event, Freddy. I think we should arrange a charity fundraiser to support your river swim all the way to, wait for it, the North Sea, which is a mere hundred miles downstream. I know it sounds extreme and slightly mad, but that seems like a good match for you, old chap. I'm not being funny, but you're not the stay-at-home type."

He's right. If only I'd recognized this obvious truth earlier in my life.

"I hear you."

"Daph, Alice and I could help arrange everything. We're blessed with strong local support through a community group who helped with the search for Georgie when he was lost. And they helped us deal with the aftermath of his passing. I know they'd love to be involved in this project as it's right up their street. And I think it would be helpful for Daph to be involved in some way to help get her through her current funk. If you're OK with it, I suggest we arrange the event in little Georgie's honor. It would allow both Daph and I to focus on something positive while we work at saying goodbye. And that's the genius of this idea, if I do say so myself—

we all help each other to get what we need. What do you think, old chap?"

A hundred miles to the North Sea! How did the me of yesterday find himself at the center of this mad dream?

I think about all that Willard, Daphne and Alice have done for me: the way they've forgiven me without a second thought, the way they've helped me when I most needed help, saved me when I needed saving, their brave honesty with me, their trust in me despite it all. It's a no brainer. I nod like I've never nodded before.

The Idea Becomes a Thing

After I've had a few quiet hours to recover by the fire, there's a loud knock at the living room door. Willard walks in, followed by Alice, and then a few seconds later Daphne follows, dragging her heals like a naughty teenager who's been told to join a family outing against her will. They sit down at a nearby table.

"Over here, old chap. We've got some planning to do."

Willard sounds like a duke for the first time since I met him. This persona must be lying there beneath his mask, genetically ready to emerge when he's excited about organizing something.

"I'd like to welcome you all to our inaugural planning meeting for Project River To Sea. In this meeting we'll cover what needs to be done to kick this project off as soon as possible, and to get Freddy on his merry way downstream."

It's off-putting to hear my river movements being talked about so formally. Willard makes it sounds so normal, so not what I was thinking when I threw my body into the dangerous river without a second thought. Despite my reservations, I nod and smile as surely I owe this to Willard after all he's done for me.

"But first, a brief recap on what this idea is all about. Freddy here is going to swim all the way to the North Sea in little Georgie's honor to raise money for charity. It's a do or die mission which will allow us to say goodbye to Georgie while making a difference. Freddy's insanity will hopefully inspire others to make positive changes in their lives, although we probably need a large-print disclaimer saying we don't endorse river swimming in the Scottish winter. Yes, now I think about it, let's disclaim the hell out of that. Does anyone have any questions about the idea?"

"Is Freddy feeling right in the head?" asks a concerned Alice.

No, but I live in hope this dream will end soon.

"Never better thanks," I say with all the cheerfulness I can muster despite the fact I'm drowning in Willard's sub-current.

"Right, key action points," Willard continues. "Alice, are you happy to round up the Project Lost Child group for a music festival at the river the day after tomorrow? There must be a local band or two we can drag along to enliven the mood."

The day after tomorrow? This is very sudden all of a sudden.

"Aye, roger that, Captain," replies Alice with a salute.

"Daph, are you happy to organize the setting up of a small stage, streamers, and a banner next to the launch spot? Your creative input will make all the difference."

Daphne nods without an iota of enthusiasm.

"Superb, thanks darling. And Freddy and I will head into Coldstream this morning to buy Freddy a wetsuit at the adventure store, as well as the other equipment and provisions he'll need to stay alive. A hundred miles in the Tweed at this time of year is the equivalent of hiking a thousand miles in the Arctic, so let's make sure old Freddy here makes it there alive. What say you to that, sir?"

I say this current is moving a wee bit fast for me, Captain.

"I say count me in, and yes, surviving would be a welcome bonus. Thanks for factoring that goal in."

"Well said, old chap. OK, unless there's anything else, let's make Project River To Sea happen. Thanks for your time, crew. Meeting adjourned."

Alice and Daphne march out of the room in platoon formation.

"Righty-o, Freddy, let's drive into town to sort out that wetsuit for you."

"Okey dokey, boss."

Willard and I get into his massive tank of a four-wheel drive, and drive the few miles into Coldstream. I'd forgotten that the rest of the world was still going about its business while I've been in my own world the past couple of days. As we drive through town, it's fascinating to watch the Coldstream locals toing and froing about their lives. This part of the world appears to be filled with smurf-like people who wander around looking twee, but who don't do much else. I wonder if they're all actors here to complete a scene which showcases what an engaged community they are. Or maybe they're just props to help my dream find the right tributary to take me wherever I need to go.

Willard parks in front of an adventure equipment store and leaps out of the car. We enter the front door at a pace of knots as Willard's frenetic energy is unstoppable now that he has a cause to focus upon.

Before I know it, Willard whistles loudly to get a sales person's attention. His piercing whistle scares the living daylights out of me, and makes me wonder where the nearest toilet is. But no sales person arrives. Unperturbed, Willard whistles again, this time louder and with growing agitation. His whistle grates like fingernails clawing across a blackboard, and I wince with embarrassment. Once again, no one hears him, for which I'm grateful. Sadly, this inspires him to whistle even louder. Someone please get me out of here. This time he's more successful in gaining someone's attention. A large scowling woman approaches us swiftly and without a spring in her step.

"Are you the whistler?" the shop assistant asks me without saying hello.

"That's me. I'm the whistler," explains Willard proudly. "We're customers in need of service, or have you not met a customer before?"

Beam me up, Scottie. This inner aristocrat in Willard is scaring me.

"You certainly got my attention, *sir*. Next time I'll kindly ask you to keep your whistling to yourself. You're not our only customer, *sir*," she explains, clearly ready to punch Willard in the face. It's apparent we've found ourselves another angry Scot. If only Scotland could bottle its anger, it would have an export industry to rival its whiskey sales.

"Now you're here, we'd like your best wetsuit for this fellow, please."

She stares me up and down with disdain.

"Sorry, *sir*, we don't have any wetsuits in the gentleman's size. I bid you good day."

She gives us both a fake smile, which translates into "Fuck off!" in all languages without the need for an interpreter, turns, and walks briskly away.

"Well I'll be," Willard says, shaking his head.

"Not to worry. There are lots of adventure shops around here, Willard. Let's go somewhere else."

Willard throws me the car keys and winks.

"Good idea, old chap. I'll meet you in the car," he whispers as he tiptoes off like an autistic Bond villain.

Eager to escape further embarrassment, I head out to the car and await Willard's return. It's not a surprise when Willard runs out of the shop a few minutes later with a brand new wetsuit in his hands.

"Drive! Drive!" he shouts as he jumps into the car.

Oh great. My new friend is a bona fide thief. I sure know how to pick 'em.

I drive like a lunatic away from the store and out of Coldstream, hopefully never to return again. It was one shopping trip that little town will never forget. I expect we'll be reading about two outlaws with a whistling problem in the newspapers in the coming days.

"I can't wait for Miss Uppity Ass to discover the little message I left her where this wetsuit used to be displayed," Willard says proudly.

I can only imagine.

The Madding Crowd

The next day is a dreamy blur. The house becomes a hive of organizational activity in preparation for the start of my swim. Alice rounds up a cast of thousands from across the community with her typical finesse. She's even been handing out flyers in the street in Coldstream which read: "Swim to the North Sea for Georgie. Join us at the river for an event to remember." She must have been a marketing genius in another lifetime because almost everyone she's connecting with is reading the flyer, raising at least one eyebrow, and confirming they'll be there to witness the mayhem. Roll up, folks, I am the mayhem.

Daphne is also busy, although I doubt her heart is really in it. She's spent the morning in the kitchen baking some cookies for the launch festival. The cookies smell OK but not great, and represent the bare minimum viable product, just like the amount of effort which went into baking them. Let's hope the punters are so hungry they won't notice.

Willard is dividing his time between researching every nook and cranny of the river's pathway to the North Sea, and giving me pep talks as if we're both characters out of *Chariots of Fire*. He clearly thinks he's the coach and I'm one of the budding athletes, but I'm not sure if I'm the one who won't run on Sundays. Launch day is on Sunday, so it's a detail which seems to matter. I prefer it when Willard sticks with the river research, as the pep talks are a bit over the top. This morning he said to me, "You can glorify God by peeling a potato if you peel it to perfection. Imagine what you can do with a river!" The little fish would like Willard as they both enjoy handing out customized motivational quotes at regular intervals. I sometimes wonder if they are one and the same person, or, rather, fish. Anything is possible in this dream, in this place.

Sunday arrives in no time, and a long line of us march towards the river carrying all that's needed to set up the launch festival. Willard catches up to me like an enthusiastic puppy.

"Exciting day, old chap. What a wonderful opportunity we have to make a difference: you with your swimming, and us with the charity. Today is a gift, I tell you, a gift!"

So why does it feel like I'm the one inside the wrapping paper?

When we arrive at the river, we find a small crowd already huddled together, talking in hushed tones as if something big is about to happen. They all seem to know one another.

"Morning, old team, cracking to see you all!" Willard bellows. "Today is going to be epic; epic I tell you. Everyone, this is Freddy, the hero of the hour. Freddy, this is everyone, legends, each and every one of them."

"Morning guys!" I call out with as much enthusiasm as I can muster, following Willard's boisterous lead.

"Thanks for being here, team," Willard continues. "Now we've got a wee bit of setting up to do. It would be stupendous if you could all lend a hand please."

Alice takes control of affairs, and before we know it there's a stage in place as well as a coffee point, and a portable toilet. It's fast evolving into a miniature version of Glastonbury. However, there's just one problem: I'm the star of the show. This thought hits me like a ton of bricks. What was I thinking saying yes to an event where I'm the center of attention like this? Have I not met myself? Ever since school I've been one of those people who are more scared of public speaking than of death.

The shock reminds me of my first time in the limelight when I was a six-year-old at school. I was to play the part of one of the seven dwarfs in a performance of *Snow White and the Seven Dwarfs*. My role was Speedy the dwarf. All I had to do was to cycle out onto the stage on cue, and to keep cycling across to the other side of the stage when the other dwarfs called out "Where's Speedy going?" in unison. The idea was to create the impression Speedy was so busy speeding around that he couldn't stop to talk. My role was written into the play to instill some light-hearted comedy into an otherwise dry school production. It all sounded so fun and simple. However, my moment in the sun backfired spectacularly when I misjudged the layout of the stage. On cue, I sped out from behind the curtains at the right time but in the wrong direction. With excitement in my heart, I cycled towards the front of the stage rather than across it. This resulted in disaster when l cycled off the front of the stage, and landed on top of the unsuspecting front row of the audience. I'll never forget their screams when Speedy the dwarf attempted to fly, but crashed head first into their laps. Along with a few of those poor audience members, l had to be carted out of the theater for urgent medical attention. l know they'll always be emotionally scarred from coming to watch the school play that year. l was. And ever since, I've tried to avoid the limelight at all costs—for my own sake and that of innocent by-standers.

Large numbers of people are now arriving along the river pathway. Each new arrival adds to the energy of anticipation, making each member of the crowd more interested by what all the other members of the crowd must be waiting around for. It's like a British queue forming in which no one really knows what they're waiting for, but, by god, it will be amazing once they get there.

The band start unpacking their instruments on stage. l wonder if they're unemployed locals as there aren't many talented bands available with only two days' notice.

"Who's the band?" l ask Willard, who's bouncing around talking to people like a sociable ping-pong ball.

"Oh, l think they're called Friends of Frightened Rabbit. Alice knows their story, old chap."

I'm floored. I've heard about these guys. They're a group of musicians who came together to play Frightened Rabbit's music to celebrate the life of Scott Hutchison. The subtext to the tribute band's mission is to promote singing your troubles away as a powerful strategy to deal with mental health challenges. The river DJ will be happy to hear their music, and is no doubt a part of this scene in some way.

The band's lead singer, whom I don't recognize, is already talking with the crowd.

"Hey, guys, welcome to this unusual but epic event. We only got the call about it a couple of days ago. We happened to be touring this part of Scotland anyway, so as luck would have it, here we are."

The crowd are still talking amongst themselves, so this fellow's comments are going largely unnoticed.

"We were told that there's a guy here today who's going to swim all the way to the North Sea to honor Scott's memory."

Scott's memory? Well, it's now clear how Alice managed to round up so many people so fast. These people are gathered here to celebrate someone far more important than me.

"What a grand idea. What an amazing journey. We knew straightaway we needed to be a part of this. Where is this crazy fellow? Harry, I think his name is."

I glance around for an escape route. As Sod's law would have it, the crowd is now tuned into every word the singer is saying. Countless nameless faces are searching for Harry, the freakish star of the show who's here to make everyone laugh with his crazy novelty idea. One woman nearby says, "He must be mad swimming to the North Sea.

You wouldn't catch me doing that for all the tea in China." She must have a much higher IQ than me. The six-year-old child within me is preparing to cycle onto stage from behind the curtain, to deliver the world whatever it wants from me even if that is a crazed river swimmer on a mission. The adult in me acknowledges the six-year-old child within me, but still suspects this won't end well.

Oh fuck it. I walk out onto the stage. The singer greets me with a warm friendliness, and genuine excitement.

"Nice to meet you, Harry. So what inspired this crazy journey? And were you sober when you came up with the idea?"

Drunk Harry. Maybe this is my mask? Or maybe I'm a different person in this dream.

"Sadly, yes I was sober. My inspiration for this journey is a long story but, in the words of Sir Edmond Hilary, 'It was there,' or, rather, 'It is there.'"

The audience is silent. Tough crowd. At the very least I thought that deserved a few pity laughs.

"Oh yes, what's that?"

"The river, the Tweed, it's there," I say, pointing at the river as if this makes everything clear.

The crowd's awkward silence cuts the air like a blunt knife. I'm not the star of the show the crowd wants or deserves. It's like *Snow White and the Seven Dwarfs* all over again, and this time I'm starring as Dopey. And, once again, I'm crashing off the stage when the job description requested a leading man. I want to cover my face and walk backwards off the stage. Maybe no one will notice if I do.

"Aye, that it is," replies the singer in full knowledge that I'm not the full quid. "OK, let's hear it for Harry, everyone."

Thank you. My time on stage is cut short for the greater good.

I limp off the stage, searching for somewhere to curl up and die. Willard greets me at the bottom of the stairs and is still smiling at me despite it all. Did he not see my onstage performance? He puts his arm around my shoulder with parental care, and hands me my new wetsuit.

Swim for Scott

I put one foot into my wetsuit, then the other, and I pull upwards as hard as I can. However, it quickly becomes apparent that my wetsuit is a few sizes too small. Why do I get the feeling the angry shop assistant is getting the last laugh here? If she were here now she'd no doubt explain, "I told you, *sir*, that we didn't have anything in *sir's* size. The wetsuit you are wearing makes the gentleman look like a pregnant pole-vaulter, *sir*." And she'd be right. This wetsuit is made for an anorexic dwarf with a small willy, and I'm not anorexic. Note to self: I'll need to explain to everyone involved how cold the river is.

With a final heave, I lift the wetsuit up onto my shoulders and stretch it in ways its creator never imagined possible as I forcibly insert my arms. My upper body is in. I stand taut like a water bomb ready to burst. My chances of zipping the wetsuit all the way up at the back are thin to non-existent. It's clear I need to get used to the idea of a having a cold back when I swim off into the sunset.

Willard has noticed my dilemma and walks over to help.

"Turn around, old chap. I'll zip you up so you can be on your way."

Willard starts with the softly softly approach, but the zip remains firmly in place like a stubborn child who won't listen. I know that zip isn't going anywhere anytime soon, but Willard's innate optimism won't let him see this. He steps up the force and pulls it with all his energy. However, there's still no movement, apart from additional pressure on my already pulverized groin area.

"It's stuck!" I squeal like a soprano.

"It sure is!" Willard squeals back like a soprano.

Willard's incessantly bad jokes are growing on me. He's like a comic cavoodle bounding around trying to please everyone no matter what they think of him. The thing about cavoodles is they find everything life-enhancing. Every person, every object, every dog biscuit. However, truth be known, if there were a subtext to cavoodle communication it would read something along the lines of: "Please like me, please like me, please like me!" For all Willard's aristocratic mannerisms, he just wants to be liked and patted on the head by everyone he meets. He wants to be told "Well done, boy," and thrown a biscuit every now and then. It's lucky I understand cavoodle.

"Well done for trying, Willard, but that zip is staying put. I'm already exploding out of this thing, so more pressure won't help. It's not your fault at all. It's just the wrong size."

"Right you are, old chap. I blame Miss Uppity Ass for this. Sorry it's on the wee side."

'It's all good. I may wee inside later," I respond, playing his bad-joke game, which is also my game.

We giggle together like naughty schoolboys.

"Righty-o, old chap, it's time to send you to the ball. The river beckons."

The band are playing a song to the now adoring crowd. "Swim Till You Can't See Land" is rearing its head again. Of course it is. I'm about to live the lyrics; well, apart from not seeing land. As the band reaches the chorus, the crowd join in and bellow out in unison, "So Swim Till You Can't See Land, Oh Swim!"

That's my calling. It's time to give these words the meaning they deserve. I walk out into the crowd in my far-too-tight wetsuit which is not quite done up at the back, and I attempt a natural smile. The crowd gaze at me perplexed.

"Well, that's a new look," I hear a woman nearby whisper. "I wonder who his personal stylist is?"

"The hero of the hour really needs to take it easy on the cheeseburgers," contributes another charitable crowd member.

The oh-fuck-o-meter has maxed out. I have two options: run for my life, or make like the emperor in his new clothes. But I still can't see an exit route, so I appear to have only one option. "You are a fish happily returning to water," I hear the little fish's voice whisper in the wind. As if reading my thoughts, the river gushes welcomingly in the background, and I feel the tension leave my body. A smile emerges from the shadowy corners of my face, and I manage to wave at the crowd. The moment I drop the sourpuss impression, the crowd starts to clap me on. Is that all there is to it? Just go with the flow, and the flow goes with you. That little bloody fish does know a thing or two. Like a wave building, the clapping becomes louder and louder as the crowd's excitement builds. And before I know it, the crowd is going wild for the hero of the hour.

With a final wave, I walk down to the infamous beach where Willard found both Georgie and I, and I wade out into the river. Moving in any direction within this wetsuit is close to impossible, so I let my body drop into the slow-moving current which carries me away with the gracefulness of an old tug boat. The crowd cheer with the same enthusiasm an Olympic Gold medalist would generate while doing a lap of honor. On the nearest riverbank, a few of them are walking alongside me as I drift away. One of them is holding up a banner which says "Swim for Scott." Another is holding up a banner which says "Swim for Georgie." But where's the "Swim for Freddy" banner? The one I was hoping for.

These signs read like warning signs from above, here to slap me in the face. I get it. I've once again become caught up in a sub-current. A part of me isn't surprised. If I'm being honest with myself, it's been a theme all my life—putting my own wants and desires beneath those of others who need help. Willard is a case in point. He needs help, and I believe he needs my help. He needs to grieve and accept that he isn't to blame for Georgie's death. Daphne is another one. She needs help, and I believe she needs my help. She needs to forgive herself, Willard, and everyone else for Georgie's passing. Alice also needs help, and I believe she needs my help. She's been carrying the weight of Willard and Daphne's problems on her own shoulders for far too long, and she's suffering vicarious trauma. And that's just the living. The dead have just as many needs. Little Georgie needs to be remembered as the happy boy he was, rather than as the cause of so much upset. One more for my "to do" list. And then there's Scott from Frightened Rabbit, who needs to be remembered for all the joy he gave others through his wonderfully honest lyrics. His music needs to be celebrated to allow his valuable lessons to continue making a difference for people who need an empathetic ear. So many people are in need of help.

All of these people are important characters in my story. All their stories matter. However, once again I've made the main character of my story a supporting character when he deserved the leading role.

"Do it for Scott. Swim till you can't see land for Scott!" calls out an enthusiastic supporter as I drift away.

Two Steps Back

Floating at the same pace as a crowd of at least a hundred people who are walking along next to you is like flying to the Moon while being attached to planet Earth. One of them is ringing a loud Swiss cowbell as if this were a downhill skiing event in Europe. From where I'm floating it rings out like a warning signal, crying out, "You are living someone else's life again!" What part of goodbye did these people not understand?

Why do I always allow this to happen? How do I end this cycle? I feel something shifting inside me, and it isn't breakfast.

I've had enough of this dream. With a final wave at the adoring crowd, I take a deep breath and dive underwater. It's time to turn this group outing into a solo mission. I change direction underwater and start swimming away in a different direction, my direction, upstream. I swim and swim until I'm far from the madding crowd, and then I swim some more. The freedom of escaping the crowd and heading towards whatever is coming next is exhilarating. The joy of my escape inspires me to jump out of the water as I'd seen the Jimmy Carr the salmon do the other day. Flying high above the water, I can see the crowd in the distance, searching the riverbank for any signs of the mysterious Harry who's disappeared into the river. Good luck with that, guys. Harry has left the building.

My underwater movement is free, fast and easy. Swimming towards my freedom is empowering, and ... unhuman. Remembering my fishy dreams of the past, I turn around to check which species I am, as you do. And, lo and behold, it's a fish tail I see wagging away at my rear. Whatever! This minor detail no longer surprises me. I close my eyes. Fish or human, the main thing is the peace I feel all around me. The river feels like home.

Everything becomes silent. I allow myself to float along without any more effort. I've exerted too much energy already, and I'm ready for some easiness from now on. The water caresses my scales like my grandmother tickling my back before bedtime when I was a child. This place is much better than life above water. A voice reverberates through the water and into my mind. "You can't go back and change the beginning, but you can start where you are and change the ending." Is that a line from *Alice in Wonderland*? Am I in Wonderland? Little fish, is that you?

I open my eyes in the hope of seeing the little fish's smiley face, and hearing his words of wisdom. He'll no doubt be able to direct me to where I need to go next. However, I discover I'm once again a dry human! I'm sitting beside the river near the pathway where the launch festival was held. There are no crowds around. It's as if the launch festival never happened. It's as if I never happened.

I'm dizzy, and the river is unusually quiet. I feel as discombobulated as a lost shaman in the Scottish winter searching for someone to heal. I gaze at the river's shiny surface and see my human face reflected back at me. It's just me. There's no one else's face in there.

How did I get here? Working my way back through my memories of the launch party, the past few days at Willard's house, the charity swim planning, and the river incident with the duke, the answer strikes me like a bolt of lightning. I've been in a deep slumber since I sat down next to the river after escaping from the house. Everything that's happened since that moment was just a dream, a very realistic dream. And that means the last contact I had with Willard was when we bid each other goodnight prior to my ungracious exit after Daphne scared the bejesus out of me. As far as he's concerned, I've done a runner on him and his family after he opened his doors to help me. So I haven't made anything right at all. What a mind fuck.

A feeling of intense disappointment washes over me. My dream contained answers to so many of my problems, and, contrary to my initial reaction, the idea of swimming to the North Sea for charity excites me. As a next step, it's a lot more enticing than my non-existent list of alternatives. I should no doubt take note. The one thing I've got is time on my hands, so it's about time I learnt some lessons from my dreamt past which never happened.

The good news is my dream showed me where I've been going wrong—the patterns I keep repeating time and time again which are holding me back. So it's no longer a mystery that the mother of my problems is putting others ahead of myself. It's become so natural for me to repeat this pattern that other people have become comfortable incorporating me into their plans as though I'm an innocent bystander who's only there to help them. That's my fault, not theirs. I'm not giving a clear enough message to the world of what I want from my life. And, in the absence of my own clarity, people rightly assume I'm a piece of driftwood, built to go with the flow. It strikes me that people in my life even think they're helping me by generously incorporating me into their plans. I feel as though they're hijacking my life, but I do nothing to correct them. I go along with the whole charade without saying a word. And, worse, it occurs to me that I may have been actively searching for sub-currents which take me in new and interesting directions—always away from somewhere I don't want to be, rather than towards where I want to go.

On cue, the river DJ starts playing the Travis song "Driftwood," which I once saw performed live in concert. Even then, the lyrics of this song were important to me, but I didn't realize they were targeted at me. The words "Rivers turn to oceans / Oceans tide you home" cause a ripple around me, and then drift away with the current.

Thanks, river DJ, I get it. I'm a piece of driftwood, and my life is in pieces as a result of my aimless drifting through life. And I'm now unreachable. The only bridges which could have been used to get to me don't reach as far as I've wandered. I'm as alone as a human can be. I may as well be sitting on Mars.

I need this message to sink in. Hang on, I suspect there's something else in this message for me, but I'm not sure what it is. Little fish? Before the little guy can straighten it out, the words suddenly mean something to me, something big. Rivers turn to oceans, oceans tide you home. It's only the river DJ helping me in my hour of need by telling me what I need to do next. This river meets the North Sea which is an arm of the Atlantic Ocean a hundred miles downstream, so the river is telling me that reaching the North Sea will take me home. The idea of reaching the ocean excites me. It awakens something deep inside. Maybe this is why I jumped into this freezing cold, deadly river without a second thought. To find home. To find me.

It's time to say goodbye to the pattern I've been repeating. It's so damned simple. I've always wanted to help others, but I have a track record of finishing last when I do. The mistake I've been repeating, which has led me off course time and time again, is not having a clear plan for my own life. Here's my truth with its mask removed. It's time for a plan.

Man with a Plan

A sense of relaxation descends upon me once I realize what I need to do next. What a burden being lost has been! I'm tired of carrying the burden of a million potential pathways for my life, all of which may be right or wrong for me. All these potential lives have weighed heavy on my soul for years. I'm ready for the joy and simplicity which deciding upon one pathway brings.

With purpose in my stride, I march up the river pathway towards the house. I wonder how Willard will react when he sees me. Will he tell me to sod off like I deserve? If I were in his position, I'd be angry. I'd probably even use a few choice expletives to tell me where to stick it. After all, that's what swear words are for: moments of uncontrolled upset when ordinary words don't have enough kick. This is Willard's moment to rightfully pull a few heavy-hitters out of the bag.

I approach the front door, shaking with trepidation. I press the doorbell which rings out like a call for the hounds to attack the intruder at the gate. I hope their rifle isn't loaded.

Within seconds, Alice swings the door open with her usual gusto and welcomes me with a smile.

"Morning, shipmate! Where have you been? We thought you were still asleep after yesterday's exertions."

"Morning, Alice. Brilliant to see you," I say with a relieved smile. "I awoke early, so I went for a river stroll. It was dreamy down there this morning."

"What a wonderful idea. The river is a special place full of secrets."

"It is indeed. Oh, and by the way, Alice, I'm very sorry for singing that silly song last night. What a poor choice it was. Next time, I promise to stop drinking well before the karaoke machine is rolled out."

"Och, that's fine thanks, laddy. I'll tell you the story about why that song upsets me some time," replies a surprised Alice. "But for now, let's get you inside and I'll dish you up my famous black pudding and tattie breakfast. I guarantee you won't leave the breakfast table hungry."

"That sounds fabulous!"

Alice escorts me through to the living room where Willard is enjoying a lazy coffee and a newspaper. Being loaded and not having to work has its upsides.

"Morning, old chap!" he says, smiling.

I walk over to Willard and pull him out of his chair with a handshake. To his surprise, I give him a hug.

"I wanted to say a proper thank you for saving my life, Willard. I'll always remember your kindness, and I'll always be in your debt."

"You're welcome, old chap. It made my day being able to help you."

"And thank you for last night. I haven't laughed so hard in ages, although I'm sorry for upsetting Alice. That was the last thing I wanted to do."

"Ha, me too. I feel like I've run a marathon after all that laughing. You weren't to know that song would upset dear Alice. Besides, both of us clearly needed a good laugh."

I'm lucky. Willard didn't notice my escape efforts, or maybe he just has the good grace not to dwell upon my failings. Finally, I seem to have found the promised land of second chances. I hope no one noticed I didn't wipe my feet at the front door.

"Willard, an idea struck me last night which I'd like to run by you, Daphne and Alice if I may."

"I'm as interested as Pandora with a big shiny box in my hands. I'll go and round up the troops. Meet you back here in a jiffy."

The fire is still blazing like a controlled wildfire. There's no wood to replenish it anywhere in sight, and I've never seen Willard or Alice put any timber on the fire. How it remains so well fueled is a mystery to me. Maybe it uses things unsaid as its fuel of choice. There's an abundance in this household.

Willard marches in with Alice, and is followed by a tired Daphne who's dragging her feet and looking mighty unimpressed. This scene is starting exactly like the scene in my dream, with the one difference being I'm the one who initiated the scene rather than Willard. It's me in the driver's seat, and it's a big change.

"Morning, Daphne," I say with a smile.

Daphne nods without saying a word. There's no judgment from me this time. I now understand this is a woman in more pain than I'll ever comprehend.

The three of them sit down around the living room table and look up expectantly.

"The floor is yours, old chap."

"Thanks, guys," I begin. "I've got this idea I want to discuss with you."

"Get to the point, laddy. I've got jobs to get on with," hurries Alice with typical impatience.

"Good idea. I will, Alice. So, the background to this idea is …"

"Laddy, I said get to the point, not please bore the pants off us with a long backstory. My grave is waiting."

"OK, got it. My idea is I jump back into the river and swim all the way from here to the North Sea, which is one hundred miles downstream."

I pause to gauge their interest like a magician who's just done the big reveal. They'd make brilliant poker players, as they aren't giving much away, although Daphne looks like she's about to cry. Maybe I should put the rabbit back in the hat where it belongs, and awkwardly change the subject. It's a skillset I've perfected over the years, so it would take minimal effort. No, this is important. I need to think like the little fish.

"And there's more. I was thinking the four of us could turn this river swim into a charity fund-raising event for a local charity. In fact, I have one in mind."

I pause for someone to ask me which charity, but no one does.

"I have in mind an as yet unformed charity which helps families who've lost a young child to deal with the grief and pain, and to help them experience joy again after their loss. The reason the Little Georgie Trust is destined to be so successful is because it's run by two incredible people who understand what it's like to lose a child."

The three of them continue to stare at the table in a contemplative silence. Spindly things have rolled through the desert with more energy, so this could still go either way. I hear the little fish's voice emerge from somewhere unknown: "With confidence, you've won before you start. Keep going." OK, little fish. I smile at the three of them, and allow my enthusiasm for the idea enlighten my face.

"And it will be fun. We could organize a music festival at the start and end of the event; well, assuming I make it all the way to the North Sea. We could invite the locals along for some music and dancing. As you guys keep telling me, the social scene here is slow, so let's turn it up to eleven."

My enthusiasm is once again met by a wall of silence, which is starting to feel like an opposing current.

"What does everyone think?"

Willard and Alice glance towards Daphne for a sign. They're waiting to see how she reacts before saying anything. Daphne is the game-changer here. But it remains unclear whether she'll recognize this opportunity for what it is: a doorway to change for all of us.

Oh no! Tears are welling up in Daphne's eyes. I must have done too much hitting on nerves, and too little inspiring positive action. Note to self: the Little Georgie Trust idea was a step too far for Daphne. I should have thought more about her perspective as a grieving mother in pain.

But after the world's longest and most pregnant pause, Daphne nods ever so slightly. It's the most beautiful gesture I've ever seen. Willard and Alice high five me, and each other, before putting their arms around Daphne.

"Count us in, old chap," says Willard. "You tell us what you need, and we'll make it happen."

In the Driver's Seat

The idea takes on a life of its own. It's unique enough to attract interest from most people we engage with across the community. And most people have lost someone close to them, or know someone who has lost someone close, so there's a strong connection to Willard and Daphne's plight from the get go. What's more troubling is the mental-health angle. As we speak to more and more people, we discover that mental illness is a true pandemic behind closed doors. More people are in trouble out there than any of us realized.

We speak to one lady who is talking very fast, too fast for us to fully understand everything she's saying. We ask her if we can please join her for a cup of tea in the hope it will help calm her nerves. However, she sits right on the edge of her seat while we sit with her. She seems to think we're there to assess her mental health.

"Please don't send Mary back. No one understands Mary there. They just want to prod Mary with their instruments, looking for answers. There are no answers, only questions."

My heart breaks a little for Mary as it's obvious she's been on her own painful and treacherous journey. I wish I could stop her being poked and prodded at in the future, but I now understand only Mary can make those changes in her life.

"You're so right. Questions are the only answers, Mary. You are very wise. Hopefully we'll see you at the river to celebrate asking the right questions together," I say, while holding her hand. A tear runs down her cheek as she nods through the pain.

One older fellow we mention the river swim to asks if he can please join me for the swim. He wants to show all his fellow retirement village friends that he still has it, whatever it is. I'm tempted to say yes, why not, but the thought of a ninety-year-old passing away while swimming with me isn't the picture I'm aiming for, and this picture is about what I want this time. When we explain to him that it would be unsafe for him to join, he smiles and explains that the more unsafe it is the more enthusiastic he is to come along. I like him all the more for saying that. I hope I'm like him when I'm ninety.

With the memory of the wetsuit-buying fiasco from my dream fresh in my mind, I decide to take the lead when buying a new wetsuit in Coldstream. Willard asks if he can tag along. I'm unsure about the idea at first, but I figure it's best if we rewrite my dream for the better together, so I say yes. We drive into Coldstream in Willard's four-wheel drive like the one in my dream, and we park at the outdoor adventure store from my dream. The shop assistant will no doubt be the same gruff Scottish lady from my dream, so I prepare myself for the worst. This business of rewriting imagined history is not for the fainthearted.

As we enter the store, the lady in question is dealing with a customer, and she is indeed: a) Scottish, b) grumpy, and c) ready to vent. We walk over to the wetsuit section where a small wetsuit is displayed on the mannequin. My manhood shrivels knowingly. The memories of the pain that wetsuit caused will live on. Within seconds Willard is becoming impatient, and he's waiting for the shop assistant with growing agitation. If only I can get her attention first. Oh no! Willard is whistling for someone's attention, just like in my dream. Groundhog day at the shops has begun. And it continues, with Willard whistling louder and louder to get someone's attention.

On cue, the sales assistant, who's now finished with another customer, marches towards Willard with the same angry energy I remember in my dream.

"Yes? Are you the whistler?" she asks with venom.

"I am indeed. We'd like some help over here if that's not too much trouble. We're customers. Nice to meet you." I wonder if he realizes he's pushing her buttons. I suspect he does. Even the best of us have our faults.

The little fish's voice fades in from wherever the hell he is right now. "Focus on your race and your race alone if you want to win it." Thanks, little fish, I hear you. I'm a key participant here, so I don't need anyone else's permission to step in before Willard can wreak any more havoc. Permission granted, Freddy. It's time to rewrite this scene the way I'd like it to play out.

"Thanks for coming over. Is this your shop?" I ask with a smile.

"Nay, it's the big boss's, the Duke of Sutherland. He lives on an estate nearby," responds the shop assistant in a hurry.

The penny drops. Donny the Duke of Sutherland is the lunatic Willard fought with—well, in my dream— and is also the cause of so much upset across large swathes of the community. He was even the one who upset Alice at the karaoke event.

"Aha. Well, I wanted to say what a great job you're doing managing this huge store all by yourself. The Duke of Sutherland is a lucky man to have you working here, and I'll let him know as much the next time I see him."

The shop assistant is speechless. I'll warrant she's not been paid a compliment in many a year, and she's forgotten how to take one.

"Um. Thank you, sir," she responds. "And how can I help you?"

From that moment on, she provides us with exemplary customer service. When we're paying for the perfect-fitting wetsuit she helps us choose, she offers to donate her commission on the sale to the river-swim charity fundraiser. She even manages to smile throughout our dealings, which must be a major achievement after her long winter of discontent. By the end of our visit, her face is transformed like a crumpled piece of paper which has been lovingly unfolded to reveal a beautiful picture. Without her grumpy mask, she has a lovely face.

I'm in the driver's seat. One moment fixed—just thirty something years of moments to sort out.

Launching on Purpose

The rest of the launch planning proceeds smoothly. Willard rounds up all his aristocratic buddies, who appear keen to outbid one another with their donations to the Little Georgie Trust, recognizing an opportunity to appear to be the most generous members of the community. We thank them profusely for their kind and generous support, knowing full well they are really exclaiming to the world, "Look at me. You may be interested to hear that my willy is bigger than all their willies put together. You are welcome to measure it if you have a long tape measure handy. Oh, you don't have one? What a shame. Well, feel free to let everyone know. Tell the world. Massive is the only word that does it justice." The male ego is one of the most reliable catalysts for action the world has ever known.

Alice organizes the music and event logistics. I ask her about the possibility of rounding up Friends of Frightened Rabbit, and she says she'll do her best. When Alice says she'll do her best, I know she'll make it happen come hell or high water. I'm hoping for my sake it's high water rather than hell that's coming my way, although I understand now that both at the same time are more likely.

The most surprising development is that Daphne is making herself busy with the planning activities, and with far more gusto than in my dream. She's even in the kitchen sewing a banner which says "Swim for Georgie." To say she's happy would be a step too far, but she's getting involved and is sewing energetically. Maybe there's life in this old dog yet.

Launch day arrives in no time. The mood at the river is buoyant, as is the river, which gushes at everyone who gazes its way. If it were a person, it would make the perfect maître d' this morning, greeting everyone with: "Welcome all of you into my magical kingdom. I love all of you, and will be here if you need anything."

Alice over-delivers as usual, and has, of course, convinced Friends of Frightened Rabbit to join us. She wanted to surprise me, and the band are already setting up on the rough and ready river stage. The band members are real people, and they're far more personable in real life than in my dream, although I still suspect they may be the same people with masks on. The lead singer in particular looks, sounds, and moves like the lead singer in my dream, and despite being friendlier than in my dream, he peers at me with knowing glances every now and then.

It's time for me to kit up for my swim. I slip easily into my new wetsuit, and it fits like a glove. This is too good to be true.

The band are now talking to the crowd, and a sense of déjà vu washes over me. Is this really happening?

"Hi, guys, thanks for joining us today for this very special event which will raise funds for the Little Georgie Trust, an incredible cause which will make many people's lives better in their time of need," says the band's lead singer with warmth and confidence.

The crowd applauds.

"Would you believe today is happening because of one person, the hero of the hour. This man is bravely putting his body on the line to make a difference for real people who need help. Everyone please put your hands together for Freddy!"

At least he got my name right this time.

The crowd cheers. I'm struggling to shake the memory of the car crash that was my last onstage interview, even if it was in my dream. I tell myself to think little-fish-worthy thoughts. I am Freddy, the confident grown man who loves his life. That six-year-old who played the wayward dwarf cyclist cycled off a stage into an abyss never to return. It's a long walk, but I eventually arrive on stage next to the singer as the hero of the hour I was meant to be. It's been a long hour.

"Freddy, what inspired this craziness? And were you sober at the time?" he asks with a smile.

I collect myself, and remind myself that I'm in the driver's seat.

Honesty will set me free. It was one thing to take my mask off in the river, but I sense it is now time to take my mask off in front of other humans. It's too heavy to keep wearing, and I'm ready for better than yesterday.

"Thanks. Yes, I was sober, but I was feeling crazy. I knew something serious was wrong with my life, and I was as lost as a person can be. So I jumped into the river hoping it would take me somewhere better, somewhere away from where I was."

I gaze down at the audience. I'm surprised they aren't running away from me in fear. It's so unnatural to speak my truth like this from upon a pedestal. My heart is racing.

"But things turned out very differently that day than the disaster I was on track for. Because I was saved in every way possible. The river kept me alive for some reason, and then, my friend Willard saved me when he found me lying beside the river unable to move."

I wave at Willard who's welling up.

"So I'd been granted a second chance, even though I didn't believe I was worthy of it. I started asking myself how I could honor this second chance, and help repay Willard and Daphne's kindness. Step by step, I pieced together a plan to help me and a few others. So while we're raising funds for the Little Georgie Trust, and the funds will make a huge difference, today is also about me doing what I need to do to live a better life."

The crowd is silent. I assume they're judging me for being a suicidal freak. Hopefully someone will clear the exits to allow them to get away from me in an orderly manner.

"That's epic, Freddy," says the singer. "We're thankful you turned a dark day into something so positive, something so aligned with our mission to help people suffering from mental illness. Like you, Scott was a special guy, and he'd want his music to help as many people as possible. He would have supported this event one hundred per cent. Of course, being Scott, he would have had something self-deprecatingly funny to say about his role in all of this."

"Yes, he would. On that note, I'd like to explain to the ladies present that today is a very cold day. That is not a justification—just an explanation and an apology."

Applause and laughter erupts from the crowd. I even notice a few kindly smiles beaming in my direction.

That's my cue to exit. I high five all the band members, take a bow, and jog over to the river with a buoyant spring in my step. I wave goodbye to the crowd, and dive into the river with purpose. The cold water is cleansing, like a fresh new day full of limitless potential. I swim towards the main current, which is moving with strong but smooth momentum today. I allow it to take me where I want to go.

Freedom

I drift away. The cheers coming from the riverbank echo around the river, making it sound like a Wembley audience applauding an encore from a big-name act. I send a royal wave or two towards the adoring crowd. Unlike my dream, no one is following me this time. I am free. Escaping in my dream felt like my last roll of the dice. But today I've been released *en route* to somewhere better, somewhere I'm meant to be. Life is great when you're in an up cycle.

I relax into going with the flow because I finally understand this particular flow is heading in my direction. The river's warm and welcoming sounds replace the fading noises coming from the folk on the riverbank. I am home.

My body is in good hands. I imagine what it's like to be a molecule of water attached to all the other water molecules, operating as one large flowing entity. The amount of trust each molecule must have in the bigger entity is hard to fathom. They're all sacrificing their individuality for the greater good, without even knowing what the greater good is. It's comforting to be carried along by something which only exists because of the faith of its individual constituents. Carry me forwards, all ye faithful.

I'm shaken out of my relaxed state all too quickly. I'm barely out of sight of the crowd and the river is moving faster all of a sudden, a lot faster. I don't remember anyone warning me there were any dangerous sections around the bend. But I'm sure it's nothing to be worried about. Willard did all that research into how safe each part of the river is between here and the North Sea, and he didn't find anything noteworthy. Although I do wonder about his attention to detail. He's become a wonderful person, but if you've been waited on hand and foot all your life, you may overlook minor details—like where white-water rapids are located! So the chances of Willard missing a life-threatening risk around the corner are well above zero. It's time to double-check.

I push off the riverbed beneath me to reach a higher vantage point. It's hardly a Jimmy-Carr-the-salmon-worthy leap in the air, but immediately I can see that there are white-water rapids approaching, and serious ones at that. As Mark Twain once famously said, "It's not the things you don't know that get you into trouble, it's the things you thought you knew which ain't true." Life can turn on a dime, and it's turning on me right now.

My theory of relaxing into the flow as the best survival strategy when floating through white-water rapids has only been tested once upstream. And, if I'm honest with myself, I think lady luck played a major role in my survival that time around. As I approach the voluminous mountains of white water, I can't escape the nagging fact that these are larger than the rapids upstream. Much larger.

I weigh up my options in a hurry. Should I try to escape the current and exit stage left? There's still time to do that if I move fast. The benefit of this strategy is that it will probably save my life, a not insignificant advantage for a normal person. Or should I continue going with the flow? Maybe this is all part of the fun, part of my journey. The benefit of this strategy is that moving forwards has been working for me ever since I jumped into the river. The downside, of course, is that death is likely. Let me think.

It's a no brainer. I can't recall a time in my life when escaping something has worked for me, even though that's been my default setting for many years. Relaxing into the flow is all I've got.

The rollercoaster begins. So far so good. I'm a few meters in, and I've avoided hitting the rocks beneath me, although I'm drinking a lot of river water. The ups and downs are growing in size. Relaxing into the flow is becoming harder as I guzzle more and more river water. It's like being told to meditate when someone is operating a jackhammer next to your head.

As I rise towards the crest of the next wave, I catch a glimpse of what's to come. Oh shit! The rapids come to a grinding halt only meters ahead of me, which can only mean one thing: I'm hurtling towards a waterfall! I'm about to join the other water molecules on their journey into the abyss.

I'm strangely relaxed. Maybe it's adrenalin, or maybe I just trust that everything is going to be alright despite the evidence to the contrary. As I approach the waterfall, l put my arms on my chest and suck in a large breath of air. The water that was carrying me forwards so faithfully jumps into the nothingness. I'm launched into the great unknown with the entire community of water molecules which momentarily separate from one another in shock.

l feel myself falling, falling, falling.

Finally, l crash into the water below. My body is forced deep below the surface with unimaginable power. I'm hurtling into the depths of a dark pool. The good news is l haven't hit a single rock in this watery world, but the bad news is I'm fast running out of air and energy. I'm now hostage to powerful centrifugal forces which are twisting and turning my body in every direction, apart from back towards the surface. They refuse to let me go. Fighting against such immense power is useless. And then there's the inconvenient elephant in the room: I'm all out of air. Bugger. My only hope is that l eventually spin out of the circular motion, so l can make my way back towards the surface. But I'm now light-headed and dizzy, and on the verge of a different kind of relaxation. My eyes start closing of their own accord. It's like struggling against sleep in front of TV, no matter what you're watching.

Hang on, what's happening? Someone grabs my hand and yanks hard. I'm being pulled out of the pummel zone and towards the surface. l must be dreaming again.

Finally, l—we—reach the surface. l suck in some air. I'm already full of river water, so there's not much room left for the air, but there's enough to bring me back from the brink. I take another breath, and another. My eyes remain closed as I'm too exhausted to open them.

But I'm breathing, and I'm alive.

The hand that saved me gently puts my arms on my chest and helps position me next to the river on some soft sand, which molds around my body like the world's most comfortable memory-foam mattress. I may be imagining things, but I think someone is stroking my forehead like my grandmother used to when I was going to sleep. It never failed to send me into the most peaceful sleep when I was a child, and always made me feel loved. I whisper a thanks to my savior as I drift off to sleep.

The Magic Pool

I open my eyes, sensing movement nearby. Aha, I'm once again underwater, once again a fish. Part of me, a big part of me, is exhilarated. This is fast becoming my favorite place to be, the place where I'm safest, where I feel most accepted.

Swimming as a fish is now instinctive with no thinking required. After swimming around in a few swift circles it's clear I'm in a deep pool, much deeper than the river. The water is cooler down below, and the cooler the water, the more sensitive my scales are. As I become more aware of my surroundings, I recognize this place. There's the familiar sound of water hurtling down from the waterfall above and dancing energetically in a circular motion around the impact zone. I'm once again swimming in the waterfall pool I was pulled out of by my mysterious savior.

I sense I'm not alone. However, I can't see anyone amidst the intense blackness which owns this world like a thrifty landlord who doesn't enjoy paying the power bills. Oh well, I am in Scotland.

Then something approaches. I'd now recognize that charismatic fishy face anywhere. It's the little fish! I'm overjoyed to see him. His smile beams bright amidst the dark waters we find ourselves in.

"Hello and welcome."

"Hi, little fish."

"How are you?"

"Great, I think."

"You think?"

"Well, I'm once again a fish, and I'm talking with another fish knowing full well that fish can't talk."

"Oh yes, I see your dilemma," says the little fish with concern. "Who told you fish don't talk? I'd like a word with them."

I laugh. The irony is not lost on me.

"People, people in general."

"So why do you think you're swimming as a fish in a river while talking with another fish?"

"I'm very good at dreaming."

"And what purpose do you think your dreams serve?"

It's a good question, and one I'm not sure I can answer. I think I preferred the little fish when he was dishing out the free advice—he was less threatening in those days.

"I don't know. Can you tell me?"

"OK, let's take a step back. Why did you jump into the river in the first place? The real reason this time. Swim deep."

"I'd had enough."

"Of what?"

"My life, the modern world."

"Oh yes? What about the modern world?"

"The way people have become obsessed with money at the cost of everything else, everyone else, everything I consider meaningful. The way people would rather look at their phones than at another human being, even when they share a meal together. The way humans have stopped caring about other humans, and are focused upon taking all they can from any given situation at the expense of all other forms of life. The way the gap between rich and poor keeps widening and no one cares. The way our political leaders have no ethics, no soul, no empathy, no compassion. The way humanity's soul has died a slow death over the past couple of decades."

"So only a short list of issues then?" says the little fish, smiling.

The little fish still has a sense of humor. That's why he's wheeled out for the toughest cases.

"Ha ha, yes."

"And why do all those things affect you so much?"

"Because I'm a member of the human race. Well, when I'm not a fish," I say, smiling.

"Do any of those global issues resonate with any other issues in your life?"

He's a clever one this one. A thought strikes me the instant he asks this question.

"Well yes, there is something."

"Go on."

"They resonate with the way I was treated by my father when I was a child."

"In what way?"

"The long and short of it is my father regularly beat me, and then he left all of us behind. When he was around I was always in trouble. I was always being shouted at. I always felt in the way. The only time he showed any interest in me was when he ordered me to bring him a beer, and even then there was never a thank you or any sign of affection. I guess you could say his anger, aggression and violence towards me was similar to the disconnection, disillusionment and loneliness that's spreading like a virus around the world. In fish language, the world is reflecting back at me how terrible it is not to be loved by your family, the people who should know better."

Shit. The penny has dropped, and it has made a great big splash.

"So what's going on beneath the surface is connected to what's happening above the surface? Do you think this connection is permanent? Or can you imagine the above and below surface currents separating?"

"I like the idea of the two worlds separating, because I'd then be free to be who I want to be regardless of what's happening in the world. But, to be honest, I'm not sure I know how to separate those two worlds. They seem to be connected on so many levels."

"That reminds me of a mood lightening joke," responds the little fish, grinning.

"Go on."

"Did you hear about the car theft in the multi-story car park?"

"No."

"It was wrong on so many levels."

You've got to love the little fish. He's a character. I laugh at his bad joke, and appreciate his warmth.

"Yes, on so many levels," the little fish continues. "We all exist on so many levels, and what's going on beneath the surface is always far more significant than what appears to be happening at the surface level. What if I were to tell you that you have the power to cut the cord, to disconnect your internal issues from the external issues you see in the modern world?"

"I'd say count me in, little fish."

"The answer is deceptively simple. It's similar to when you were a child and discovered that the Bogeyman didn't exist. With that knowledge and some time to grow up, you let the Bogeyman go on his way somewhere else. He lost his residence inside your head. That's it. So all you need to do is recognize that millennials and iPhones and all those other things are not responsible for your problems. And in doing so, you need to let them drift off into another part of the river while you continue onwards within your own current to where you want to go."

"If only it were that simple."

"It is. I promise," replies the little fish, who swims closer to me and stares deep into my eyes. "It's as simple as wishing for more time in the river after you jumped in."

"Pardon?"

"We both know the way you kept going after you leapt into the river was an act of faith. You were trusting that somehow everything would be alright, and you'd be able to let go of everything that wasn't working for you. That's why you kept wanting a little bit more time in the river in your darkest hour. You were calling out for answers to the problems which have been holding you back. That's an act of bravery in my book. By taking action to change, you've already become the hero of your own life."

I nod silently.

"So if you can jump into the river like you did, you can do anything you need to do to heal yourself. You can become a master of letting go of all that you need to let go of, leaving it all behind in a cesspool while you swim forwards in the river of your life."

"I love this idea."

"It's one of my favorites too. You can leave whatever you want in there, and you'll never see it again."

"I'm calling it the Cesspool of Discontent," I explain to the little fish.

"Great idea, although can you add the word Modern in there please. I feel like it adds something."

"Yes! The Modern Cesspool of Discontent. How's that sound?"

"Yes, you're hitting it now. So what would you like to throw in there?"

"OK, the Modern Cesspool of Discontent best prepare itself because I've got a lot to leave behind. For starters, I'd like to dump smartphones, social media, narcissism, chauvinism, inequality, environmental abuse, extractive agriculture, climate change, global pandemics, the wildlife trade, animal cruelty, whale hunting, overfishing, tree clearing, and anyone who's abusive to anyone else."

"It's a solid start. Can I please add the dolphin hunt in Japan to the list? From a fish's perspective, that's up there as one of the worst problems. It makes me sick. Those dolphins deserve much better."

"Yes, throw it into the cesspool. Let it stagnate with the rest."

"It feels good, doesn't it?"

"It sure does. You're one clever little fish. How do you know all this stuff?"

"Well, this is a magic place where the veil comes down just enough for people like you to peep over. So this is more about you than it's about me."

"I'm not used to it being about me."

"That's why you're here."

"That's becoming clear to me."

"So now that we've dumped all those external frustrations into the Modern Cesspool of Discontent, let's delve deeper. Follow me."

The little fish swims deeper into the dark pool we're in, and I follow him. As we swim deeper it gets even colder and darker, and my senses become further heightened as the cold water tickles my scales. This pool appears to be bottomless. The sound of the waterfall's pummel zone is becoming quieter and quieter, until it can't be heard at all. The little fish hovers in the darkness. I allow myself to hover next to him, to listen to what's coming next.

"Now, let's both stay quiet for a moment and consider what's going on beneath the surface of your story. Close your eyes and open your mind."

Life underwater is so beautifully simple compared to life in the madness above the water. It's almost too peaceful and serene in this magical world to believe this is the right place to delve deeper into my mundane life challenges, but the little fish knows best. I trust him.

Upon closing my eyes, memories from different points in my life start appearing in my head as if they're playing out as a film in front of me.

The first memory is of my mother and father disagreeing over something. It appears to be an argument about an affair my father has admitted to. My mother is crying and distraught, but she isn't saying much between her sobs. It's as if she's not surprised, as if this was the life she signed up for so she's decided she needs to bear it, warts and all. However, as I peer closer at her face, I see it's not acceptance I'm witnessing. It's the downtrodden expression of someone who's given up believing they deserve better. I'm floored.

Next up, a memory appears of my father hitting me hard across my face while he's driving and I'm sitting in the passenger seat. He's exasperated by something, by everything, me included. I watch myself being hit, and the emotions which follow on my little face are clear: shock, then pain, then confusion, and finally sadness. I can see myself trying to figure out what I've done to deserve this latest beating. Then I watch myself move beyond my own sadness towards acceptance of what my father has done.

Rather than blaming him, I can see myself ascribing responsibility for his actions onto myself, and thereby normalizing being hit as a part of life. What a weight to carry for an eight-year-old! I feel deeply sorry for the bright-eyed boy in the scene who deserved so much better.

"What do you see?" asks the little fish with concern on his face.

"Memories from when I was a kid."

The little fish nods.

"And what do you notice in those memories?"

"I see myself taking responsibility for my father hitting me."

"Oh yes?"

"He kept blaming me for making him angry. So I ended up blaming myself for his actions even though I could never figure out what it was that I'd done wrong. I think I learnt that from my mother. I always assumed that because I was only a kid, I was the one in the wrong."

"Were you the one in the wrong?"

"Of course not. I was an innocent little kid trying to figure the world out."

"Do you notice anything else?"

"Yes. At the time, I never noticed that my father's face was so stressed. To me, his behavior seemed angry, aggressive and inexplicable, but I can now see that he was extremely stressed. He was beyond desperate."

"And why do you think he was so stressed?"

"Well, from my experience of the world as an adult, I'd say most men become stressed for the same fundamental reason."

"Oh yes?"

"Loss of freedom. When they believe they've been captured, men transform into wild animals who'll turn on those nearest and dearest to them, including their children. The more vulnerable the victim the better from their perspective."

"Why's that?"

"Because vulnerable people can't fight back."

"So it was your father's own unhappiness that led to his mistreatment of you?"

"Yes."

"And you're now feeling some empathy for your father's situation when you were a child. You're understanding he was a deeply unhappy man."

"Exactly."

I think about this. My father didn't set out to be the world's worst father. He was just struggling to cope with his own life. He was trapped in a life he didn't want, which all probably started when his own father mistreated him when he was a little defenseless child like I was. The problem was no one in this picture took the time to say stop, wait a minute, let's take a look at ourselves. Let's sort it out so the next generation doesn't need to go through the same pain again, so the cycle doesn't need to continue ruining lives.

Enough already. The cycle stops now.

"Time brings perspective, reflection brings clarity," says the little fish as though he's following my thoughts.

I'm ready to heal.

"I know you are," says the little fish.

I hadn't spoken that out loud.
"I get it."
"I know you do."
"This very moment I am healed."
"I know you are."
I forgive you, Dad.
"Thank you."
The little fish disappears.

Tiny Changes

The gushing of the waterfall awakens me like a loud alarm clock on a morning when waking up seems like a mad idea. I'm soaking wet, lying half in and half out of the waterfall pool. Thank god for my wetsuit. It's kept my body temperature warm, so the freezing cold water hasn't done bad things to me. Against the odds, I feel like I've had a long and restful sleep. I'm feeling better, much better—all thanks to the little fish and his wisdom. Back up. I also need to congratulate myself for my bravery. Well done, Freddy, I'm proud of you.

It's time to get moving. So I crawl back into the waterfall pool and swim across to the other side. There's a small series of cascading waterfalls on the other side of the pool which appear to signal a watery pathway towards the North Sea, the promised land. I climb down this section as it doesn't appear to be swimmable. The rocks are slippery, so it takes some time to navigate them safely, but eventually I make my way into a new section of the river. It's wider and deeper here, and it's remarkably calm in comparison with where I've come from. "Plain sailing ahead, Captain," I say out loud to myself. But then I correct myself. "Come what may,

Captain, come what may." I'm fast learning that I have no idea what's coming next, and that's alright.

Amidst the calm, I can hear the river DJ is cranking a song up. It's another easily recognized tune for me: "Heads Roll Off" by Frightened Rabbit. The lyrics echo all around. "While I'm alive / I'll make tiny changes to earth / tiny changes to earth / tiny changes to earth."

Yes, I get it river DJ. What are the tiny changes to earth I intend to make before my head rolls off? What will my scorecard say at the end of my innings? One thing is clear to me straightaway. I want to make these tiny changes happen sooner rather than later because I understand that time is incredibly short. The truth is anything that's not at least starting to happen now in my life is never likely to happen. So what am I to do? Well, as a starting point, this river swim will help raise some money and awareness for a worthy cause, if I'm lucky. However, I know the river is suggesting I need to be thinking bigger about my place in the world. The little fish's voice drifts into my mind. "Small changes eventually add up to huge results." I hear you, little fish. How's this sound? I promise to have a game plan in place to make bigger tiny changes in my life by the time I arrive at the North Sea. In the meantime, feel free to throw any ideas you may have in my direction. I'm all ears. Happy? Good.

The river is flowing smoothly. It's a mighty relaxing way to travel after the body pounding I endured upstream. I'm able to lie back and gaze up at the sky, knowing I'm safe for the moment. As I do, my gaze is attracted by the sky's magnificence. Scottish skies are almost always gray, but what most people don't realize is that there are subtle differences in the tones of gray, depending on the time of day and when the next rain is due. Of course, rain is always due here. I once heard that Scottish tourism numbers are benefitting from booming demand for rain tourism experiences. I couldn't help but laugh. If you're traveling to a dark and rainy country like Scotland to watch the rain fall, the good news is you must have an excess of sunlight in your life already. The darkening clouds above me suggest the next downpour is fast approaching. As I'm already wet it doesn't bother me in the slightest, but I'm also aware that it's almost evening. Being cold and wet come bedtime is not a good idea in these icy climes.

I hear the sound of a man clearing his throat nearby. There's no one around, so I may have imagined it. But there it is again. And it's a familiar sound.

"Willard?"

"Surprise, old chap!"

Willard steps forward from behind a tree and smiles. It is great to see him; to see a genuine friend.

"Hello! What on earth are you doing here?"

Willard holds up a backpack he's carrying.

"We couldn't have you getting cold and hungry out here, old chap. I'm the cavalry with the supplies," he says while pretending to jump out and surprise me. "Supplies, get it?"

"I get it," I say, laughing. "Thanks for coming. It's super to see you."

"You too, old chap. Are you ready to call it a day?"

"Your timing couldn't be better. I was just about to stop for the evening."

I haul myself out of the river and give Willard a wet hug, which he accepts graciously.

Willard starts setting up our campsite for the evening in a clearing next to the river. In his supplies bag he's brought the Taj Mahal of tents and a feast fit for a king. My evening is looking up. I get changed out of my wetsuit into the clothes Willard has brought for me. There's something magical about wearing warm dry clothes after being wet and soggy.

Willard attempts to get a fire going next to the tent, and I'm using the word "attempts" kindly. The way he's botching up the fire lighting makes me wonder if he's ever lit a fire before in his life.

"Willard, who keeps your fire blazing when you're at home? It's the best managed fire I've ever seen, so I always assumed you were a closet pyromaniac."

Willard pauses, then laughs. "Not me, old chap. That's bloody obvious, isn't it?"

"Call it a lucky guess."

"Ha! Would you believe Daph insists on tending to the fire every day. She hasn't let it go out since little Georgie passed away. I think she sees it as special because Georgie used to love sitting in front of the fire when he was playing his games, especially on cold and rainy days rather like this one."

"What a special way of keeping Georgie's memory alive."

"The bonus is the rest of us get to keep the icicles away during the winter months. Between you and me, that old house gets pretty damn icy."

I take over the fire-starting duties with more success than Willard. We soon have a warming fire going, and start cooking dinner.

Willard unpacks the feast. Alice has somehow fitted inside the backpack a vast array of food, including: chunky sausages, burgers, jacket potatoes, carrots, bean salad, tomato salad, a cheese platter and some posh red wine. Alice is a great wonder of the world. We warm the meats over the fire, and set out the salad on the ground. Once the dinner is ready, we toast one another and take a big gulp of the wine. We eat, nay, devour the meal. After the day I've had, this is the most delicious thing I can imagine eating. Having rich and well-catered for friends has its benefits.

"I'm lucky to have you as my friend," I say to Willard.

"We're both lucky, old chap. It's a two-way stream."

"It is."

"And it's my turn to be the lucky one tomorrow."

"Oh yes?"

"Didn't I tell you? I'm joining you in the river in the morning."

"Are you sure that's what you want?"

"As sure as the devil is in London."

"Great, that works for me. By the way, promise me the devil will stay in London. I don't fancy meeting him in these parts."

Team of Two

The next morning is glorious. The river glistens brightly as the sunlight does a tap dance across the smooth glassy surface of the water. A large salmon jumps out of the water upstream with majestic prowess. Could it be my old friend Jimmy Carr the salmon? If it's him, he'll no doubt have a good fishy joke to share. I imagine today's tickler is something along the lines of: "Why didn't the hippie swim in the river? Because it was too mainstream." Ha ha. It's almost as if he swam over anyway to brighten our morning.

Willard is buoyant as he packs up the camping gear. He could be preparing for a sailing trip around the world with the level of excitement he's exhibiting. He pulls out his wetsuit and puts in one foot. As an expert in wetsuit sizing, I can see straightaway that he's facing an unsolvable mathematical challenge. Rather than fighting the impulse to laugh, I feel his pain, and try to help him zip it up.

"These things must shrink when you don't wear them for a while, old chap," Willard exclaims with a higher than normal voice.

"I'm sure they do," I respond with a nod.

"OK, so maybe I suffered a bit of furniture disease over the years."

"Furniture disease?"

"Yes, my chest has fallen into my drawers."

We both laugh. It strikes me that Willard and I have something major in common. We both crack wise to help ourselves fit in, particularly in awkward situations. We'd both like to argue that we do it to entertain others, but it's all a smokescreen to divert attention from the truth. The mask-off reason people like us crack jokes is to make others like us more. But the irony is most people subconsciously pick up on the true motive behind our poorly timed jokes, so our little smokescreen isn't hiding anything. And, worse than that, by showcasing our insecurities through our jokes, we're sitting naked as friendless losers for the whole world to see. Of course, this makes it far less likely anyone will like us. What a major inconvenience it is that people always see us much more clearly than we see ourselves, no matter how hard we try to hide. I'm sorry Willard has been losing the same battle as me. I see him as a brother-in-arms.

Willard leaves the backpack full of camping equipment next to the river for one of his crew to pick up later. Having a support team is growing on me by the day.

We're both ready for action. We wade out into the river together.

"Ouch. That's rather nippy, old chap."

"'Tis indeed, but you'll be fine in that wetsuit once you get used to the temperature. You'll find that there's a small layer of warm water inside your wetsuit which will become warmer throughout the day. And no, you don't need to top up the warm fluids yourself."

Willard laughs as we drift off as a team. Despite how close I feel to Willard, it's strange to have someone with me on what has become such a personal journey. However, I've learnt that my river journey is always evolving into something different. The one constant is change. I've also observed that once I begin to understand something, the next challenge arrives and I'm back in the dark again. Willard and I are silent for the first few minutes as we ease into the flow together. Rather than swimming, we're floating on our backs next to one another, letting the current propel us forwards with minimal effort.

"Who'd have guessed I'd be in the drink here with you when I pulled you out of the river that day, old chap?"

"Not me, no way."

"Aye, life has a funny way of surprising you with what's around the corner."

"I'm glad it was you who was around the river's bend for me, Willard."

"Me too, old bean, me too."

"So what inspired you to join me in the river? I wouldn't have guessed this was up your street, or anybody else's street for that matter."

"You inspired me, old chap. When you got up on that stage and talked about knowing something was wrong with your life so you jumped into the river to sort it out, you made it sound like a bloody pilgrimage, and one that I need in my life."

"Really? There was me thinking that everyone would view me as some sort of freak for jumping into a river that would almost certainly kill me. Suicide is a prickly subject at the best of times."

"That's exactly why everyone was so enthusiastic. You were being one hundred per cent genuine in a world in which authenticity is such a rarity. Who talks honestly about suicidal thoughts? I'll tell you: no one. And yet many of us, or, more likely, most of us, have them pop up from time to time in our lives. I know I did after we lost Georgie. I couldn't imagine life without the little fellow, so I considered ending it all. It was touch and go at one point, and I pulled myself back from that cliff just in time. And yet, even though I've survived these thoughts, the idea of standing on a stage and telling the world that I've considered topping myself in the past seems even crazier than this river-swimming lark."

"I hear you."

"What you're doing with this river swim is something totally unique in a world in which everyone is doing the same thing. Most people are staring at their mobile phones like zombies, hoping for something better to happen in their lives. But very few people are taking action to change their lives. You, my friend, are a rare inspiration."

I've never been good at taking compliments, and this one takes me by surprise. I want to swim away as a fish, so I can hide in the depths of the river. If only I could change species whenever I wanted to. But the river only offers up that opportunity when the time is right. I realize I'm drifting away from Willard, so I ease back into the present moment.

"How much wine did you drink last night?" I eventually respond, laughing.

"You know I'm right, old chap," Willard replies without laughing.

"Thanks. But what about you? Do you want to talk about your stuff?"

"I don't want to bore you, old chap. Being here is enough for me."

I understand Willard's position so well.

"What if I were to tell you that you can't bore me because I accept you as a friend?"

"I'd say you drank too much wine last night."

His barriers are as well constructed as my own were.

"What if I were to tell you that the healing process will take work on your part?"

"I'd say I didn't drink enough wine last night."

"And what if I were to tell you this river is special and has healing powers?"

"I'd say once again you drank too much wine last night."

We both fall silent and drift on, knowing full well that Willard's light-hearted flippancy won't help either of us. Oh well, it's his door to open when he's ready. In the distance, a bird sings a song which ambles along slowly like the river. It's a warm and soothing sound which gently encourages the bright colors of the day to shine brighter. Nothing seems to matter while the bird's song guides us through the water.

"Righty-o, old chap. I'm going to take your advice, but only because it's you giving it. Pull up a chair because I've got something to say," says Willard with renewed enthusiasm, as if he's listened to the bird's encouragement.

"Roger, Captain."

"Here goes then. My story."

I nod, and lie back into the river's flow.

"Like most titled families, I grew up in a cold world of discipline and responsibility. My father was the cliché of the rich aristocrat with too much time and money on his hands, but not enough common decency. He was a violent drunk who used to walk around the house slamming doors closed whenever he wasn't screaming abuse at my younger sister and me. He was a real charmer you could say, old chap.

Anyway, as you'd expect, the drunken violence ended up destroying any love my mother had for him, despite her tendency towards compassion and care which became her second nature during her time working as a nurse. My sister Laurie and I used to pretend we were escaping from prison by hiding in far flung parts of the property where we hoped no one would find us. But find us they did, and we'd know about it for a long time afterwards. Of course, my father's life of misery and abuse was destined to be mine because I was born first. Numero uno. As my reward, I was presented with a title and a big cold house, and not much else. But I'd have gladly given it all up for a loving family. My father never hugged me, not once."

"I hear you," I say, feeling Willard's pain.

As Willard regathers himself to continue, I can tell his story hasn't seen the light of day like this before. He's opening up and speaking his truth. The river has slowed down to give him the space he needs to continue. The bird has stopped singing, but it's still flying along next to us.

"As I grew older, I stepped into the shoes that were meant to be mine from the moment I was born. A smelly pair of old slippers they were, old chap. I took on the title that comes with the role, as well all the responsibilities which come with being the duke, the largest of which is to manage the estate without collapsing under a pile of debt like most of my peers have done throughout the ages. That's one of those stereotypes that lives on, with each generation borrowing more than the last. While I've been tempted to hit the bottle as hard as my father did on occasion, I'm proud to say I never did, not even during the whole Georgie business. Yes, I enjoy a glass or two of good whiskey, but I knew if I started drinking in earnest at that time, I'd soon be sliding down the world's slipperiest slope *en route* to oblivion. I'm proud of dodging that bullet."

"Well done, Willard. That would have taken a lot of strength."

Willard takes a deep breath in preparation for what's to come.

"Thanks, old chap. But I've suffered in other ways. As you know from our chat around the fire, the light in Daph's eyes went out some time ago. She walks around as a ghost of her former self. And I have that small issue to deal with of Daph looking at me with pure hatred in her eyes. It kills me. Do you know how it feels to have someone you love look at you like that?" Willard asks with a quiver in his voice.

"It must be beyond difficult."

"It's like she's cut the cord between us. Game over, kaput. The situation makes me feel like a little boy again, the little boy whose father used to become furious with him whenever he made even the slightest noise. The little boy who was afraid to open his mouth for fear of how his father would react. The little boy who'd often have the living crap beaten out of him after his father had a few too many drinks."

"I hear you, and I can relate to this part of your story. You and I have this in common."

"Sorry to hear that, old chap, but it's comforting to know I'm in such esteemed company."

"So what you're facing up to is your relationship with Daphne, but what you're dealing with at a deeper level is your relationship with your father?"

The little fish would be proud.

"I guess so. That makes sense, old chap. We're strange creatures, aren't we?"

"Indeed."

"And you know what I want most of all?"

"What's that?"

"To learn how to be the man my wife needs and wants, and the man my father would have been proud of. I need help to become that man because he's not looking back at me when I look in the mirror these days."

As I listen to Willard's story, an epiphany strikes me. We're all the same, and we're all struggling with the same things. And yet, through our suffering we all feel alone and separate from one another. It seems so simple. All we need to do is connect with one another to share the pain, to lighten the load. Why aren't we all doing this?

"I'd say the majority of the men on planet Earth, including me, aren't seeing the man they want to when they look in the mirror."

"We're hopeless, aren't we?"

"No. Hope is one thing we have in abundance, and it's all we need."

"I hear you."

"I have an idea."

"Oh no, not another one!" Willard smiles.

"A good friend of mine recently asked me to step into my own shoes as a young child to observe what was really going on in my formative years. It helped me to understand my childhood better from different perspectives, and it allowed me to make more sense of my life."

"Have you become a hippy, old chap?"

"I don't know what I've become, but it's working. Are you in?"

"Righty-o, but I draw the line at singing Kumbaya."

"Thank god. With your singing ability, let's stick with the talking." I smile.

"You're hardly an up-and-coming Pavarotti yourself. In fact, my ears hurt in remembrance of your last performance." Willard laughs.

"Ha ha. OK then. If you close your eyes and allow memories from your childhood to float in, what do you see?"

Willard closes his eyes.

Willard's Childhood

"Funnily enough, a memory is popping into my head, old chap. It's of when my father received notice that his father, my grandfather the Duke of Roxburghe, passed away. The official cause of death was listed as cardiac arrest, but we all knew it was booze that killed my grandfather. He was rarely sober. In fact, he was almost always so drunk that he couldn't speak properly. So, in this memory, my father has just inherited the title and the property, which is worth a fortune, driven in no small part by the coal-seam gas reserves discovered on our land. My grandfather had allowed the miners in without a second thought, despite the disastrous environmental impacts. He was all about growing the family wealth at any cost, growing the brand name at any cost, being an asshole at any cost."

Willard is angry. The river has almost slowed to a stop.

"Rather than crying or showing any emotion at the news of his father's grisly end, my father pulled out a copy of our family tree and efficiently crossed out the words Duke of Roxburghe next to his father's name, and rewrote them beside his name. There wasn't even the hint of an emotion on his pre-programmed robotic face."

"Why do you think your father was so emotionally detached?"

Willard closes his eyes and watches the scene again.

"Because he was—I think the technical term is—a dickhead, old chap."

I can't help but chuckle.

"And why do you think he was a dickhead?"

"Because he didn't receive an ounce of love in his own life from anyone. He was viewed as a museum piece, a member of the British aristocracy who was expected to live his life as the history books wanted. He was nothing but a source of sperm to create the next level on the family tree. And beyond producing an heir, his only role in life was to be the duke. So he had nothing to do but to play an outdated role from a theater production no one was watching anymore."

"Yes, if he didn't receive any love, he wouldn't have known how to dish it out."

Was that me or the little fish talking?

"Exactly."

"So while the world reached the conclusion that your father was a bone fide dickhead, in reality he was more lost than you are now."

"Yes! He never learned how to love or be loved."

"I can once again relate. If only our parents had sorted themselves out when they had time ahead of them."

"Indeed. And now I find myself in a situation where my wife doesn't appear to love me, just like my father. History is repeating itself in a most unwelcome way."

"It has a way of doing that."

"Bear with me, old chap. I'm thinking the question I need to ask myself is: Have I done anything to inspire Daph's anger? Something inside me is telling me the present may be connected with the past."

"Yes, I think you're on the right path, Willard. Everything in my life seems to be connected, as you say. From listening to your story, I also wonder if there's a deeper connection to Georgie's passing. How did you react at the time?"

"Gosh, old chap, that's all a bit blurry in the memory banks. It was a living nightmare as you can imagine."

"I hear you."

Willard closes his eyes again.

"Hang on, something else has popped up. I can see Daph and I standing next to one another at Georgie's funeral. We both look distraught. Daph turns to look at me, but I remain fixated on Georgie's coffin. Daph is putting her hand in my hand. Oh no! It's me who moves my hand away. And my face looks furious. It was me. It was me."

Willard stops talking and punches at the water with venom. He seems to be experiencing the anger he saw in himself in the memory, but this time it's directed at himself.

"OK, I see," he finally says. "It was me who withdrew from Daph, which in turn caused her to withdraw from me. The truth is I was furious with her for letting Georgie out of her sight that day. And between you and me, in my heart of hearts, I still haven't forgiven her for it. I don't know how to."

Another penny drops for Willard. He seems to be in shock.

"I can't believe I didn't see it before, old chap," he continues. "I've been largely responsible for the whole shooting match by virtue of my own dickhead tendencies. The easy option was to blame Daph, and to withdraw from her at the very moment she needed me to be her rock. So that's what I did, the easy thing, the weak thing. I blamed her."

The river seems to be moving slightly faster, and its mood has changed. It's evolved from quiet and soothing into supportive and encouraging.

"Not many people ever have to go through something as stressful as losing a child, so how's about some kindness towards yourself before you beat yourself up too much."

"I'm not sure I deserve any kindness, old chap. I let my wife down at the very moment she needed me, for god's sake."

The river continues to speed up.

"So if you're responsible—along with Daph, of course—for the current state of your relationship, how do you think you can help to make it better at this point?"

"I'm not sure. The best thing would be to go back in time and restart the past year or so. Have you got a time machine handy, old chap?"

"I wish. Is there anything you can do in the present moment?"

"Well the obvious answer is I could forgive Daph, but I don't know how to do that."

We're both silent for a few minutes as the river carries us forward. I know the river is way ahead of Willard and me, and always will be. I try to channel some of its energy, the little fish's wisdom, my wisdom.

"I have a crazy idea. What if we were to wash away all your resentment towards Daphne? Cleanse you until you're left with nothing but forgiveness."

"Well, it's a novel idea, but we're already in the river and I don't feel cleansed yet. In fact, I feel worse now I realize I'm the one who's responsible for the right old mess my life has become. I'm so annoyed with myself."

"I hear you."

"What did you have in mind?"

"We're cruising along like holiday campers right now. You haven't yet experienced the sensation of being pummeled by the river's infamous white-water rapids. Believe me, those bad boys have a way of cleansing you deep in your soul, while you're not able to breathe and are struggling to stay alive."

"So you're suggesting a near death experience may help? You're loco, old chap."

"Trust me. Trust the river."

We drift forwards, knowing things are about to get rocky again. They need to for Willard.

The River Knows Best

Willard and I relax into a comfortable cruising silence. You know when you're in the company of a true friend when you can be with them in complete silence, without any overhanging awkwardness. Willard and I are at this milestone. It's not surprising given how much we've learnt about and from one another in such a short period of time.

The river remains wide and smooth-flowing with no signs of white-water rapids. However, the moment I expect something from the river, something else generally happens, so there's no point speculating about what's coming next. Que sera sera.

An unusual birdsong drifts along with us as we float under some majestic willow trees. It sounds similar to the bird we heard earlier but also different, like an expert flautist who's interweaving each note with the river's current. The song is mystical, reflecting the river's mood in this section. Or I wonder if it's the other way around. Does this little bird possess the power to influence how the river behaves? One change in the bird's tune may control how fast the river flows, and how volatile it is. The idea of one tiny change triggering a world of much bigger changes is comforting to me. It means the tiny changes I'm aiming for have the potential to change everything in my life. I thank the little bird for singing its mysterious song, and helping us on our way.

However, the moment is cut short. The river is changing, and we're heading into rougher waters. More worryingly, Willard seems to be drifting away from me, and fast. I try to bridge the growing gap between us by swimming towards him, but he's being pulled away from me by a force far more powerful than my swimming.

In a matter of seconds, Willard has drifted all the way across to the other side of the increasingly turbulent river. He's too far away for me to be of any use to him if things turn bad. Willard waves at me anxiously, and I wave at him, but we can't hear each other's calls anymore above the deafening sounds of the river. The river is expanding in width, and it's now a seemingly impossible mile from one bank to the other. It's as if the river is growing into a vast ocean in which Willard and I are merely two tiny boats skirting around the nothingness in the middle. An entire world has opened up between us. I'm scared.

But there's no time to dwell, as the river is changing yet again. I'm now being pulled diagonally across the river towards Willard on the other side. Willard is also being pulled across to my side of the river, but he's still a long way away from me. And the water is starting to rush around in a powerful circular motion. If it weren't impossible, I'd say we're caught up in a gigantic whirlpool.

There's no point fighting the whirlpool's power. The more I oppose it, the more likely this will end badly for me. The whirlpool is in control. All I can do is play my best hand with the cards I'm dealt. I remind myself I'm in safe hands, and relax into the flow letting the whirlpool take me where it will. This is easier thought than done as the whirlpool is still speeding up, and I'm spinning out of control towards its deep center. Each spin seems to be double the speed of the previous rotation. I'm now moving so fast I've lost my bearings, along with my better judgment. As I spin closer and closer towards the center of the whirlpool, a voluminous dark mountain of water rises around me. It has an ominous foreboding energy, like a gigantic wave building on the horizon which could wipe out life as we know it. I can't see Willard anywhere. I just hope that, like me, he's relaxing into the flow, rather than fighting against it.

If I'm not imagining things, there are soap suds gathering in the center of the whirlpool, like a gigantic washing machine in the middle of a spin wash cycle. The overpowering smell of washing detergent reminds me of the detergent my grandmother used to use. It's a comforting smell, a smell of being at home, a smell of not being spun towards oblivion within a whirlpool. I'm moving beyond dizzy. I don't know how much more of this I can take.

Cleansed

The spinning finally subsides, and I find myself in the normal free-flowing river as if nothing happened. My head is still spinning, so I take a moment to regather my senses. I search for Willard, but he's nowhere in sight. This is worrying. Willard could easily have drowned in that whirlpool given his lack of experience in handling the dangerous curve balls the river throws at you. I can imagine him fighting gallantly against the powerful whirlpool, only to discover that his efforts were in vain, and ending with a brief "Oh bother" before drifting underwater, never to be seen again. It's all my fault. I said yes to bringing Willard along, knowing full well what the river is capable of. He came to me in a time of need, and, rather than helping him, I led him into a place he could never understand or survive. He deserved so much better than a grisly end like this.

I swim to a beach area at the side of the river. I lie down on the beach and gaze up at the sky. Despite my concern about Willard, I have to fight a feeling of relaxation, as though nothing serious could ever go wrong in the river since it's a place of healing, not of death. If only that were true. This strange relaxation only compounds my feelings of guilt. What sort of person chills out at the beach after their friend has just died on their watch? I must be some kind of monster.

"Hello, old chap."

I glance around, but there's no Willard in sight. The river is playing with me again. I deserve it this time.

"Hello, old chap. Up here!"

Glancing skywards, I see Willard's familiar face peering down at me from the willow tree above. He's safe and sound, and is smiling down at me like a cheeky child who's been discovered while playing hide 'n' seek. The immense relief takes my breath away for a moment.

"Willard! You survived! Are you alright?"

"Never better, old chap, never better."

"Great, I'm so glad. What happened to you?"

"Things started spinning out of control. We were caught in some sort of whirlpool, and I never thought I'd be saying that out loud."

"Yes, it was a whirlpool, if you can believe it. That's where I lost you."

"That's where I lost myself as well. It was too much. I started to drop underwater as the damned whirlpool was moving so fast. I fought as hard as I could, but to no avail. It was obvious I couldn't fight it. And do you know how I felt as it dawned on me that my time was up?"

"Tell me."

"I experienced intense sorrow for all the things I wanted to do and never achieved. And there are many. But there was one thing in particular I haven't done which circled urgently around me in that whirlpool as I was drifting underwater."

"And what's that?"

"Give Daph a big hug and tell her I'm sorry. If my life were to end before I do that, the whole shooting match would have been a big old waste of time. That's what was running through my mind as I thought I was off to meet my maker."

Rather than looking desperate as he'd done at his realizations earlier in the day, Willard smiles with a new lightness.

"Wow."

"Then, when I thought all was lost, I had no choice but to accept my fate, and accept it I did. So I closed my eyes to let the inevitable happen. However, the inevitable didn't happen. I opened my eyes and found myself sitting here in this tree awaiting your return. God knows what happened, or why it happened. It's a strange place, this river."

"Welcome to my world."

"Do you know something even stranger, old chap? I'm feeling very different since the whole whirlpool experience. I feel lighter, and would you believe I'm experiencing joy at the idea of being alive. I haven't experienced joy like this for the longest time, since before Georgie left us. I've missed it. And now I can't bloody wait to get on with the rest of my life. Facing death like that has a way of shaking things up, doesn't it?"

"There was me thinking you were a goner, and you've only emerged from the whirlpool in much better shape than you went in."

"It's a win, old chap, a big one. I don't even care to discover how this happened."

Willard gets it.

"That's wise. I've also reached the conclusion that letting the river work its wonders is all that matters. You can only do that by letting go, and trusting that everything will be alright."

A few days ago I was ready to give everything up, and now here I am talking like the little fish about the river's powers. What's happened to me?

A memory drifts into my mind from many years ago when I worked with an extremely religious man. I arrived at work one day to find a small bible sitting on my desk with a note on top saying, "I've highlighted the sections I think are relevant for you." I remember thinking at the time: thanks a lot for being so presumptuous. Sure enough, the bible was filled with highlighted sections and notes which this fellow had meticulously compiled on my behalf, with lessons in mind for me. There was one section he'd both highlighted and circled which he no doubt thought was particularly relevant. It was all about trust, and it went something like: "God is waiting for us to trust him so he can guide us forward and act with our best interests in mind." OK, so maybe the quote was spot on for me now that I think about it. But that's beside the point. Who was this guy to dare to assume he knew what was going on in my world? I'll never forget how condescending and uninvited it felt. It was an intrusion on my thoughts, and a judgment on me as a person. Of course, his strategy backfired royally because I've never been so unmotivated to read anything in my life.

With this memory in mind, I check myself for the way I've started talking to Willard about my newfound love for the river's healing powers. I don't want to go anywhere near the cliff of condescension which my overbearing colleague had jumped off without a second thought. Note to self: please avoid becoming a sanctimonious wanker.

"I agree with you, old chap. I'm here to trust in the river, in you, in me. And you know what else I'm here to do?"

"Tell me."

"I'm here to forgive myself for everything I've done since Georgie's passing. It wasn't anyone's fault, including mine. For all the mistakes I've made, and I've made many, I was just trying to do my best as his father and as a husband."

"That's huge, Willard."

Willard climbs down from where he's perched in the willow tree and walks over to sit next to me on the beach. He does indeed appear lighter, less stressed, and more human. His frown lines have all but disappeared, and he's moving with an easy flow which he didn't have before, at least since I've known him. He appears to be a new man who's finally forgiven himself after years of fighting against the current—a man who's accepted that sometimes bad shit happens, and we all need to deal with it and move on.

I may be imagining it, but I can hear whistling approaching us from some unknown direction.

"Willard, can you hear that whistling, or am I going mad?"

"I can indeed, old chap. It sounds like ... No, it can't be ..."

"What?"

"It sounds like that bloody song we were singing which upset Alice the other night."

On cue, Alice appears from behind one of the trees. She's whistling the Alice song as Willard suspected. I wonder if she's lost, in all meanings of the word. She has an expression on her face of determined resignation, but despite that she looks as though she's meant to be here. She strides forward with purpose towards us.

"Alice! What are you doing here?" asks a surprised Willard.

"Hello, Captain, hello, Freddy. Well, I was bringing you both some food supplies for the evening ahead, but I made my mind up on something I've been mulling over while walking over here."

"Oh yes?"

"Captain, I heard you telling Daphne that you were going to jump into the river to heal yourself like Freddy did."

"That's right."

"Well, I've decided to do the same."

"By Jove, that's a great idea. Yes, please join us, Alice."

"Welcome to our little party, Alice," I chime in.

Not Alice's Burden

Alice has brought with her a customary feast for the evening ahead. With this in mind, we decide to camp where we are on the little beach as everyone is hungry. I will never eat commoner food again. Alice unpacks the food onto a picnic rug and reveals a roast chicken with gravy, lasagna, tomato salad, feta salad, homemade bread and sweet potato chips. Everything smells incredible. I can't think about anything except devouring everything in sight.

"It's great to see you, Alice."

How long do I need to make polite conversation before we can start eating?

"Ach, you're thinking with your stomach. Let's chat after you've had your fill."

The food tastes as great as it smells. Alice has brought copious quantities of everything, so we're able to enjoy multiple courses to our heart's content.

"You're a legend, Alice. Thanks for dinner, thanks for thinking of us, and thanks for being here."

"You're right, laddy, it's my pleasure. I hope it's OK that I decided to join you in the river tomorrow. It's just something I need to do."

"It's more than OK, Alice. It will be our pleasure to have you join us. Why do you think you need this?"

"Well ... that little incident the other day with the karaoke song showed me that I've got a lot of healing to do. And at my age time is short. So here I am, ready to heal."

"You're in the right place. Tomorrow will be a day you won't forget."

"I'm good at not forgetting."

We all relax into a deep sleep after dinner, and morning arrives in the blink of an eye. We prepare for the day ahead by packing up camp and donning our respective wetsuits. Alice puts her feet into her wetsuit and pulls upwards, but to her shock her wetsuit makes a loud sound like a fart which echoes across the river. Unlike a normal echo, the fart sound is not diminishing with each rebounding echo. It's as if the river wants to make a point of lifting our moods this morning. Poor Alice is the butt of its joke.

"It was my wetsuit I assure you!" insists Alice, looking embarrassed.

I can't hold back a schoolboy giggle. Any fart noise or even mention of fart noises is too hard to resist, a remnant of a childhood spent laughing at bodily functions at every available opportunity.

"I believe you, Alice. These wetsuits make a whole lot of funny noises when you least expect it."

"Thanks, Freddy."

The three of us leave a bag full of dirty plates and camping equipment to be collected by one of Willard's team. We wade out into the river free of stuff, and what a glorious experience it is to travel this light. I feel as free as a bird. The water is fresh and alive as we submerge ourselves into its exhilarating world.

"Alice, you are in for a treat today," explains Willard. "This river is a special place."

"Aye, Captain, if you say so."

"There are no captains here today. We're all crew members in the river, Alice."

It's a cloudy morning, so the water is particularly dark and mysterious. The river appears to be in a thoughtful mood today. I assume it's related to Alice joining the group and turning this into a three-person mission. The challenge afoot for Willard and I is to bring Alice into our newfound circle of trust. The me of a few weeks ago would have jumped straight in with a few questions for Alice to help the process along. However, I now understand that timing is everything, as is the power of listening from a position of total acceptance. The wise old tree taught me that. It's time to get into the flow as a group of three.

"Alice, how have you been?"

To my surprise, Willard has started the ball rolling.

"Och, you know, fair to middling, fair to middling."

"I see. And which parts are middling?" continues Willard with genuine interest.

"I'd say the happiness side of things needs a wee bit of work, Captain."

"Oh yes?"

"Since little Georgie's passing I feel like I've been carrying a heavy weight around my neck. They say time heals everything, but it isn't getting any lighter. If anything, it just gets heavier with each passing day."

"Right."

"I can't stop dreaming about that dreadful day, and remembering each of my movements in slow motion. I keep questioning why I wasn't there to help Daphne with Georgie on that day of all days. If only I'd been there, I'm sure I could have made a difference to the way it all turned out. Little Georgie may still be with us."

Willard is silent for a long time. I consider interjecting, but this is an important moment for both Willard and Alice. It's not part of my journey. What a joy it is to be silent and respect energy which is flowing in the right direction, and out of my control.

"Alice, Daph and I have both been going through the same what-if analysis you've put yourself through. And it's been killing all of us bit by bit. I want you to understand that this horrible thing which happened was not your fault. There was nothing you could do to stop Georgie's passing that day. And another thing. I think you've been carrying some of our guilt for us. Thanks for the offer, but no thank you. That's our burden to carry, not yours. It's not your burden, Alice, do you hear me? You need to let it go."

Alice is quiet for a long moment. Then she starts to cry. Initially, she fights it and her tears flow slowly, but the dam eventually bursts. An unstoppable flood of tears forces its way through as she lets go.

Willard is the next domino to fall, and he starts crying alongside Alice. He has a huge backlog of repressed grief to unload, and unload it he does. His tears are flowing thick and fast like an uncontrollable river rushing downstream to a better place.

I'm the last domino to fall. Who knows if I'm crying for Alice, Willard, Georgie, or myself, or for all of the above, but my tears are flowing strong.

Lightening Up

"We're a cheery bunch, aren't we?" says Willard, smiling.

Alice and I glance at Willard, and can't help but laugh. Of course, now the pendulum swings the other way, and we can't stop laughing. It's such a fine line between laughter and crying, and we're all more than a little loco at this point. The way I see it, the crying cleansed away the things we needed to say goodbye to, and the laughing is us saying hello to whatever is coming next.

"Holy smoke, I needed that!" exclaims a more relaxed Alice.

"You and me both, Alice. Let's make that compulsory whenever you feel you're carrying our stuff for us," says Willard.

"Aye aye, Captain," says Alice with renewed enthusiasm.

The heavy, dark-gray Scottish skies are clearing up to reveal a stunning blue sky beneath. I'd almost forgotten how beautiful a blue sky can be. This one reflects back the deep blue of the North Sea as though it's cheering us on from afar. I wonder how many miles we have left before we greet it in person.

"Alice, another question for you. When was the last time you had fun, proper fun?" asks Willard.

"Remind me, what is fun? It's been a while, Captain. A long while if I'm honest. Since before Georgie's passing, so that's well over a year ago."

"I thought so. Do you remember what it felt like?"

"Sort of. I remember having a right laugh at a pub karaoke night a few months before we lost Georgie. I was as drunk as a skunk, and I was up on stage singing 'Livin' on a Prayer' at the top of my voice. I'm not the world's best singer at the best of times, and I remember I cleared the pub of customers during that song. Davy, the pub owner, told me afterwards that he may need to ban me from singing karaoke for the sake of his business."

Alice chuckles, as do Willard and I. Having witnessed Willard's karaoke attempt the other night, I have no trouble picturing a pub-clearing singing performance.

"Yes, I remember hearing stories of the evening Alice's singing scared all the local cats away. It's become a part of local folklore."

An idea strikes me as I contemplate Alice's long absence from all things fun.

"You two, I've got an idea. Fun is one thing none of us can do without, no matter what sort of challenges we're dealing with. Why don't we all do something fun right now? Something silly and childish with no objective beyond the thing itself."

"Well, that sounds like being an aristocrat, old chap. What a useless waste of space we are," pipes in Willard.

"Aye, that sounds like exactly what I need," responds Alice.

"OK, brilliant. Let's swim to that rocky area over there on the right, and I'll show you what I have in mind."

The three of us swim towards the side of the river with noticeably more energy than we got in with. Alice is clearly not the world's best swimmer, but she's doing the breast stroke with frenetic enthusiasm at the prospect of a lighter moment, while Willard and I take longer slower strokes which move with the river's current. There's a whiff of excitement in the air.

Upon arrival at the river's rocky shoreline, Willard and Alice sit on a small beach area awaiting their instructions on how to have fun. It's clear that having fun is the one thing most adults don't have the slightest idea how to do anymore. Maybe I should write a book called *Fun for Dummies* which reopens this lost world to adults who believe they have to be serious twenty-four seven. Step one: start to view fun as a worthy emotion again. If in doubt about how to do this, remember some of the fun you had as a child, and aim to recreate some of those memories. Step two: when said fun arrives in your life, accept it and remember to laugh when you feel so inclined. I smile at the idea.

"Right, team, welcome to the stone-skimming Olympics. Our motto is Maximum Bounces for Maximum Joy. This is a special sport for special people. The way the game works is we'll have five throws each, and the two non-throwers will count the number of stone skims on behalf of the thrower. Of course, we expect one hundred per cent honesty and sportsmanship, so if there's any doubt regarding the number of stone skims, the decision always goes in favor of the skimmer. We're all successful unless proven otherwise in the stone-skimming world."

Alice and Willard appear amused, but also teetering on the edge of thinking I've lost the plot. They don't yet realize that I have indeed lost the old plot, but something much better has arrived in its place. I'm confident they won't be so skeptical by the end of the game. In the meantime, my enthusiasm will have to be enough to keep us all engaged.

"Righty-o, old chap, let's give it a whirl then," says Willard.

Alice nods uncertainly. "Och aye, count me in for a whirl then."

I pick up a nearby stick which I start talking into as though it's a microphone with which I'm addressing a crowd of spectators.

"Welcome everyone to the stone-skimming Olympics. Yes, it's that moment you've all been waiting for when the world's best converge in Scotland to skim stones like they've never been skimmed before. Get your slow-motion video recording equipment ready, because what we are about to witness will warrant many replays in the coming decades."

Willard and Alice seem a bit interested, and also a bit sorry for me.

"Put your hands together to welcome the world's best players: Willard, whose skimming title is the Beast from the East; and Alice, whose skimming title is the Giver on the River. And I'll be joining the game as the Rock Ness Monster."

I clap and cheer in a lonely celebration.

"First up, we have the Beast from the East. The river is yours, sir."

Willard searches for a suitable stone. The perfect stone to skim with is round, smooth and flat, and there's an abundant supply around us. It's as if the river expected us. Willard finds a suitable stone and walks to the side of the river.

"The Beast from the East approaches the river with the calm confidence he's famous for. But don't let that deceive you. Beneath that rock-like exterior, the Beast is an unstoppable force of nature who takes stone skimming to places it never knew it could go. Some would say to places it didn't want to go."

Alice is giggling in the background.

Willard bends down and throws his stone. It starts skimming across the water a few meters in front of Willard, and continues on its way across the river's surface. One, two, three, four skims, and then underwater.

Alice and I clap.

"The crowd go wild for the Beast's first throw! It's a solid start, but nowhere near his personal best. Well done the Beast from the East. Now it's time for the Giver on the River to give her best."

Alice finds a suitable stone and approaches the river.

"The Giver is her normal composed self as she prepares to throw. She's famous for making stone skimming look as graceful as professional ballet, as beautiful a thing to behold as a Swan Lake performance. Many an opponent has been blindsided by her grace as she skims her way past them to victory."

Alice bends down and skims her stone. One, two, three, four, five, six skims and then underwater.

"The crowd are on their feet. The Giver on the River has given her best, and what a start it is. She hits the front with stylish ease."

After three more stone throws each, we enter the fifth throw neck and neck at ten stone skims each. I'm grateful that we're all of a similar ability as it makes the game that much more engaging. However, what I'm most happy about is that Willard and Alice have started having fun, real, honest, genuine fun, the fun we all used to have as kids. They're smiling and laughing and looking alive. And they love their nicknames. Every time I mention them, it brings a smile to their faces. Who'd have thought something as simple as a silly nickname could have such a hugely beneficial impact on how people see themselves.

"As we enter the fifth and final throw, the score line is ten all, something we have never before seen in the stone-skimming Olympics. What a treat this is for today's crowd who are all on the edge of their seats as our contestants prepare to throw for the last time. One gentleman just fell off his seat in the excitement. Are you alright, sir? Steady yourself. The Beast is ready."

Willard and Alice have already learnt that the quality of the stone often defines the quality of the throw in the world of stone skimming. So our time spent searching for the perfect stone has increased as the competitive tension has come alive. Willard jumps in the air, fist pumps and calls out "Oh yes!" when he finds the right stone for his throw, a particularly flat and round specimen. He approaches the river, bends down, and throws it as hard as he can.

"The Beast has unleashed a monster! Eight, nine, ten, eleven, twelve skims! He has hit the lead! The crowd are going ballistic! Congratulations to the monster that is the Beast from the East. The Giver will have to pull something very special out of her bag of tricks to take the title after that. It's her turn to turn on the magic."

Alice searches for the right stone for ages, and, like Willard, she jumps for joy when she finds it. She walks confidently to the river and bends down. Rather than throwing it hard, she throws the stone with less force, but much more spin and angle than her previous throws. She's learnt the all-important lesson that it's all in the way that you use it.

"What an unusual throw by the Giver, but by god watch it go! Eight, nine, ten, eleven, twelve, thirteen, fourteen, fifteen skims! Awesome stuff! Can you believe it? The Giver has once again shown the world why she's so special, so beautiful. Well done the Giver."

As she celebrates, Alice looks as happy as anyone I've ever seen. She jumps up and down like a child who's just discovered a superpower for the first time.

I complete my final throw which makes eleven skims.

"The Giver has won the stone-skimming Olympics. The crowd are on their feet, going wild! This is a win to remember throughout the ages, a special day for everyone who worships the titans of stone skimming. Well done to the Giver from the River. Here's your Olympic gold medal."

I hum a generic national anthem as Alice walks over, and I hand her a slightly golden-colored rock I found earlier.

"Thank you all for supporting me so well during the competition. I can't remember the last time I had so much fun."

Unexpected Visitor

Our team of three is flourishing. The changes in both Alice and Willard have been dramatic since they arrived in the river. Willard was a broken man, but now he's relaxed and jovial. And when Alice dipped her toe in she was lost and tired, but now she's connected and joyful. I remember believing when I was younger that people don't change, they just get older. How wrong I was. But I hadn't met the river in those days.

After a few more hours of swimming, we climb out of the river to set up camp at a pretty bend where red and yellow flowers are blooming in abundance. Alice suspects this is the spot where the support team are due to drop off the next round of supplies, but she's not certain since, like me, she's bad with maps. Upon searching the area, we discover there are no supply packs in sight. I pretend I'm unperturbed by the lack of support, although my stomach is doing somersaults. I remind myself that I signed up for a rough and ready adventure in the Scottish wilderness, and that may involve not having a five-course meal accompanied by a glass of award-winning red wine every night. It's a tough pill to swallow.

We decide to stay the night here regardless, as we're all tired and it's a beautiful spot. We allocate the setting-up-camp jobs between us in order to divide and conquer. Alice and Willard head off in search of wood for the fire while I look for timber and foliage with which to build a shelter for the evening. I'm impressed by what an efficient team we've already become.

While I'm hunting for construction materials, my spider senses are tingling. I'm sure as sunrise someone is watching me. However, when I search around for signs of life, there's no one in sight. I carry on with the job at hand, but I can't shake the feeling that I'm being observed. There's a new energy in the air, and it doesn't match mine, Willard's or Alice's after our time in the river. It's less at peace, and more in pain.

There's a loud noise nearby which sounds like a stick breaking.

"Willard? Alice?" I call out.

There's no reply, and there's still no one in sight. I carry on searching for timber. But there it is again, the sound of a twig breaking nearby. It's almost as if someone is standing right beside me. Maybe I've drunk too much river water again. I walk around the area in ever-decreasing circles, but the mysterious noise-maker remains hidden.

I return to the area where I intend to build the shelter only to discover a large bag of supplies has been dropped off there. It's a similar bag to the previous supply drops by Alice and Willard's crew, so I assume this is the planned drop Alice was expecting. But why would one of Willard's team drop the supplies bag and run, aiming to avoid talking with us, or at least me, at all costs? My inner detective comes to life, and I focus on cracking the mystery. I surmise that the bag dropper must have approached from the nearest road since the supplies bag is quite heavy. So that suggests the mystery bag dropper carried the bag in from a nearby car park. I'm on their scent now. I walk in the direction of the nearest road, which is around half a mile inland from the river. Eventually, I discover a well-trodden footpath which must connect with the road.

I speed up as the escapee must be nearby now. And, sure enough, a few hundred meters ahead of me someone is walking quickly in the direction of the road. I start jogging as quietly as I can, and within a few minutes I'm only a hundred meters away from them.

"Hello?" I call out.

The person turns around, but is distressed by the sound of my voice. I recognize that sad face straightaway.

"Hello, Daphne."

Daphne appears to be considering her options. Should she run and pretend I'm not standing here? Or should she respond? Of course, responding would mean engaging with another human. I know that's not on the top of Daphne's "to do" list these days.

"Thanks for the food and supplies. You're spoiling us."

She continues to stand there like a lifeless doll. She has nothing to say to me, and her reptilian eyes suggest she's not really present. Remembering what she's been through, I stop myself from judging. This is a woman in a world of pain I can never understand.

"Hey, Daph, would you like to join us for a cup of tea? We're about to get a fire started. I know Willard and Alice would love to see you, as would I."

She's silent, but I can tell she's considering whether to respond. This could go either way.

"Why?" Daphne finally asks. "Why would anyone want to spend time with me?"

Good question. I'll need to think of a good answer.

"Because Willard and Alice love you, and I want to get to know you better. We want to spend time with you because we all believe there's something positive inside of you."

Daphne laughs sarcastically. "Well, I hope you can show me what it is because I can't find it."

She turns away from me as if she's decided to leave regardless. This conversation has been an epic fail on my part. The little fish's voice pops into my head. "Don't lose heart. Just keep going, keep at it." OK, little fish.

"Daph, please join us for a cup of tea. If you want to leave afterwards, no one will stop you."

Daphne considers my offer, but she still looks as if I've just asked her to fly to the moon. She finally nods unwillingly, and walks slowly towards me like a home-less dog being walked away from the homeless shelter without knowing where its next home is.

We walk back to the campsite in silence, and I'm starting to wonder if this was a good idea. There's only so much the river can do. There's only so much I can do. I catch myself, and decide to choose blind belief over sensible caution.

When we arrive back at the river, Willard has miraculously started a fire, and Alice is unpacking the supplies bag in preparation for dinner. It's a homely scene. When Willard and Alice see Daphne walk in they can't hide their surprise.

"Daph!" exclaims Willard as he walks swiftly over to her and gives her a big, purposeful hug. Willard is changing, but Daphne doesn't react. She remains unanimated, and her arms flop beside her like a lifeless doll when Willard cuddles her.

"Daph was kind enough to carry in our supplies bag for the evening. I thought the least we could offer her is a cup of tea heated up on our outdoor fire," I offer up.

"Great idea, old chap." Willard appears to be fighting some disappointment that Daphne is crashing the party with her usual morbidity after his purposeful warmth towards her.

"Daphne, come sit over here with me, and we'll get you that cup of tea," says Alice generously.

With Daphne's arrival a sub-current has emerged, a complex sub-current which is affecting everything as we attempt to navigate our way around it. I remember a piece of advice my grandmother once gave me many years ago: "If there's an elephant in the room, it's polite to introduce him to everyone. Remember there's a magic in boldness." Right now, I'm unsure whether the elephant in the room is the need for Willard and Daphne to forgive each other for the tragedy which wasn't their fault, or Daphne's deep depression. They are connected, but the cause of all of this upset is clearly the aftermath of Georgie's passing. I decide the elephant in the room is the lack of forgiveness between the two of them. However, the idea of introducing this elephant to Daphne is as scary to me as entering the uncontrollable world of the white-water rapids; more so, in fact. People are less predictable than white water.

Alice serves everyone a cup of tea, and we sit quietly around the fire allowing it to dominate proceedings, rather than facing any of the items of awkwardness which are bubbling away beneath the surface.

I know what the little fish would say, so here goes.

"Daph, it's been a great start to the trip. Both Willard and Alice have been healing themselves by addressing things which happened when they were growing up, as well as major events in their lives, such as little Georgie's passing."

Daphne's eyes flicker with anger before returning to their default reptilian state. Before running down this rabbit hole, I want to see which way the current moves next without my input. Daphne is creating an opposing force which I don't want to fight. My chances of forcing her to change direction are low to non-existent unless she decides to do it herself.

There's a long moment of silence as everyone considers what to say next.

"Freddy's right, Daph. It's been an epic couple of days," says Willard with an expression of newfound empathy on his face. Thank goodness he's taking control of this scene as he's the only leading man for this role.

"Darling, there's no point in me dilly dallying. There are things I need to say out loud to you. Alice and Freddy are a part of this journey now, so I want to say the words in their presence."

Daphne appears not to have heard. She remains silent and unmoved.

"After a lot of self-analysis with the help of my time in the river," Willard continues, "I've learnt I need to forgive both you and me for what happened to our Georgie."

Willard pauses and takes a deep breath.

"I'm sorry, darling, that it's taken me so long to say this. We both need to accept Georgie's passing was not our fault. Do you understand? It wasn't your fault, and we both have to forgive you. And likewise, it wasn't my fault, and we both need to forgive me."

Daphne's eyes instantly come to life with a flurry of emotion, ranging from surprise to hatred. I'm praying for Willard as it doesn't look like things are going his way. Willard knows it and crosses his legs. Time stops as Daphne contemplates Willard's words.

"And there's something else, darling girl, something big. I'm so sorry that I wasn't there more for you when Georgie passed away. You needed your husband to support you through the most tragic and horrific moment any parent can ever go through, and I let you down due to my own failings. It's no excuse, but I've recently discovered I hadn't dealt with some events from my childhood which were stopping me from seeing my issues. Anyway, the long and short of it is I want to take this one fairly on the chin by telling you it's my fault. I let you down. I am so, so sorry for it, my girl. Please forgive me."

I want to clap, but I restrain myself. Daphne continues to battle a vast array of painful emotions which are contorting her face in conflicting directions. It's hard to feel anything but sorrow for all she's been through, and is still going through.

All of a sudden Daphne screams! It's not the type of scream you'd hear from someone watching a horror film. It's not a scream of surprise. It's the contorted and anguished scream of a hurt animal, an animal which has been caught in a trap for too long to remember, an animal which can't handle the intense pain anymore. Her cry of pain keeps going, and going, and going.

Willard, Alice and I are as uncomfortable as if someone was scratching their fingernails across a gigantic chalk board in front of us. It's so painful to witness. Please stop, Daphne, please. Maybe the inanimate Aunt Sally look was a better look for you after all.

Finally, thankfully, her scream comes to an end when Daphne runs out of breath with which to release her pain. She collapses exhausted in a heap. There's an awkward silence in the air, as the three of us wonder what's coming next.

"Fuck, that felt good," whispers Daphne.

Willard shifts quickly from being shocked to being relieved. He starts laughing, as do Alice and I.

"Darling, that's the best thing I've ever heard you say," says Willard as he puts his arms around Daphne.

Our laughter grows like a wave, with each of us making the others laugh more. Daphne appears too tired to join in after her exertions, but eventually we hear her quiet laugh, her sweet quiet laugh, the unintroduced member of the group. Daphne's laughter grows until she is joining in like the rest of us with free, uninhibited laughter, laughter which sounds almost hysterical.

Thank god, the elephant has left the room happy to have been introduced, and the eggshells have disappeared.

"Darling, will you stay with us tonight?" asks Willard with newfound confidence.

Daphne nods with a smile. What a smile she's been hiding from the world.

Awesome Foursome

The shelter I made is plenty big enough for the four of us. The latest supplies drop off included blow-up mattresses and fluffy pillows, so we're once again on track for a comfortable night's sleep. I even notice Alice pulling out some hair rollers from the magical bag of five-star comforts as she prepares herself for slumber. I'm starting to believe that bag is like Doctor Who's Tardis, with an entire world of whatever we need in there. Alice sees me smiling at her and responds with, "At my age it takes a wee bit of work to look this good, laddy." She's fast becoming the aunt I've always needed in my life. With a grin on my face, and exhausted after our day of strenuous physical and mental activity, I fall asleep in nanoseconds.

The morning light hits my face, and I open my eyes after a gloriously deep sleep. Willard, Daphne and Alice are still asleep. I double check that I have human feet rather than a fish tail, and I'm in luck today. No, not luck. Being a fish is fast becoming one of my favorite pastimes, but, to my surprise, so is being human. Willard has his arm around Daphne. It looks awkward and uncomfortable, but I'm guessing neither of them is used to being so close to another human these days, so some retraining is required.

Willard hears me rising from bed. "Morning, old chap! Another day in paradise," he says as he turns to kiss Daphne.

The three of us pack up and prepare for the day ahead. Already, this step is becoming habitual as if we've been swimming the river all our lives.

"Daph, will you be alright to make your way back up to the road when we head off for the day of swimming?" Willard asks.

"No need. I'm coming with you," Daphne responds without a second thought.

"Really? Are you sure?"

"Yes. I'm sure. I need this just as much as you do."

"Thank god you joined us last night, darling."

"Yes, we needed last night. And I've needed the river's help for the longest time. I just wasn't ready to listen."

"Oh yes?"

"You may have noticed I've been reading that poem about the fish—well, a lot."

"Yes, I have."

"I wasn't sure why it was so important to me. And then when Freddy arrived, and I heard him talk about how the river helped him through his personal challenges, I realized the poem contained the answers I was looking for. It mentions experiencing wisdom through the river, and learning what joy is from the fish. Well, I'm ready to learn those things with you. That's why I'm here."

"Yes, that funny little poem has been guiding us back to the river for years. We just couldn't hear it."

Willard puts his arms around Daphne and holds her tight. She lets him.

"So, welcome to the crew, darling," Willard continues. "One small problem, though. The river water is close to freezing so you'll need a good wetsuit, but there aren't many shops to be found around these parts."

Daphne stands up, walks over to the magical supplies bag, and pulls out a brand new wetsuit.

"Well, aren't you a sneaky one, darling? Hooray!" celebrates Willard.

Daphne chuckles. "I packed it just in case this happened. No, hoping this would happen."

"There was me thinking we were dragging you kicking and screaming into our little party here."

And so our group becomes a family of four river wanderers *en route* for the North Sea. Once everyone is ready, we wade into the river for a new day of swimming. The current is reasonably strong in this section, so we lift up our legs and let the river do all the hard work. We drift forwards with strong momentum.

Our group splits naturally into two groups because Willard is holding Daphne's hand, which we're all celebrating on the inside. They glow like a new couple from a Jane Austen novel, and holding hands appears to be another important milestone after the immense distance between them. Alice and I sense they need some space to reconnect, so we allow the distance between the two groups to widen.

"Right, so what fun have you got planned today, oh wise river guru?" asks Alice cheekily.

"I think I might be all funned out after the past few days. Do you have any ideas?"

Alice thinks for a while.

"Here's an idea. When I was a kid, my dad and I held bad joke competitions which I'll never forget. The only rule was that the joke had to be cringe-worthy. What do you think?"

"I was born for this one."

I wonder if Jimmy Carr the salmon is swimming nearby. I hope so. He'll want to hear these.

"Brilliant. You go first then. Give me your worst bad joke."

"OK, let me think. Right, here's a bad one. A cowboy friend of mine once asked me to help him round up nine cows. I said, sure, why not: that's ten cows."

"Oooh, that's really bad. Well done," responds Alice, laughing.

"Why thank you. Your turn, madam."

"Aye, here we go then. I had an argument with a friend about Doctor Who's Tardis the other day. I thought it was a little thing, but it seemed much bigger once we got into it."

"Ha ha, genius! Would you believe I was thinking about the Tardis last night, and I can't remember ever thinking about the Tardis before as an adult. What a strange coincidence."

"Or not."

"What do mean?"

"It's getting harder for me to believe in coincidences these days, laddy."

"Oh yes. Any particular reason?"

"Take you, for example. The moment Willard and Daphne were about to part ways with the D word imminent, and just when I was starting to lose the plot, you miraculously showed up out of the blue. No one has been seen river swimming in these parts before, ever. And yet for some reason, you happened to be river swimming past our house, which is in the middle of bloody nowhere, and in sub-arctic conditions, at exactly the right moment. Then, it just so happens your strange journey is helping us heal in ways we hadn't dreamt possible with the help of the river. Not that any of this was obvious when you first arrived on our doorstep like a half-drowned cat in need of a home. But the upshot is your arrival has helped us all, and just in the nick of time. How can that be a coincidence? Please explain that one, oh wise river guru."

"So you think this was all pre-ordained? You believe I was told to jump into the river on that fateful day?"

"All I know is there's more going on here than I understand, but I do believe it's beyond coincidence."

"You may well be right."

The river is getting rougher. Let's hope we aren't approaching any rapids or waterfalls.

"Alice, let's swim over to Daphne and Willard to check on how they're doing."

We breaststroke our way towards Willard and Daphne, who are still talking intimately. As we approach them, I can hear the words "start again." The current is moving in the right direction for these two.

"Hey, guys, I noticed the river is getting rougher. Word of warning: this section is identical to an earlier section of the river which led to a waterfall and almost certain death. Long story. Can I suggest we all stay close to the left hand side of the river, so we can get out of the river if there indeed is a waterfall up ahead?"

"Solid idea, old chap. I'm all for staying alive," responds a circumspect Willard.

We round the next bend as a team. And, straightaway, it's obvious the river disappears into nothingness up ahead. As suspected, we're approaching a waterfall. But we're a step ahead of the river on this one. It's the first time that's happened since I entered the river's world, so my gut instinct tells me to remain on high alert. I'm in no mood to risk anyone else's life.

What's that noise? It sounds like music playing in the distance. Trust the river DJ to materialize again when least expected. Although, it would be the first time this has happened with other people around, so something new is afoot here. Could the river be revealing its deepest secrets to the other three?

"Can any of you hear that music?" I ask, hoping that they can. A small part of me has been questioning if I'm crazy to be hearing these river DJ songs in my head, so confirmation they're real would be welcome. Please, river, prove to me I'm not rowing with only one oar in the water.

"Aye, I hear it. Where's it coming from? What's going on?" asks Alice.

The music sounds like it's coming from the bottom of the upcoming waterfall. This is strange, since river DJ songs generally sound as though they're coming from all directions at once, like listening to headphones in your mind. Hang on, I recognize this tune. It's another Frightened Rabbit song, "Living in Color," an uplifting anthem to be sung loud at the end of a long winter. Inexplicably, the song sounds like it's being created from within the very depths of the waterfall's belly, and is exploding upwards within the water spray. I know better than anyone how unpredictable the river can be, but this latest development is mysterious even by river standards. The lyrics I know so well rise up above us as though they're addressing us from the heavens: "I am floating, I, I am floating / with my eyes closed, with no sails."

Willard, Daphne and Alice look terrified.

"What the hell, old chap?"

"I know. The river does some strange things. Between you and me, this is not the first time I've heard music playing since I've been in the river. But it's the first time I've heard the music like this with others around."

"OK, so we're in the Twilight Zone."

"Something like that."

"Hey, guys, the music sounds like it's coming from down below the waterfall. Why don't we get out of the river and walk to the edge of the waterfall to have a look at what's going on down there."

"Aye, let's check it out then," agrees Alice.

We pull ourselves to the side of the river and scamper up the slippery bank like investigative otters. The edge of the waterfall is around two hundred meters ahead of us, and the music is continuing to erupt from within the waterfall. We form a single file and cautiously make our way along the side of the river towards whatever awaits us down below. I experience a sense of dread, which I haven't experienced since I jumped into the river; a sense of foreboding. The others also look concerned. Willard is holding Daphne's hand in a protective manner. However, I notice that Daphne is walking with a newfound confidence despite it all. Alice is quieter than usual. I hold my breath. Please, river, let everything be OK. I feel responsible for what happens to these three.

As we approach the waterfall, the words of the song become clearer, and I suddenly realize that this music is not being played by the river DJ, or anything else remotely otherworldly.

We reach the edge of the waterfall and peer down. Below us there's a large school of people congregated around the bottom of the waterfall, including a band on stage playing the music we've been hearing. They sound more robotic than the band from upstream. Despite this, there's a large crowd assembled in front of them who are jumping around enthusiastically as only fans of the original Frightened Rabbit would do.

All of a sudden, someone in the crowd calls out, "They're here!" and points up at us. The crowd turns around and stares in our direction. Then they start cheering as if we are long lost heroes who are here to present them with the ten commandments from the mountain top.

From where we're standing, this all seems a bit over the top. Something is telling me these people are about to create a sub-current at a time when I was enjoying the direction the river was carrying our special little group. Our first commandment is: please leave us alone.

One Way Down

"**I**wasn't expecting a welcome party!" exclaims Willard.

"Me neither. These guys must have organized this themselves," adds Alice, who had arranged all the group events up to this point.

How's this possible? Without Alice's help, and in the three days since the launch party, someone must have calculated exactly where we'd be, and then swiftly arranged all these people to meet us here. I'm suspicious.

The crowd continues cheering at us with next-level enthusiasm. They're champing at the bit to dance, to sing, to participate in whatever is happening next. And they're wired. Without warning, they start shouting "Jump! Jump!" at the tops of their voices. I feel like I'm at the end of a high school party with a testosterone-fueled crowd of teenagers calling out dares which appear to be fun and voluntary, but are really a test. Those who don't follow the crowd's orders will be forever ostracized for being below the minimum fun standard. Today could not be going further off track.

"Ach, they can't be serious. That's too far to jump," decides Alice as she steps back from the waterfall's edge.

"I'm not jumping down there," agrees Daphne.

A few years ago, I read a fascinating book called *The Madness of Crowds* which discussed how powerful crowds are at encouraging individuals to think exactly like them, and to become one of their own. Most people are easily convinced that the many of the crowd knows much more than the lonely individual. But what if that's not the case? What if the crowd is crazy, and the individual is sane? Right now, I'm feeling about as close to the full quid as I've ever felt, but I can't say the same about the erratic show unfolding at the base of the waterfall.

The crowd are now jumping around hysterically, as if they're reacting to my thoughts. Their calls to "Jump! Jump!" are growing louder and louder like manic seagulls calling out for leftover fish and chips, or whatever else we've got.

"It doesn't look like that big a jump now I think about it," concludes Willard as if the crowd has successfully programmed a change of mind in him.

Sensing they're making progress, the crowd's calls to jump become louder again. One fellow calls out, "You know you can do it!" while staring intensely at Willard. The more he stares, the more control he seems to have over Willard.

Since Willard's change of decision, or at least his move in that direction, Alice and Daphne are also reconsidering their options, despite their initial non-jumping stance. And despite not wanting to admit it out loud, I'm in the same boat as the two girls. Up to this point, everything that's happened in the river, no matter how crazy it seemed at the time, has been exactly what was needed in hindsight. So part of me believes I should keep trusting the all-knowing river. However, another part of me is warning me this doesn't feel right. These people seem to want something from us I don't want to give them. Little fish? Where are you? Normally, I can't shut the little guy up, and now he's gone missing in action just when I need his help.

"Oh, OK," Daphne concedes. "Let's jump then. It's not that far."

"Och, alright," joins Alice, the final domino the crowd needed to fall.

I size up the powerful waterfall. It's roughly the same size as the one I went over by myself earlier in my river journey. I survived that fall, but with help. It seems insane that we're considering jumping off this one of our own accord simply because these strangers are chanting at us to do it.

Willard holds both Daphne's and Alice's hands in preparation for jumping. Alice picks up my hand so the four of us are connected. The cheering below has become a frenzy of excitement as the crowd realizes they've won this one, whatever this one is.

"On the count of three guys," guides Willard. "One, two, three …"

The four of us leap off the cliff and hurtle towards the pool below. The waterfall's pounding noise guides us downwards as we descend like stones. And from around halfway down, the fine spray from the impact zone flies up to greet us as though we're falling into an upside down shower.

We land in the water below and are forced deep into the pool. Luckily, this pummel zone is far more forgiving than the one I encountered upstream, so it's relatively easy to pull ourselves away from the circling water. We return to the surface for air. Everyone is fine.

We're met by a round of applause and more general euphoria. The crowd is acting as though we're here to receive a Nobel Peace Prize rather than having jumped a few meters into a waterhole in the middle of nowhere.

The band starts playing another song. It appears to be a welcome of sorts, but the moment is a blur to me as the water from the waterfall pounds all around us in dramatic fashion, dulling our senses to the reality of what's happening. I feel like I'm at the end of a long night of nightclubbing, and in need of my own bed. Everything moves slower than usual.

No, not this song. I know it so well: Frightened Rabbit's "Floating in the Forth." The singer doesn't even try to mumble the words which reveal what the song is really about: "Take your life / Give it a shake." He's looking the four of us directly in the eye as he almost speaks these words as if they're orders. After they've done their business, the words dissipate around us amidst the buoyant water spray. It's most definitely not the welcome I was hoping for.

Enter the Pied Piper

A welcome party approaches us as we swim to the side of the pool. I recognize some of their faces from the launch festival. However, most of them are new faces with the same inexplicably happy smile. Straightaway, I recognize the masks they're wearing. They want us to believe that they're the happiest people ever to have lived. I wonder why.

A tall man wearing a black, long-sleeved T-shirt saunters over to us.

"Welcome, team! What an entrance," he enthuses.

He holds out his hand to help us out of the water. His stance appears rehearsed, as though he's been thinking about this moment for a long time. And the forced smile he's wearing gives me the feeling he's a tour leader welcoming a bunch of tourists. Every rehearsed gesture and move communicates to us that he knows he knows more than we do. He's the host, and we're the lucky guests here to learn from the master. The rest of the crowd stand back, letting him do all the talking, all the helping.

"Guys, great to meet you all. My name's Truin," offers up our welcomer as he grabs my hand and yanks me out of the water with more force than I was expecting.

"Thanks for the welcome," is the best response I can muster as I'm catapulted up the riverbank.

One of my greatest challenges has always been my inability to smile naturally around people I don't like. I find myself involuntarily over-compensating in these situations with a weird forced smile which no doubt makes me look deranged. So, on cue, and within nano-seconds of meeting Truin, I'm smiling like an inane weirdo. Despite my facial faux pas, I'm surprised that Truin's smile continues to beam bright as though I'm coming across as one of his greatest admirers.

"Great to meet you, old chap," says Willard, accepting Truin's hand with his customary warmth.

The other three of us follow Willard's friendly lead to avoid the awkwardness of not being friendly when everyone else is. It's obvious we're all people pleasers by nature. We'll do anything to avoid being perceived as impolite, even if it goes against every feeling and intuition we're experiencing.

"Guys, once you've dried yourselves off, would you like to join us for a warming cup of tea? We've even got homemade biscuits," offers up Truin.

"Smashing idea. I could do with a hot cuppa," Willard responds on behalf of the team. The cat has my tongue and won't let it go, so I'm grateful that Willard is taking the lead here.

There's a large table set up near the band with tea and biscuits which we all congregate around. The crowd parts like the Red Sea as we approach the table, and then it efficiently reforms around us. Truin bows at each of us, and then serves us tea with the ritualistic flair of a geisha. It's remarkable how comfortable he is being the center of attention, being the leader. I'm partly in awe of his confidence, and partly terrified by it. Who does he remind me of?

"So, Freddy, Alice, Willard, Daphne, how is your river adventure going?" Truin asks the question of the four of us, but he's only looking at me. I'd say he's staring at me with more intensity than the situation warrants. Back off, buddy.

"Well, we're all learning as we go, and going as we learn," is the best light-hearted response I can conjure up.

Truin continues to stare at me with an intensity that could burn holes in fabric.

"Who organized this get together?" interjects Alice, with concern written all over her face.

"A few of us heard about what you guys are doing through the Frightened Rabbit network, which has really come together since Scott's passing. Our band, Enlightened Rabbit, are helping spread their music far and wide."

An inner giggle rises within me. Whoever named their band is either a comic genius or too serious for their own good.

"Oh yes, and what's your interest in river swimming then?" continues Alice, borderline aggressive.

"We're more interested in what you guys represent than in river swimming per se."

"What we represent? What's that then, old chap?" chimes in Willard.

Truin appears surprised. He must have thought we knew more than we do about who he is and what he's planning. The glaring subtext to his body language screams, "Could you be any stupider?" I remember a primary school teacher who made me feel stupid in the same way, and how I became scared to put my hand up to answer any questions in his class. If the little fish were around he'd no doubt tell me to always hold my head high and walk tall. I know that little guy so well now. It's almost as if he's here even when he isn't.

"Everyone's been talking about Freddy's speech the other day," Truin continues. "And when he mentioned that he jumped into the river to lose himself, which in turn led to him healing himself, quite a few of us saw similarities with other events of significance, events which are important to us."

Why am I feeling stressed all of a sudden?

"Events of significance, old chap? That's what we called drunken dorm parties when I was at uni. What are you talking about?" counters Willard.

"Think about it. A man throws himself into a freezing cold river to end his suffering. To the rest of the world, a man like that is assumed to be crazy, lost, and, let's be honest, mentally ill. However, this man ends up surviving thanks to friends he makes along the way, and ultimately he thrives. Then he ends up leading his new friends on a river journey which they hope will yield similar results. What does this story sound like to you?" Truin asks pointedly of Willard.

"I'd say it sounds like a situation of each to their own, old chap. Freddy here found something which works for him, and I say well done to him for that. And then Alice,

Daph and I found something which works for us. Bully for all of us."

Willard's confidence is growing. I'm proud of him.

"OK. Then I have another question for you. Have the rest of you noticed that the river has helped heal you on your journey so far? They could be mental or physical healings, but they'll have resulted in noticeable changes to your wellbeing. You'll know what I mean straightaway if you've experienced what I'm talking about."

The intensity of Truin's gaze hits all four of us hard as he burrows deep into our minds, hunting for the answer he wants. I'm praying the other three remain quiet, so I give them a "stay quiet" look. But from the confused expressions on their faces I think it's coming across more like "I need a toilet this instant."

"I have," Daphne finally responds. "Healed that is. I feel better after only one day and one night in the river—better mentally, physically, emotionally and spiritually. And Willard and I have connected for the first time since the death of our little boy, which is no small feat."

Thanks, Daphne. I couldn't get her to talk for love nor money a day ago, and now she's become a chatterbox extraordinaire in the one moment I wished her quiet.

"Daph's right, old chap. The river has healed me in ways beyond belief. I like myself for the first time in, well, ever. And I now understand what I need to do to rebuild my relationship with Daph, to rebuild my life."

Truin's smile extends to beyond his ears as he chows down on the information he's been searching for, hoping for.

"And you, Alice?" he questions eagerly.

"Ach, aye. I'm experiencing joy for the first time in forever. Would you believe I've started earning these laughter lines in the past few days? About bloody time eh?"

Truin smirks like the cat who got the cream. And Alice utters the words I've been praying no one will say.

"It's nothing short of a miracle to be honest."

Our Journey Labeled

Truin whispers excitedly with his minions. There's no prize for guessing he's spreading the news he's just extricated from us. He has a brief word with the band, who've stopped playing to observe what's going on. If the little fish were here he'd no doubt explain to me that no one has any power over us apart from us, so we're safe to continue on our journey.

Truin walks onto the stage with the charisma of a religious Steve Jobs here to peddle his own brand of iPhone to the unsuspecting world. I suspect he's here to change life as we know it, or to exterminate everyone while trying. The crowd claps loudly, almost hysterically. Truin gives them a royal wave, showing he appreciates the applause, and then hushes them so he can address them.

"Thanks, guys, what a great group you are, and what a special occasion this is. I'm sure most of you will have heard about these four wonderful people who dropped down from the heavens above while on their very special journey, a journey into themselves, to heal themselves, to heal the world."

To heal the world? I don't remember that being on our "to do" list. Truin pauses and steps back with expert speech-making ability to let the crowd applaud. The crowd play their part like well-versed actors. There are cheers and fist pumps everywhere you turn. One guy calls out, "The word is coming to life!" as he jumps up and down on the spot like a neurotic baboon with bottom challenges.

Truin steps forward again and takes a deep breath.

"I don't know about the rest of you, but I don't believe in coincidences. I don't believe we all made the effort to be here today just in case something miraculous were to occur, on the very day the miracle arrived. Do you?"

He steps back again, and members of the crowd start calling out, "Not on your life brother!" And my favorite: "Word up. No way José!" Whoever José is must be turning in his grave.

Truin steps forward again, this time beaming with pride.

"So I believe there's only one way we should interpret this, don't you? This is a clear message from our savior. He's talking to us from above, and he's saying, 'Go forth and join these people on their pilgrimage of healing to heal yourselves, to heal the world. Go forth in love.' Do you hear it as well?"

Oh fuck! Just when I thought I didn't need the damned thing anymore, the oh-fuck-o-meter has hit a maximum high. The crowd are buying into every word Truin is pedaling like hungry wolves who've been searching for a meal for too long to care whether it's real food or a mirage. The crowd's wild applause is a sight to behold as he expertly rouses them into a feeding frenzy.

"Fantastic. I'm so glad you're all in, like I am," Truin continues. "All that's left is to sort out the logistics of our journey. There are around a hundred of us here, and I believe a fair few of us brought wetsuits just in case we found ourselves in this position."

Just in case? So they decided they were coming with us before they even met us. That's a tough pill to swallow, but I remind myself that everything that's occurred in the river thus far has happened for a reason. Are these crazed people another important part of our journey? Or have we veered off track into a perverse sideshow in the freaks section at the circus? Where's that little bloody fish when you need him?

Truin rounds up his troops who are already donning their wetsuits, which have emerged as if out of a magician's hat. They're perusing a map of the river and discussing drop off points for food and shelter. The mood has shifted from religious fanaticism to military organization in a matter of minutes. It's scary how efficiently they can switch roles.

Willard, Daphne and Alice are as surprised as I am by this turn of events.

"These folk are proof God has a grand sense of humor," surmises Alice. "But why have they decided to join us without asking us? Am I missing something here?"

"Alice is right. This is beyond strange, old chap. Our little adventure appears to be in the midst of a slow motion party crash," adds Willard with unusual heaviness.

"Yes, it appears to be. I wonder what they really want from us."

"By the way he's rousing his rabble, I'd say they want more than we're willing to give. I've never seen so much fist pumping in my life," adds Alice.

"Indeed. I'll warrant they're after more than a quick jolly in the river," agrees Willard.

"We need to make them understand our journey is not a pilgrimage for the masses to join as they see fit," I respond.

"Yes, it's our journey, and it's by private invitation only," whispers Daphne.

"Well said, darling."

"Are we all agreed then that we need to put a stop to this right now?" I ask.

"Indeed, old chap. It's time we ask them to leave us be."

"OK then. I'll go find what's-his-face for an honest chat."

Battle of Wits

Truin is scheming away nearby with a bunch of his disciples. As I approach, he sounds like a parent talking with young children who don't know how to fend for themselves. I hear him utter the words, "Let's keep it that way!" to a sheepish young guy he's addressing. When he sees me approaching, his facial expression changes from an intense look of concentration to his famous over-the-top smile. I take a deep breath and remind myself it's my life, not his.

"Freddy, we were just talking about you guys. How are you doing? Are you feeling the love?"

"Actually, I wanted to have a quick chat with you if that's alright."

"Yes, of course, fire away."

"Well, here's the thing. I started this river swimming adventure by myself for myself. Then Willard, Alice and Daphne joined me because we all know each other, and it's become clear that our journeys are connected for a whole range of reasons which I won't go into now. The reason the river has been such a positive experience for us, and why we're healing in the way you consider miraculous, is because we're all meant to do this together as a team."

I'm aware my arms are crossed as I say this, so I uncross them and stand taller. I'm not entirely sure what my face is doing, but I hope it isn't giving me away.

"What I'm trying to say is this journey is as much about us as it is about the river's magic."

"Right you are, Freddy, that's great to hear."

Did he hear me? He's gone from understanding every micro-gesture to not comprehending a simple "Back off!"

"So what I'm getting at is we don't want to be joined by your group on our journey. We'd like to keep going as we are, in our group of four."

Truin's smile drops as fast as if I've told him his mother was a gorilla, and not an attractive one at that. A frown emerges like lightning across his forehead as he loses control of his normally watertight facial expressions for a brief moment. As I speak my truth, I know he's processing this new information as fast as he can to compute the best possible strategy to divert my energy back in the direction he wants it to go. Back in your box, Truin. I understand about sub-currents.

"Aha, that's interesting to hear, Freddy. I totally understand where you guys are coming from. It's been such a personal journey for the four of you, and you've bonded as a group through the healing process. It makes a whole lot of sense that you should continue doing what's working for you. As they say, don't mess with a winning formula."

Well, I wasn't expecting that, but I know I'm not yet out of the woods.

"Thanks, I'm glad you understand. I knew you would."

"But I have one question for you," he continues with gravity. "Has your journey thus far been based upon letting the river, or, let's say, the universe, guide you? Or have you been calling the shots yourself like, let's say, a puppet-master, would do?"

He's smart, really smart. But so am I.

"Good question. I'd say the former. We've let the river guide us on our way, but by trusting the river we've found ourselves trusting ourselves and our gut instincts more and more. You'll be glad to hear it's our gut instincts which have led us to make this decision to travel forth alone."

Truin smiles, acknowledging a strong move when he sees one.

"OK, great. That's settled then. You guys should continue onwards as you are."

Have I underestimated my opponent, or have we clarified the situation as I'd hoped?

"We'll do our own thing as well, and I promise we won't bother you guys from now on. We'll swim the river without any help, input or guidance from your group, so you can swim away safe in the knowledge that we are swimming our own way, independent of the awesome foursome. We're even planning an epic party for when we arrive at the North Sea."

Swimming their own way to the North Sea? Bugger. I did underestimate him. He knows it too, as he appears to be suppressing an inner giggle. I'd recognize the symptoms anywhere.

Exit Stage Left

I return to Daphne, Alice and Willard, who are sunning themselves next to the river.

"Guys, I explained to him who must be obeyed over there that we want to go on our merry way by ourselves. The good news is they've accepted our position. But the bad news is they're planning to travel in the same direction as us, in the same river as us, at the same time as us, and towards the same end point as us."

"So they're just a big group of old-fashioned stalkers then. What a piddle," responds Willard. "What are our options then, old chap?"

"Well, we either accept that they're coming with us, or we leave now before they have a chance to get their shit together. Being small and nimble as a group is our main advantage as we can move much faster than they can. Shall we vote on it?"

"Aye, let's vote then," responds Alice.

"All those in favor of joining forces with the religious crowd, say aye."

Everyone is silent.

"All those in favor of getting the hell out of here now, say aye."

The four of us all say aye loudly and in unison. Even Daphne is fired up about it. Willard high fives each of us in a show of enthusiasm.

"OK, I don't see any reason to make a song and dance about it. I've already told them what we're doing, so that counts as a goodbye. Let's go."

We zip up our wetsuits, and are ready to leave within minutes. Upon surveying the scene, we conclude that our best unobserved exit point is the largest river tributary connecting with the back of the waterfall pool. It's pointing in the direction of the North Sea, the right direction.

"This way, guys."

We enter the river with a running leap. As the cold water embraces my body, I'm immediately back to feeling like a fish who's been out of the water for far too long, and is now home. Daphne is floating along as if she's always been a river swimmer, while Alice and Willard are rolling around like playful otters. The current is moving slowly here, so we half swim, half drift away. And soon, we're far away from the waterhole and all those strange characters who attempted to piggyback on our adventure. Our freedom tastes sweet.

The river becomes narrow and shallow around the corner which allows the current to pick up. While swimming here is easy, we take advantage of the shallow water by allowing our feet to guide and propel us forwards as though we're jogging through the water. It's liberating to be able to accelerate forwards while moving along with the current.

"How stupendous is it to be absent of that rabble, old chap?" asks a now relaxed Willard. "That fellow was the first person I've ever met with an inferiority complex which was fully justified."

I laugh freely, and Alice joins me.

"We're free!" enthuses Daphne as she flies through the water like an eagle.

The thought occurs to me that maybe Daphne needed to be captured to achieve her freedom, just like Willard needed to survive the whirlpool, and Alice needed to have fun in the stone-skimming competition. Maybe Truin was playing a part in the river's bigger game-plan. Or, then again, maybe he was just a nasty sub-current designed to make us appreciate being back on track.

"Woo-hoo!" calls out Alice as she fist-pumps the air. "It's more fun than I thought."

However, like acid rain on our parade, we can suddenly hear Truin's band playing music in the background. OK, so it wasn't a dream. The music has an eerily haunting effect as it descends upon the river like a chamber orchestra. While it sounds as if it's coming from behind us, it's also moving forwards with us, dancing around our every movement. Surely it must be the river's strange acoustics playing tricks with us again. I ignore it, as I suspect the little fish would tell me I have the power to make it all disappear by not believing it's real.

The Show

We slow down after another bend in the the river as it widens and loses momentum. As we put more space between us and the wrong direction, the sky becomes bluer and the air lighter. It's as though the North Sea is sharing some of its gifts with us from afar.

Strangely, the latest song we can hear from Truin's band is now echoing from directly inland, rather than from behind us where the waterhole is located. A small part of me is concerned that something seriously bad is afoot, but a large part of me couldn't care less. There's no changing the fact we're free of Truin's freak show, not when we know a simple trick called walking away.

"Why can't they leave us alone?" asks Daphne.

"Their need for answers is clearly more important than their ability to not stalk us. But look on the bright side: we're clearly far too interesting for our own good," I respond.

"My ancestors would have shot first and asked questions later in this situation. Maybe it's time for me to become the old-fashioned duke, if you know what I mean," adds Willard.

The music won't let us be, and is now upon us. We scan the side of the river, which is covered with tall trees swaying in the wind, warning us there are intruders at the gate. It's unclear how our pursuers caught up with us so quickly, or how they knew how to find us. The river's current is moving much faster than the average person's walking pace, so they must have moved with superhuman speed to catch up with us.

On cue, the band emerge from within the thick forest onto the riverbank. I can't help but admire the way they're kicking their feet high in the air, as though they're in the North Korean army, while also singing in perfect harmony. It would be a sight to behold if it weren't so terrifying.

Truin follows the band at the rear as if they're leading him forward, rather than the other way around. As the sunlight hits his face, he slowly turns it towards the heavens to breathe in the sunlight as if it's a fine wine. He's wearing a perfect-fitting wetsuit, as are the band, and every other man and his dog in the group. I wonder if they were bulk purchased from our friend at the Coldstream adventure store. I hope so.

"Hey guys," says Truin with his all too friendly smile. He appears as relaxed as if he's just arrived at a Mediterranean beach resort for a casual swim. "What a coincidence finding you here like this. We decided to search for the best access point for a large group like ours along the river. Our map shows that the river widens around here, so I'm glad we've found it."

"Oh right?"

"Yes. I hope it's still alright that we do our own thing as we discussed before you all departed without saying goodbye?"

If doing your own thing means buggering off, never to be seen again, then, yes, what a genius idea.

"Of course. We'd expected to be a fair way ahead of you by now so as to leave you guys more room in the river. Anyway, we'll be on our way now. Have a great day," I say as I turn to leave.

"Yes, message received loud and clear, you can rest assured. However, isn't it lucky how we've all reconnected at a point in the river where space is so abundant, so there's no need to worry about that. We're fortunate our creator has provided us with everything we need to happily co-exist in harmony," replies Truin with another knowing smile.

Why isn't speaking my truth working in this part of the river? What's this sub-current trying to teach me? Little fish, I need some help please.

"Isn't it a little dangerous to use one's entire vocabulary in a single sentence, old chap?" asks Willard, whose inner aristocrat is coming back to life.

"What a wonderful sense of humor you have, old chap," responds Truin with a weak attempt at a smirk. "But what a shame it is you're not the strong man your family line is famous for. It must be challenging to be a sensitive soul amidst the hard world of the aristocracy. I suppose that's why a fellow like you needs a little help in becoming a real man."

Willard is clearly thrown by Truin's cruel retort. His entire body has stiffened.

"What do you know about it? You'd best stick with your knitting, and be on your way," Willard responds with a quiver in his voice.

"Touchy one, isn't he? And yet, I know more about you than you may realize, Willard, Duke of Roxburghe. Surprised? My father was the minister at the church your family used to frequent when you were a child. And do you know what he told me about your father?"

"To be honest, I'm not interested in anything you have to say," responds Willard as he turns to leave.

"He told me your father always appeared as happy with your mother as a gypsy with a mortgage. A gypsy with a mortgage! Goodness I chuckled when I heard that."

Before our eyes, Truin is transforming into something far scarier than we ever imagined. Willard is stopped in his tracks. He turns around to face his tormentor with the same anger I saw in my dream when he half-fought, half-danced with Donny, the Duke of Sutherland. I pray he doesn't attempt something similar.

"Yes, you may be right about that. But one thing you've clearly not picked up on is that I've forgiven my father. I know he was doing the best he could with his life. Sorry, but you're barking up the wrong tree."

Truin is silent for a brief moment, which we all relish.

"I hope you're right about that because you never know how much time you have left to make your peace," he finally responds.

"Leave Willard alone," interjects Daphne with more backbone than I've seen from her. "And let me spell this out for you: please sod off."

Willard whispers, "Thank you my darling," to Daphne. Thinking that's finally the end of this uninvited conversation, the four of us resume our journey forwards. But, alas, we hear more words directed in our direction from behind.

"Well said, Daphne. I love watching a wife protecting her husband, and turning the whole weaker sex thing on its head."

"Ach, you're giving me the boak. I'll need a sick bag if you continue talking crap like this," Alice interjects matter-of-factly.

Truin laughs out loud, a not-quite-right-in-the-head laugh.

"Ah, shut your pie hole!" Alice shouts at him with the same anger as when she threw that glass at the wall after my karaoke performance. That memory seems to be from another lifetime.

Truin keeps chuckling away in the background. But out of the corner of my eye, I notice something more concerning. His cast of thousands are lining up alongside the river as though they're preparing to jump in.

"Into the river!" Truin shouts, pointing at the river section we're swimming in.

Inundation

The four of us turn towards the riverbank in time to witness Truin and his people leaping in unison into the river. Already there are at least fifty of them splashing happily around us, and there are more coming. There's no slow entry needed for these people to become accustomed to the freezing cold water. They wade in without fear as if they've always existed in the freezing cold water. And they're quickly spread out around us as if in a pre-agreed formation, an intricate web no doubt designed to prevent us from escaping. Each of their moves is so trained and controlled, I half expect them to start a synchronized swimming performance at any moment.

Despite the vast array of bodies which have appeared around us, there's a heavy, suffocating silence in the air. None of them are talking anymore, not a single word. Even Truin is lying back in the river gazing up at the sky in silence, and it's not often he's short of a word.

Willard, Daphne and Alice swim closer, so we're just out of earshot of the floating stalkers around us.

"What's our plan here, old chap?" whispers Willard. "How can we make them understand?"

"Yes, that's the right question. It's clearly time for a plan. Willard, you gave me an idea by the way you handled Truin just then."

"I gave you an idea? Who'd have thought it."

"He was trying so hard to push your buttons, and he hit you below the belt. But you bravely rose above it."

"Thank you, old chap. I hardly recognize myself these days, although between you and me I was tempted to man-slap that smug face of his for a split second."

"You're only human."

"Indeed."

"What I saw was you taking control of what his words did to you rather than allowing them to cause the intended damage, almost like a game in which you had the power to neutralize your enemy's weapons."

"So what's your idea, laddy? In case you hadn't noticed the intruders at the gate have turned amphibious," adds Alice with urgency.

"My idea is we start to view these stalkers as characters in a game which has been constructed for us by the river for a reason."

"Now you're talking my language, laddy. As the Giver on the River I haven't got time for anything less than fun and games," interjects Alice. "How do we play this particular game then?"

"I'd say we get to make up how the game works ourselves."

"Ach, you've lost me," says Alice. "What do you mean?"

"Well, for example, let's make it a rule that we're in charge of our own destiny in this game. Translation: we da boss no matter what." I smile.

"Aha, I like it," responds Alice. "Oh, I've got one. We get to keep it light-hearted regardless of what's happening around us, or what's floating around us, no matter how unpleasant it is. In fact, the darker the moment, the more lightness is needed," says Alice. I know Jimmy Carr the salmon would love this one. In fact, he'd love Alice.

"Well done, Alice," responds Willard. "Here's one from me. We reframe any less than perfect situations to make them more palatable. I remember when I was at boarding school, if I didn't like the dinner I was served I'd mash it all up together and give it a funny name. Toad in the Hole always tasted much better when it was called Toad on a Mediterranean Holiday. Hey, I had a lot of spare time on my hands."

I give Willard a quick high five for that one.

"I have one," whispers Daphne. "We love all aspects of our lives no matter what, no matter what."

"Well said, darling." Willard takes Daphne's hand. "And what a wonderful idea, Freddy. I almost hope these twats stick around a while longer so I can reframe that fellow's verbal diarrhea into something more socially acceptable, although that's a big ask."

"We're ready for whatever's coming next, team. To the North Sea," I say as we start picking up pace alongside the vast array of silently floating bodies.

Almost the moment we conclude our team talk, Truin swims over with the expertise of a fish. I'd recognize that fish-like swimming movement anywhere now. I wonder if he's somehow tied up with all my fishy dreams. It wouldn't surprise me.

"Hey, guys," Truin says warmly, as though it's the first time he's seen us today. "Since we've all reconnected in this glorious way, we want to invite you to a special event. Will you be our guests at a river banquet this evening? A few of our friends are setting it up a short distance downstream as we speak. It would be our pleasure to serve you up a feast in celebration of what you're doing, even if it is separate to our journey."

"Listen, I'll spell this out for you, old chap," Willard responds on behalf of the team. "There is indeed one thing we'd love from you that only you can provide."

"Name it," responds Truin.

"A postcard from anywhere but here," says Willard.

My inner giggle rises to the surface, as does Alice's. However, Truin doesn't react. He just lies back and gazes up at the sky. It's as though he was listening in to our game-playing strategies, and is already playing by the same rules. I can't comprehend how he's always a step ahead of us. Unfortunately, he doesn't swim away from us. He's floating alongside the four of us as if he's a welcome member of our group.

"It really is time for us to part ways now," I say to Truin. But his ears are underwater as he floats along, so he can't hear a word I'm saying.

"Guys, let's climb up the riverbank over yonder," I say to the other three, remembering the "we da boss" plan. "We can rest up, and leave all these people to swim on their way."

As we float towards the nearby shallow river bank, I have an overwhelming desire to crack a joke to lighten the mood.

"Alice, did I ever tell you about the time I visited a monastery?" I say with a slightly louder voice than normal to show these stalkers they aren't affecting our ability to enjoy ourselves.

"Nay, laddy."

"As I walked past the monastery kitchen, I saw a man frying chips. I asked him, 'Are you the friar?' And he replied, 'No, I'm the chip monk.'"

It's a Jimmy Carr the fish classic designed to shine a light into dark places, and Alice appreciates it. She laughs a little louder than usual.

Someone suddenly appears out of nowhere on the riverbank we're aiming for and calls out. Truin's team start waving madly at the caller-outerer, who's standing on a rock like an explorer who's finally found what she was hunting for. As quickly as they entered the river, Truin's drones exit the river *en masse* and in unison, scrambling up the riverbank like hungry spiders desperate for a kill after a long dry patch. So much for our escape plan.

Alice, Daphne, Willard and I form a huddle in the river like rugby players who are meeting at half-time to discuss how the game is going. Right now, it's hard to tell if we're on the winning side or not.

"Guys, we can swim with the river's current for another couple of hours before nightfall. That's likely to get us a few miles away, and far enough to be clear of these people for the evening," I suggest.

"Great idea, old chap. Let's just keep going. It's simple, but I like it."

As we're talking, I sense we're being watched. The girl who called out to the group from the riverbank is pointing at us from the same rock she was standing on like an overly diligent meerkat on patrol. "They're over here!" she calls out in her meerkat language, which is customized to notify as many people as efficiently as possible. A few of Truin's crew are running over with ropes in their hands. Where did they find rope so fast? Who cares. Four ropes land with a thud next to our heads in the river. They're as thick as pythons. Truin stands on the rock next to his meerkat to watch the scene unfold.

"You guys must be exhausted after all your swimming today. Grab the ropes and we'll pull you in," he calls out to us.

Without a second thought, Daphne starts swimming frantically away from the ropes, away from Truin and his drones. There's no mistaking she has escape on her mind. Willard follows Daphne as soon as he sees her move. Alice and I aren't hanging around either.

Of course, the moment you start fighting against the indomitable power of water, you're dead in the water. So within seconds, we run out of steam. Our escape effort becomes nothing but a slow-moving drift along with the current, while the shark in the river stalks us in ever-decreasing circles. Truin and his crew must be finding this bloody hilarious.

Ouch! Something hits me hard on the head. It's that damned rope again. This time it's been lassoed around my neck and is being pulled tight. It hurts.

Hanging Around

The noose around my neck becomes tighter and tighter. The life is being choked out of me as I'm yanked back towards the shore. The other three have also been caught, and are being hauled in alongside me.

A few of Truin's faceless jailors lurch forward to disentangle us from the ropes just before I black out. I breathe in a deep breath of air and let it bring my body back from the abyss. They drag our limp bodies out of the river and lift us to our feet with unnatural speed and superhuman strength. In short order, all four of us are being supported by two of them on each side. They speed-walk us up the riverbank towards a large table set up in the middle of the forest. The joy of being able to breathe again combined with passing the point of exhaustion is so overwhelming that I almost forget I've been captured against my will. I'm even starting to feel grateful that these people helped us out of the river after a long day of swimming. The line between friend and foe is so blurred when you're this close to the edge. Truin approaches us as we near the table.

"Guys, I'm so sorry for the clumsy attempt at saving you with the ropes. We concluded you were too exhausted to pull yourselves out of the river. The ropes were meant for you to hold onto while we pulled you to safety. What a clumsy bunch we are."

His smile doesn't quite reach his eyes, and is customarily inconsistent with an apology based upon empathy. We all know that things are going exactly the way he wants.

"You might have thought of that before you started choking us to death!" responds Willard.

"Indeed. As I say, I'm dreadfully sorry for that."

"What's your game, old chap? Bullshit aside, why are you all so damned desperate for us to have dinner with you? We never even met you before today. Are you that short of friends?"

"What a great question. I promise to explain everything over dinner if you can stand to join us for a feast of all your favorite foods, cooked by our talented chef. I got my team to do some research beforehand to ensure we could accommodate your respective tastes. Daphne, we've prepared an Italian tricolore salad as a starter with you in mind. Alice, we have a cullen skink second course concocted for you. Willard, we've brought in your favorite red wine, the Viña Tondonia Rioja. And Freddy, we've prepared a spaghetti Bolognese course exactly how you like it, full of garlic and herbs, and with a dash of Willard's favorite red wine thrown in for good measure."

My mouth starts to water as my stomach does a little dance. Damn it, Truin, stop commanding our stomachs' attention as if they're members of your crew.

"How on earth did you find all that out about us? Have you got spies running around for you?" I ask.

"Well yes, if you call the world of social media a spy. All of you have divulged information online over the years about your likes and dislikes, as have most members of the human race. It took us less than five minutes to ascertain what you'd like most for dinner, and, voila, your dreams are appearing as if by magic."

On cue, Truin waves his arm at a group of his people who are standing at attention like well-trained soldiers. They start carrying out plate loads of food.

"Thank you, Facebook, thank you, Google, thank you, Instagram. You may even want to thank our little team at the end of the meal, but we shall see," says Truin like a proud father.

"There's one small problem with your dinner plan, old chap. We don't want to be here. In case you hadn't noticed, we've told you more than once to sod off." Willard eyes off a bottle of his favorite red wine, which is heading in his direction like an arrow flirting with its target.

"Guys, I understand where you're coming from. You don't know us, and out of nowhere we appeared as if out of a puff of smoke. But have you considered the notion we may be a positive part of your journey? Maybe this is all meant to be."

The four of us respond with silence. I assume the others are going through the same battle between head and heart as me on this one. My heart is currently winning this battle hands down, and it's not pleased.

"Why don't you at least try some dinner while you're here?" Truin suggests with less force.

"Och aye. Since you've dragged us here like drowned rats, let's say we believe that phish. Let's have a wee bit of dinner, and then we'll be on our way," Alice finally responds in her typical no-nonsense manner, driven by her no-nonsense appetite for a tasty meal. My stomach agrees. Surely, we deserve a good meal after another long day in the river, and then we'll finally be on our way.

Story Telling

The four of us sit at the dinner table. Oh. My. God. There are no words to describe how delicious the food smells. The garlic dances through the air, and deep dives into our nasal passages to sing the arrival of the spaghetti Bolognese. The herbs in the Bolognese sauce pirouette into our senses shortly thereafter, led by the oregano which moves with the grace of a ballet dancer in perfect tune with the garlic's dancing. Next up, the sage zigzags like a synchronized swimmer who's working its way around the other herbs, making them better at their craft. It's a performance to behold, and the indomitable smells are taking control of our senses without our permission.

Willard looks like he'd say yes to eating dinner while handcuffed and standing on his head. Alice is relaxing into the moment as she eyes up the large bowl of cullen skink with her name on it. Daphne is the exception. She remains in control, despite the alluring food offerings.

I'm snapped out of my smell-induced dream-like state by movement around the table. Truin sits down opposite us with four people in tow. After a few moments trying to place their faces, I recognize them as the band members. The five of them ooze the relaxed and trusted vibe of old friends who know everything about one another. I'm conscious that there are five of them, and only four of us. Somehow this seems to put us at an important disadvantage, but I have no idea why.

"Welcome to our little feast here, guys," starts Truin with his customary Cheshire-cat smile. "I'd like to introduce you to the members of our very talented band, Enlightened Rabbit. This is Shannon, who sings, Wilco, who plays drums, Sinclair, who plays guitar, and Ewan, who also plays guitar. We're so proud of the way these guys are breathing life back into Frightened Rabbit's important music at a time when the world needs to heal like never before."

"Hello, yes I recognize each of you from when you were stalking us earlier," responds Willard.

"Guys, please help yourselves to dinner before it gets cold," says Truin, ignoring Willard's retort.

Willard doesn't need to be asked twice. Within seconds, he's piled his plate high with food and has a glass of red wine at the ready. Alice and I help ourselves to dinner, although with less abandon than Willard. Alice dishes out a serving of cullen skink and breathes in its aromas like a fish soup connoisseur. Daphne, on the other hand, doesn't help herself to anything. She remains uninterested, despite the seductive smells which have taken control of the rest of us. Is she being excessively cautious? Surely we all deserve to enjoy a decent meal together after a long day in the river. I shovel the food into my mouth as though I haven't eaten for months. And the more I eat, the hungrier I become.

Across the table, Truin and the band are watching us intently rather than eating. Truin clinks his glass with a spoon and stands up as if he's about to give a speech. I wish him silent.

"Guys, I wanted to say a few words if I may."

There's no response from our side of the table. We couldn't care less what Truin says or does while we're gorging ourselves on the feast at hand.

"Great, thanks. One of the reasons we're so excited to have you join us on this special journey is connected with the notion of facing life's difficulties through song—sharing the individual's pain to alleviate the group's pain. It's amazing how many people respond positively to singing their problems away, and yet it's also startling how few people in the world realize this. So we had an idea. What if we were to create a movement around music which helps millions of people turn their problems into opportunities. And the biggest opportunity of them all is to help them heal and become whole again. Sounds pretty exciting, don't you think?"

Truin pauses and glares intently at the four of us like a leopard stalking its prey. What does he want from us beyond an Oscar nomination?

"You'll know that all good music is based upon stories, and all good stories start with real people. And the best stories grow over time to become far more powerful than the seed from whence they grew."

He stands like a tree with his arms out when he says this.

"When a human life transforms into a powerful story," he continues, "and many people tell it over time, each layer of retelling adds more meaning to the original tale. What starts as a simple but honest story can evolve into a global movement. And there's only one absolute requirement for this to happen."

He waits for us to ask what that may be, but we remain focused on dinner. I chump down on a big mouthful of Bolognese sauce and try to ignore the background noise otherwise known as Truin's chatter. But he continues unperturbed.

"The original story must be one hundred per cent original, unique, and, most importantly, it must mean something to the common man. And that's the challenge. After so many billions of human lives over the centuries, how many human stories can be described as truly original these days? As the Beatles sang sixty year ago, 'There's nothing you can do that can't be done / Nothing you can sing that can't be sung / Nothing you can say but you can learn how to play the game.' Never were wiser words penned. Most people are retelling the same stories over and over again like groundhog day, and we've all become used to the merry-go-round working like that. It's hardly surprising we've all become so jaded. We've overdosed on the same boring tales of human existence for too long."

Truin pauses as if to contemplate his own genius.

"So you can imagine how excited we all became when we heard of a truly original story involving real people. Consider for a moment the tale of the man who jumped into a freezing-cold Scottish river to end his life because it wasn't the life he wanted. But this man doesn't die as he hoped. Instead, he's saved by the river, and then by a local man grieving for his son whom he lost to the river. Can you see the remarkable circularity in this story?"

Truin's hands move in a circular motion so as to reinforce his point. All I notice are circles forming in my spaghetti as I twirl it around my fork in preparation for another juicy mouthful.

"Over time, our hero realized that the act of giving himself to the river was the very act that saved his life. So this man was saved by something far bigger and less explicable than the world we humans can see and understand. There's something far more mystical at play here. Can you see that this story proves that having faith is indeed the one and only answer to fulfilling our potential?"

Truin glances around. Alice, Willard and I stop gorging ourselves for a moment when we hear this. What Truin is saying suddenly seems to mean something, and even in my food-induced stupor I can tell it is bad news for us. I take a deep breath and remind myself that nothing bad can happen on the river's watch.

"It's clear that this story, your story, is one of those important stories which could make a difference. This man and the people who joined him in the river are uniquely qualified to become important historical figures, leaders for others to follow on the pathway towards healing. I believe this story is the start of an important movement which will build over time as the myth around it grows through each retelling."

"Och aye, whoopty-do. Pass me the wine," responds Alice.

Orchestra Conductor

The effect of gorging myself full of food is taking its toll. I feel the sort of sleepy I used to experience as a child when sitting in the backseat of the car with my head rolling from side to side while being taken hostage by the forces of slumber. I wonder if we'll make it home before I fall asleep.

I open my eyes. I'm back in the river. And I'm not surprised that I have a fish tail. I know this drill so well now. I'm overjoyed to be back where I belong, and also far away from the incessant noise of Truin and the human world. I start swimming fast and free, and let the cold water wash away the memories of a rather strange evening.

I'm not alone in the water. Up ahead, I notice a large school of fish engaged in what appears to be some sort of group exercise. They're swimming fast in circles around something in the middle, which I can't see. But something is wrong. They're swimming erratically around one another without the stylish finesse of fish who know how to swim together as a school. They're bumping into one another at key turning points, rather than changing direction in time with the fish near to them. It's like observing a fish school for dummies on a training outing. It sure ain't pretty.

1 swim closer as I'm curious. Up close, the awkward bumping into one another is more brutal than it appears from a distance. These fish are whacking hard into one another, and at high speeds. Each hit must be causing serious pain, and yet they keep doing it over and over again. If anything, they appear to be speeding up as they go, hitting even harder into one another. Amidst their fast and erratic movements, 1 catch a glimpse of the thing they're circling. It's large and shiny. 1 suddenly realize what it is: a big fish.

Not just big, it's a monster. It must be around fifty times the size of these smaller fish. It's hovering in an almost stationery position while the smaller fish swim frantically around it. The big fish seems to be somehow communicating with the smaller fish, like a conductor in charge of an orchestra. There are no words or sounds being exchanged, but there's something about the big fish's unerring confidence in its position as the center of the action which confirms some form of communication is indeed occurring.

All of a sudden, the small fish come to a grinding halt. And, after a momentary glance in my direction, the big fish turns around and starts swimming slowly downstream, away from me. Nice to meet you to, oh great leader of my kind. The small fish form an orderly queue behind it, and follow the big fish away. Their swimming is so slow and orderly, and so contrary to how it had been only seconds earlier.

Involuntarily, 1 start following the line of fish without understanding or wanting whatever lies at its end. Maybe this is the exception to every rule I've ever learned, and everything the little fish has taught me. Maybe these fish are leading me somewhere better than where I was, and maybe my gut instinct is just plain wrong. But, deep in my heart, where the little fish used to live, I have no idea why I'm following them, or what the hell I'm doing here.

As I swim behind them it's becoming clear these fish are very different from the little fish I know so well. Their eyes are dead and fish-like, and soulless. The more time I spend here, the more I feel their dead-eyed-ness creeping into my soul, where it hangs damp and heavy like wet clothes on a cold day. The big fish never turns around to check on their progress, on my progress. It swims forward with the smallest possible tail movements, as if it's trying to conserve energy. And like a master puppeteer, it seems to know for certain that the smaller fish will follow its every move.

Finally, something appears to be happening up front. We're adjusting course, albeit very slowly. The big fish stops using its left pectoral fin and swims harder with its right pectoral fin. It's gradually moving its gigantic body to the left, like the *Titanic* changing direction ahead of an iceberg. The small fish continue to follow, driven by their blind faith in the big fish. They don't seem to care about where they're going anymore, just as long as they don't have to think about which direction they're heading.

Ahead there's something on the side of the river which the big fish is aiming for. It's a gate. As we approach it, the gate opens slowly like a toll gate after the toll operator has been paid its dues. Through the gate we swim in our orderly line, following the big fish into a world of darkness.

I sense the panic of short and sharp movements all around me. The other small fish are still swimming nearby, but for some reason they've lost their sense of calm. More and more collisions are happening around me as the small fish become frenzied. If I could speak whatever language the little buggers understand, I'd try to calm them down. However, I'm no calmer than they are. They may not be able to swim properly in a fish school, but at the end of the day we're all the same. We're all trying to survive. And we all want to be one of those magical fish who make it all the way upstream despite the evidence to the contrary. None of us want to hear what David Attenborough would have to say about our prospects of success at this point—please keep it to yourself, Dave.

Suddenly, a bright light beams down through the water to reveal the world we're part of. The abruptness of the change is even more terrifying than the darkness itself. I scream an underwater scream which emerges as small bubbles of fear. Luckily, the small fish are too busy panicking to judge me for it. After blinking my eyes a few times as they become accustomed to the intense brightness, the reality of our situation comes into focus. We're swimming in a large fish tank within a military building or compound. But the big fish is nowhere to be seen. It's just me and the other small fish swimming frantically around one another. Thanks, big fish, for leading us astray and then buggering off like that. You're a real leader of your species.

A face hovers above us. Someone is peering into the tank from the standing area where the lights are shining down from. Hang on, I recognize that face. I swim closer for a double take.

I'll be damned. It's Donny, the Duke of Sutherland, the charming fellow who pulled me out of the river as a fish in an earlier dream, and the fellow Willard attacked on my behalf. Where's Willard when you need him? I didn't like Donny when I dreamt he tried to kill me the first time around, and I like him even less now. I watch him suspiciously from below. He's pushing some buttons on a device attached to a long cord. And out of the blue, music starts playing in the tank.

Oh no. It's the same Frightened Rabbit song the band were playing at the bottom of the waterfall, "Floating in the Forth." The words "And the door shut shut / I was vacuum packed / shrink-wrapped out of air" reverberate throughout the tank and force themselves into my fishy ears against my will. The tank suddenly feels very small.

This does not bode well for me. I always suspected this song would drift into my consciousness at a moment exactly like this. In fact, I seem to recall having lived through this moment in a dream when I was younger. They say that you become your thoughts, so that must be what's happening. All those times I've dreamt of ending it all are rushing back to me in white-water rapids of pain. Am I any further ahead in the river of life than when I jumped into the river?

The other fish around me are reacting to the song, although not as I would have guessed. Having been unable to swim properly as a fish school only moments earlier, they've started swimming in unison as though they're a single body. They've finally evolved into the expert swimmers they were meant to be, and are swimming together beautifully as a school. For a moment, I forget where I am, and I'm captivated by their stunning performance.

Out of the corner of my eye, I notice one of the small fish darting fast towards the water surface. Then it disappears out of the tank into whatever lies beyond. What the? Another fish follows in short order, rushing at the surface and jumping out of the water. And another follows, and another. It's as though they're all jumping out of the tank towards where the duke is standing. But this doesn't make any sense. Why would they do that? Like a bunch of lemmings who've witnessed a few of their comrades jumping off a cliff and then communally deciding it's a brilliant idea to follow, the other small fish are now charging towards the tank's surface as a school. I watch them disappear into the nothingness beyond the water's surface. In seconds they're all gone, every last one of them.

I've never felt so alone. Without the small fish swimming around me, the tank seems like the end of the world, a vast gap of emptiness where life enters only to disappear into nothingness for eternity. The desolation seeps deep into my soul. I hover without purpose.

The song continues to play in the tank. The volume is rising relentlessly, and my fish ears are starting to hurt. My rational self knows this nightmare will end because the river's momentum ensures all things will pass. But my less rational self feels an overwhelming need to follow the other fish towards the surface, through to the other side. It would all be so simple. All I have to do is swim as fast as I can towards the surface, and maybe everything will be OK. Maybe life is better on the other side. All I have to do is jump, jump into the great unknown which is staring at me from above, screaming at me to follow the small fish like the little fish I am. If it's good enough for them, surely it's good enough for me.

Even though the little fish isn't in the tank with me, I know he'd recommend some thinking time. I can just imagine him saying, "Gathering more information can only be helpful before all big decisions." So I swim to the water's surface and squint at the bright lights to ascertain what's really happening above the surface. No, it can't be! The duke is holding open a large freezer box full of motionless small fish. Mystery solved. As if responding to orders from above, the small fish all jumped out of the safety of the water straight into the duke's open freezer. It was strategically positioned to collect their soon to be dead bodies as efficiently as possible. He just asked them to jump, and they willingly gave up their lives for him without a second thought.

The duke stares down into the tank, directly into my eyes. He sees through me in every possible way. I can feel him feeding on my fear. I'm just another fish for him to

capture and consume—his takeaway fish 'n' chips awaiting pick-up. He gestures towards me to "Come here," as
he points at the freezer enthusiastically. "You know you
want to, Freddy," is the message I'm receiving loud and
clear. Who cares anymore.

However, something small and hidden inside me is
stopping me from jumping. It's fighting against my urge
to throw everything away. This tiny something within
me is wondering if there may be a better outcome for
me by not doing what I want to do, and by being dis-
ciplined for once in the face of my emotional turmoil.
"Think about it," says my subconscious interrogator
deep within. "Rolling the dice randomly has not worked
for you in the past. Why would you repeat a pattern
which has always been a road to nowhere?" It continues
with, "What about learning a lesson or two along the
way?" Did I hear the words "you idiot" at the end of that
question? Hang on, I recognize that voice. It's only the
know-it-all little fish. Hallelujah! He's returned to help
me in my time of crisis by attaching himself somewhere
in my subconscious. He's an inventive one, and he's
most welcome.

What's that, oh wise one? His next words come clear
and loud. "Yes," he continues, "life is all about rolling the
dice as you have done so many times in the past, but you
need to know what you want the dice to land on before
you roll the damned things. Otherwise you're driving
blind like one of those lemmings running off a cliff,
hoping you can somehow defy gravity and avoid the
sharp rocks below. But no one avoids the sharp rocks

below once they've accepted the wrong unknown." Did he just call me "stupid"? I was hoping for a little more empathy. "More importantly," he continues, "the river, the universe, whatever you want to call it, can't deliver to you whatever it is you want because you don't know what you want. You're destined to live a life of disappointment if you keep insisting on living your life like a piece of driftwood." He's getting quite worked up now, and asks his next question with venom. "What the fuck do you want from your life? It's time to make some decisions. And the more specific your answers, the more likely it is they'll emerge in your life as if by magic."

Alright, little fish. Jesus, I hear you.

Heavy-Footed

The first thing is, you over-talkative little bastard, I want to live. And by the way, I fucking love my life. The words come out of my mouth while I'm looking at the duke, but I'm thinking of the little fish and his annoying know-it-all head-nodding habit. The duke appears to hear what I'm saying as though we're sitting across from one another in the same room. He nods his head in the same way as the little fish. With disappointment in his eyes, he turns away from me, away from the water tank. He slams closed the freezer full of dead fish with a bang which reverberates throughout the tank as the music comes to an end. The lights in the facility turn off as if it was the freezer which was providing all the light. Day has once again turned to night, and I close my eyes to become one with the darkness.

There's a strange smell in the tank. It reminds me of spaghetti Bolognese. Of course it does. I open my eyes to find I'm back at Truin's dinner table with my head lying on the table. I've been asleep. I lift my head up off the table and gaze around. Daphne, Willard and Alice are all fast asleep next to me, and there doesn't appear to be anyone else around.

But something terrible is going on. My feet don't feel right, and not in a now-I'm-a fish-and-have-a-tail kind of way. I peer under the table to discover that I'm wearing what appears to be a pair of ski boots. I try lifting my feet but nothing happens. The boots are weighted to the ground, and I'm stuck. As if to reinforce the point, I've also been tied to my chair. What has Truin done to me?

Willard starts to stir. He lifts his groggy head.

"Whoa. What on earth happened, old chap?"

"We've all been drugged."

"I had the craziest dream," Willard continues.

"Let me guess. You were a fish, and you were caught in a tank with a bunch of other fish who all committed mass suicide by jumping out of the water?"

"Who gave you a view into the inner workings of my crazy mind? It was intense, old chap. I'm so glad to be alive."

"Me too. I had the same dream, but we have bigger issues to deal with right now. Look down at your feet."

"What on earth is going on?" hisses Willard as he discovers that his feet are also weighted down in these strange ski boots and his body is tied to his chair.

Alice and Daphne both start stirring when they hear our voices. They look down at their feet to discover their feet are also trapped inside the same boots, which can't be moved.

"What have they done to us?" asks a spaced-out Alice.

"I'm afraid we've been captured. These nutters have more serious issues than we thought. Everything will be OK, though. Won't it, Freddy?" Doubt vibrates throughout Willard's being.

"Yes, if we want it to be. Remember, we're in charge of the game," I respond, trying to convince myself it's true.

"I do want everything to be OK. I'm ready for happily ever after, old chap, for the first time in my life."

Daphne remains silent. Willard tries to reach her to put his arm around her, but he can't quite reach.

"Everything will be alright, darling. We didn't come this far to only come this far," Willard says to her.

Willard tries to remove his feet from the boots like a wild animal caught in a trap. But the more he fights, the more trapped he becomes.

Truin and the band suddenly emerge out of the darkness as if they've always been at one with the color black. Have they been listening to us? Truin's smile remains plastered on his face as usual, but the band members appear downcast and tired.

"Morning, sleepyheads. Did you enjoy your slumber?" Truin asks as if we're family members who've been staying over at his home for the weekend.

"What are you playing at? What have you put on our feet?" asks Willard furiously.

"Oh yes. You'll have noticed that we've given you all a pair of our specially crafted river boots. Don't tell anyone. The whole world will want a pair."

"What? Why can't we move, you scoundrel?"

"Yes, sorry about that. It's a technicality we haven't mastered yet. The good news is they're great for river swimming, as you'll soon discover."

"River swimming in these? Are you mad?"

"Guilty as charged, old chap, but aren't we all? As much as I'd like to, I'm afraid I can't sit here chatting with you lovely folk all day. I must prepare. The band will help ready you for your next river-swimming adventure. Don't worry, we won't be joining you. We'll respect your wishes to continue forwards on you own pathway."

"Listen, old chap, I'd prefer a battle of wits but you appear unarmed, so I'll just say this once: release us now if you don't want to spend the rest of your life in jail," responds Willard.

"I love your gusto. It's the thing about you we'll all remember the most fondly." Truin smiles.

"Ach, you're the reason God created the middle finger," interjects Alice.

Talking with this maniac is a waste of time, so I remain silent, as does Daphne. Truin walks backward into the darkness. The band members march off with him like a fearful platoon following its dreaded leader.

"Guys, our fun day out has officially turned into a kidnapping situation," surmises Willard.

"It's worse than that," adds Daphne. "They want us dead."

"Well, they can't have us dead, darling. Freddy, they can't have us dead, you hear me?"

"I hear you. What do you suggest we do?"

"I'll offer them bucket loads of cash to free us. For once in my life, my family's fortune will be useful," responds Willard.

"Aye, offer 'em some dosh. It's folly to live poor and dee rich," adds Alice.

"What do you think, honey?" Willard asks Daphne.

Daphne remains silent for a long time while she considers our perilous position.

"This is not about our bloody money. It's much more serious than that. But we'll be alright. Trust me."

"I do, darling."

Before we can devise an escape plan, the band members march back towards the table. Three of them are pushing what appears to be an old-fashioned horse cart. The other one, the drummer I think, is pushing a crate-lifting machine you'd normally find on a factory floor. He approaches Willard's chair from behind and places the lifting machine underneath it.

"Hello there? Hello, I say! Can we talk for a moment?" pleads Willard.

There's no response from the emotionless drones. The drummer is focused on operating the machine, which is now lifting Willard's chair off the floor while beeping the customary industrial machine warning signal. The beeps come slow and loud. If only we'd recognized the warning signals earlier for what they were, and there had been many along the way.

Willard's chair is maneuvered with the lifting machine onto the horse cart, which the other band members have positioned next to the table. He's rooted onto the horse cart by the weighted boots, once again unable to move. Willard catches my eye from above. I understand the expression on his face: he's fighting against the need to fight. And, as he takes a few deep breaths, he's reminding himself it's all but a game. He's reframing the situation and is starting to relax into the current's flow.

The band members methodically capture Alice, Daphne and me in the same way. They lift the three of us and our weighted boots onto the horse cart next to Willard. We're stranded next to one another on the edge of the darkness, peering down on the human race from above.

The band members stand back and gaze up at us. It seems for a brief moment as though we're sitting high on our thrones addressing our loving subjects who'd do anything for us, even roll us around in a horse cart if we want them to. However, their eyes tell a very different story. While they're devoid of the human emotions which would ordinarily provide a clue as to what they're thinking, their masks are wobbling. I try to put myself in their shoes. I imagine they've been gradually downtrodden by Truin over the years. He would have no doubt crushed their spirits, and forced them to see the world the way he sees it. And there's only one word to describe Truin's perspective of the world: cruel. He takes joy in taking control of others' lives to allow him to become the big fish he wants to be. Bit by bit, Truin would have worn them down with his incessant lectures about how they're creating an important movement which will change the course of history forever. He would have talked to them about how their names will fill the history books for future generations because, just like a well-trained school of fish, each of them is playing an important role for the bigger whole. And whenever they had doubts about Truin's ideas, he would have talked them back around with the power of well-reasoned words, just like Socrates in his heyday. It's hard to say this is really their fault. They're victims just like us. No, not like us. The V word is a word I erased from my vocabulary earlier in my river journey.

One of the band members smirks. Yes, it's a definite smirk. That's the cruelty bubbling to the surface through the dead-eyed depression. With their pre-programmed perspective in mind, I imagine they're looking at us as if we're circus freaks who people come to watch to feel better about themselves. Go ahead and smirk. But you're the ones wearing the masks. We shed ours a while back. As this awareness descends upon me I realize I'd still rather be in my shoes, however heavy they appear, than the shoes of the people staring up at me. No, more than that. I'd rather be in my shoes than anyone else's in the entire world. Being Freddy is all I want. What a time for this epiphany to strike.

The band members move to the back of the cart and start pushing us towards the river. The horse cart stops moving a couple of feet away from the river. Truin appears once more out of nowhere. He's not smiling anymore.

To the Riverbed

I watch the river from the horse cart above. It's like seeing an old friend who knows you're screwed and is trying to change the subject to avoid discussing the elephant in the room. But it's still like seeing an old friend, even now. The river gurgles loving sounds in my direction.

They've thought of everything. Their system is unbreakable. The horse cart has been positioned next to a side pool which is out of the river's main current, so we have no chance of being saved by the river's current. And the water below us is dark black, which means it's a deep pool. There's only one way this is going to play out. And yet, I feel strangely relaxed as I know nothing bad could ever happen here.

Truin steps forward. Without his fake smile plastered on, with his mask removed, he looks like a schoolyard bully who hasn't evolved since his glory years of inflicting pain on defenseless children. He's David Attenborough's arch-nemesis. Just when the audience expects some empathy and compassion towards the poor dying salmon who were trying to swim upstream, Truin's voice overrides David's famously sympathetic tones with: "These fish deserve to die. They knew they had to swim upstream to fulfil their life's mission, but they didn't make it. Let me spell that out for you: they failed. And that's how nature works. If you're a fish who fails, I'll look forward to frying you up on my barbeque for dinner, because that's the best place for you. No, that's the only place for you. Yummy."

Truin's minions congregate around him like a perfectly attuned fish school. They turn to their great leader as if he's about to address them. Of course he bloody is.

"We are gathered here today to give thanks," he begins, "thanks to these four wonderful humans for all they've done, all they've given, all they will give. The world needs inspiring stories like never before. The world needs heroes and heroines like never before. Look around. We can all see that the human race has lost its way, and is now drifting aimlessly towards destruction. Today, we are here to say that change is needed, and change is possible. A new movement is emerging which values human lives and human needs, while recognizing that humanity is inherently flawed."

As Truin pauses to draw breath, I notice Willard, Alice and Daphne are all relaxed and watching Truin as if he's nothing but an actor in a film. He may be a straight-to-DVD type of guy, but all four of us are well and truly in the moment. Knowing how hard it is to relax into a dangerous current, I'm beyond impressed by the three of them.

"The story the world needs today is one of sacrifice. It's always been the way. But not just any sacrifice. We need the sacrifice to come from the people who have connected with others through their pain, those at the center of the story that matters. Remarkably, these people have shown the world that moving to just beyond the maximum point of pain is where the real growth begins. I'm talking about the heroes and heroines who started this movement based on dreaming that life can be better, should be better, will be better."

He's on a roll. I wonder if anyone has ever talked themselves to death by overdosing on bullshit. We may need to call an ambulance shortly.

"Freddy, what an inspiration you were. You jumped into the river only a few weeks ago because you'd lost all hope and were ready for your sacrifice even then. Yet somehow, against all odds, you were saved. Through that process of being saved, you then became a savior for others to learn from and follow. Rest assured, we shall mourn your passing, and you shall become a key figure, the key figure in our movement. People shall remember your name throughout the ages."

"Isn't that's Sod's law at work?" I respond, without planning to speak my thoughts out loud. "I've been wanting my less than memorable name remembered for as long as I can remember, and here it is being offered to me on a plate for eternity by a deranged psychopath who wants to kill me. What were the chances?"

Alice giggles out loud. Truin is perplexed by my response, and moves on without responding.

"Willard and Daphne, what an extraordinary amount of pain you two have experienced. It's hard to imagine how difficult it was to lose Georgie to the river like you did. For you both to recognize the opportunity for grieving and redemption that Freddy brought to your front door on that fateful day is inspiring. You have shouted to the messiah, 'Bring on the pain; life can be better through the pain!' Rest assured, we shall mourn your passing, and you shall always be remembered as the best of parents, the best of people."

Daphne's quiet resolve is unchanged despite it all. She and Willard catch each other's eye and hold it for a moment. But they remain resolutely silent.

"And Alice, your positive energy helped countless people, both within your household and across the local community. You were always there for others when they needed help. Rest assured, we shall mourn your passing, and you shall always be remembered as a light bearer for future communities."

"Ach, you've got a face like a well-skelped ass," Alice directs back at Truin.

The band step forward from the nameless, faceless crowd, carrying their instruments and looking as down-beat as ever. They start singing the all too familiar "Heads Roll Off" by Frightened Rabbit, but they're playing it far more slowly than the original as if they have all the time in the world to sing it. If only that were the case. The song's significance is not lost on me as the words "Jesus is just a Spanish boy's name / how come one man got so much fame?" are sung pointedly at us.

A tear rolls down my cheek. Ever since I jumped into the river, I've been living in hope I'll make those tiny changes this song is all about while I'm on earth. I was running for the line to make it happen. I even promised the little fish I'd make a plan for what those tiny changes would be. However, as I face the prospect of my head rolling off, I'm not sure if I've made those tiny changes. What have I accomplished? I didn't make it to the North Sea. And the world looks very much the same as before I jumped into the river. Here I am awaiting my grisly fate, just like those poor salmon who didn't make it upstream. Worse than that, I've brought down three people with me, three people it turns out I love. What a time to realize that! I love Willard, Daphne and Alice. They've only gone and become my family through this experience. And rather than saving their lives, and helping them heal like they needed, I've brought them into the lion's den via the front door. My impending death is irrelevant in the face of these realizations.

A few of Truin's faceless minions step towards the horse cart we're perched upon. They start tipping the cart backwards towards the river with predictable efficiency. There's nothing for any of us to hold on to, so as soon as the horse cart's angle steepens, our chairs start sliding towards the river.

I take a deep breath as we slide off the cart and plunge into the dark deep pool below. The cold water feels like knives penetrating my vulnerable body. We all sink like stones.

Movement in the Dark

I hit the bottom of the river with an abrupt thud. My weighted boots find their pre-ordained place on the dark muddy riverbed below, resulting in an eruption of disrupted mud around me. With that final deep breath, I've got anywhere between one and two minutes before it's game over since I'm nothing but a human today of all days. I start counting the seconds and praying for a miracle. Any ideas, little fish? I need more than clever words this time. One, two, three, four, five ...

Out of the corner of my eye, I sense something is moving. Or is it? It's so dark down here, it's hard to see much at all. Yes, there's definitely movement happening nearby. Someone or something is swimming around. I can't be sure, but maybe there's more than one thing moving.

Suddenly, what appears to be a large fish and a little fish swim right up to me and look me in the eye before swimming down to my boots. No, maybe they're not fish. It's murky down here, so I squint for a better view. It's a person, possibly two people. Yes, two people: one adult and one child. And they're fiddling with my boots. The adult seems to be focused on unlocking my boots while the child is helping. The child is also intermittently patting the adult on the back. In a matter of seconds, the two of them have unlocked my right-hand boot and are helping pull my leg out of it. And a few seconds later they've unlocked my left-hand boot and are once again helping pull my leg out. My feet are free! I hope this is not a dream. I need this to be real. I push off the riverbed with all my might.

However, I'm not out of the woods yet. I'm not sure if I can make it all the way to the surface. It's such a long journey, and I have an overwhelming desire for a quick nap. I hover for a moment and notice there's still action afoot down below.

Beneath me, the adult and child who set me free are still swimming around the riverbed. Should I go back down to help them? Since they saved me from the jaws of death, I'm morally obliged to help them. And if the adult is from our group, this is also about saving someone I love. Yes. Without a second thought, I turn back around and swim towards them.

The two of them are now helping the other two booted people out of their boots. They're struggling with one set of boots, so I swim over to help. However, the lock is stuck. I can tell the adult helper is tiring and the child is weak, so I take the lead by putting both my hands around the lock's key while positioning my feet on the riverbed for leverage. I turn the key with everything I've got, and this time the key moves and the lock opens. However, the person in the boots is on their last legs and is unable to release themselves from the opened boots. As I stand up to help them, a little of the unsettled mud clears, and I can see the face of the boot-ed person. It's my father's face. I recognize him through the murkiness. What's he doing here? This was about saving Willard, Daphne or Alice. My people, the people I love. But I know what I have to do. I help pull his feet out of the boots and lift him upwards so he has a chance at swimming away. The movement reanimates him and returns him from the abyss for one more shot at life. As he starts swimming, I push him as hard as I can to help him on his way. It's beautiful to watch him swimming towards the surface like a salmon *en route* for success.

I know I should be joining him on the upwards jour-ney, but something is stopping me. And it's not the little fish this time. It's me. I know I'm needed down here for just a moment longer. The idea of dying doesn't scare me in the slightest, but the idea of not living my life to the full terrifies me. And that's what's keeping me here in these murky depths.

As the mud clears, and a degree of visibility returns, I notice that the adult and child are still underwater with me. Inexplicably, they're just sitting on the riverbed together as though it were the most natural place in the world to be hanging out. I swim over to them and signal to them by pointing at the surface that we need to swim upwards now. "We all need to live!" I bubble in their direction. I can no longer tell if I'm a fish or a human. It doesn't matter anymore.

But the mysterious adult and child still refuse to move. They're holding each other's hands as if they're waiting for something or someone. If they refuse to save themselves, I'll give it my best shot to help them. That's clearly what I'm here for. To make the positive difference I've always dreamt of making. To live a life with meaning. I take hold of one of each of their hands in preparation to push off the riverbed with both of them in tow. However, the child becomes agitated and tries to swim away from me the moment I hold its hand. Bizarrely, the adult helps the child disentangle itself from my hand and pushes the child away from us. Away from us.

"No, come back!" I bubble in the child's direction. "Please come back." But the child keeps swimming, and the adult is just waving at it. Letting it go. Then the adult signals to me that it is indeed time to head upwards, and pushes off the riverbed.

"What about the child!" I bubble in the adult's direction, but to no avail. The adult is already swimming towards the surface, and the child is waving frantically at the adult as it swims away. The adult pauses and waves back at the child, appearing to reconsider which direction to swim in. But it's too late. The child has disappeared, and in its place is a little fish happily going about its business. I must be dreaming again. The adult waves once more at the little fish, and then continues upwards toward the air above.

But I'm still sitting on the riverbed trying to figure my life out. I'm aware my time is nearly up. As my eyelids become heavier, the little fish swims nearer, and I hear an all too familiar voice. "It's got to be you, Freddy. Only you can save yourself. You have the power within you to do what needs to be done. Now wake up and swim hard!" OK, OK, little fish, I hear you. I push off the river-bed with all my remaining energy and take a few strokes towards the surface. I'm about halfway up, but the urge to take a break is intoxicating. What's that? The little fish has something else to say, but I'm not sure I've got the energy or patience to listen to the little chatterbox right now. OK, OK, no need to be rude, speak up then. "Imagine no limitations on what you can have, be or do. Be you, do you, for you." Alright, little fish. With that, I wake myself up and pull myself towards the surface with everything I've got. Finally, I break through the water's surface like a baby born into a new world.

I take in a deep breath of the good stuff. It's the sweetest feeling in the world as life flows through my body again.

I can't believe it. Willard, Daphne and Alice are all at the surface, all alive. Like me, they're all coughing and spluttering and sucking in deep desperate breaths of air, as only people who were on the brink of drowning can do. I check that there's no one else around beyond the four of us, and there isn't. Time has slowed almost to a halt as we breathe in new life.

With our almost non-existent remaining energy, we instinctively swim away from our would-be assassins towards the opposite side of the river. Luckily, the river's flow is almost stationery, so we can glide slowly to safety.

I turn back to glance at Truin and his cast of ghouls, who are still in view near the riverbank. They're dancing along to the music around a gigantic fire, without a care in the world. For a brief moment they look genuinely happy, particularly Truin, who is kicking his legs the highest of them all. You'd think they'd just won the lottery rather than becoming serial killers in the name of creating the religion of their dreams. I catch one last glimpse of Truin's face, and I see a big fish who has mastered the art of feeding off the little fish who love him, or, rather, believe they should love him. But there's no more time to dwell on that particular sub-current. I've got my own journey to continue on with now, my own family to spend quality time with.

Willard swims closer to Daphne.

"Honey, was that you down there?" he whispers.

Daphne is quiet for a few moments as she's still struggling to breathe.

"Yes," she answers quietly.

"But how?"

Daphne continues to breathe deeply as she contemplates her words.

"When you were all drugged and fast asleep, I pretended to be asleep like you. However, I was really watching them doing their dirty work."

"Genius."

"One of them left the key to the boot locks on the table while he was helping with the horse cart. So I grabbed the key when he was busy and went back to pretending to be asleep when he next turned around."

"Well done, darling! But how on earth did you manage to find us all in the murkiness down there? I couldn't see my own feet."

"I was guided by a little fish who wanted to help us."

"A little fish?"

"None of that matters now."

"You're right, my darling girl. All that matters is that you saved all our lives. We owe you everything!"

"It was nothing."

"It was everything, Daph. You are everything, and should be proud of that," I add. "But there's no time to talk about this until we're safe. Our best bet is to swim with this current until it hopefully picks up pace downstream. Oh, and the all-important second part of the plan is: we keep going."

"Right you are, old chap, right you are."

We swim slowly until the river's current gradually increases. We allow it to carry our bruised and battered bodies forwards in silence. The joy of being alive is exquisite. The awareness of how close we were to losing everything is humbling.

To the Estuary

Within a matter of hours, we're drifting along in a relaxed silence as if nothing has happened. But I know everything has changed.

Daphne and Willard have been holding hands ever since we left Truin's murderous camp. Willard is gazing lovingly at her as if he's seeing her for the first time. All of us are in awe of her bravery. She has emerged from the experience as the heroine for the ages Truin was describing. Of course it would be a woman. That should have been obvious.

"Daph, what you did back there was beyond heroic. It was a miracle. You are a miracle. Thank you," I say to her, knowing full well that no words will ever be able to express what she has given us.

"Thanks, Freddy, but I'm not the only one who deserves thanks. I saw what you did down there."

"It was nothing."

I know it was everything. I helped save my friends. And I saved myself, the most important job any fish has on their "to do" list.

Daphne understands better than anyone. And her eyes are alive once more. Before us is the woman in the painting at Willard's house, the woman whose eyes sparkle, the woman whose smile lights up any room, any river.

"Och aye. I've always said that good gear comes in small bulk. Thanks, lassie. You're a wee legend." Alice winks at Daphne. "And thanks to you, Freddy, as well. We all know what you've given us, even if you're too modest to admit it. If you hadn't arrived wet and bedraggled on our doorstep that day, we'd all still be in a right old pickle. You're pure dead brilliant."

For the first time in my life I agree with a compliment about me. I'm pure dead brilliant, minus the dead.

With that said, our mission continues towards the North Sea. No one knows how far we have left to go, but distance doesn't matter anymore. Just the direction: forwards.

The four of us are quiet for a long while as we swim onwards. We're all on the same journey now, the journey to let go of everything we need to let go of. Amidst the peace, I focus on letting go of Truin and all he brought into our lives. But then it strikes me that it's more important each of us allows Truin's story to help us, because he's given us so much to work with. There aren't many teachers around who could teach us how not to live our lives as well as Truin. He has a role to play in our journey after all, but I won't be telling that smug bastard.

After a while, Alice comes up with an idea.

"Right, you three. After all we've been through I think it's high time we talk about the future rather than the past."

"Count us in, Alice. What do you have in mind?" asks Willard.

"OK, great. So let's play a game called 'My Life in ten years' time.' The only rules of the game are: you need to be honest about what you really want from your life, and you need to talk about an action plan to achieve what you want. And if you don't come up with an action plan, you'll be forced to pay a forfeit."

"What would that be?" I ask, smiling.

"You'll be forced to sing 'Who the Fuck is Alice?' with me at every pub karaoke night for the next ten years."

We all laugh nervously.

The little fish would be proud. Correction, the little fish is proud.

"Righty-o, I think it's a great idea. I'd like to kick off please, Alice."

"Please do, Captain."

"I see Daph and me making a difference in ten years' time through the Little Georgie Trust. I see us helping other families who are grieving the loss of their children. And I see us deeply in love."

Willard takes Daphne's hand.

"And my action plan to get there is to build the Little Georgie Trust charity by sharing the lessons the river has taught me with grieving families, as well as listening to their stories from a place of acceptance. Oh, and I plan to start looking after my lovely wife the way she deserves to be looked after."

"Thanks, darling," responds Daphne. "I agree, the Little Georgie Trust is in both of our futures, as is a loving relationship between the two of us. But I also hear something else in my future, our future."

"Oh yes?"

"I hear the pitter patter of little feet once again," says Daphne confidently. "And the action plan to achieve that ... Well, that involves more than just holding hands, Captain."

"Some retraining may be required, me matey, but count me in," responds Willard, laughing.

"And Alice. What's on the horizon for you?"

"I see myself with a fella in the next ten years. I can't say what he looks like, but he'll enjoy my black pudding and tattie scone breakfast. And he'll enjoy a laugh. If he's seeing my face first thing every morning, he'll need to. I may even take him stone skimming one day. As the Giver on the River, I have a lot to teach the bugger."

"Brilliant. And what's the action plan to meet this fellow, Alice?" asks Willard.

"Well, for a start, I'll start saying yes when I'm next asked out for a date. Call me a wee genius, but it's about time I allowed some love into my life."

We all call out "Hooray!"

"And Freddy. What's coming next? What say you, sir?" asks Willard.

"Well, I finally know what I need to do. I'm going to make a career change. I want to become a nature documentary presenter. I want to tell stories about rivers and the fish who make it all the way upstream, for the simple reason that's what I love. Oh, and I'd like to move to the Borders to be nearer you guys."

"It's about time you came home, Freddy," says Daphne with warmth.

"Thanks, Daph. I'm lucky to be returning home to such a wonderful family."

"So what's your action plan to make it happen, old chap?"

"Beyond moving house as soon as possible, my action plan is to stay where I'm meant to be from now on, right here. And let's just say I won't be jumping into any rivers I don't expect to be surviving ever again."

"And for your career? How are you going to make that change happen?" Willard asks.

"I'm going to start by telling the world I want to be a documentary presenter. As someone very clever once told me: the world can't deliver me what I want unless I start making it clear to the world what it is I want. Isn't life simple when it's not so complex?"

"Well said, old chap. I think we've all learnt that same lesson. You'll be great at the nature documentaries. I can't think of anyone better qualified for the job."

This current feels right.

Then, one day, out of the blue, we arrive at the estuary which connects the Tweed River with the North Sea. After all we've been through to get here, the North Sea doesn't disappoint. The meeting of fresh water and salt water is like a party where old and young are invited, white and black, tall and short, happy and sad, anything and everyone. I feel something deep inside me being released. I am one lucky fish to have made it all the way here.

We look towards the shore. There's a crowd of people awaiting us. Oh fuck, reads the oh-fuck-o-meter. Has Truin tracked us down? But as I consider our options of either swimming six hundred miles to Denmark, or facing up to and accepting whatever, whoever, is here to greet us, I reset the oh-fuck-o-meter to "Come what may." It's official, we're done with swimming till we can't see land. It's time to swim towards land.

"Hang on, I recognize those lassies over there," says Alice. "It's the same group of friends and members of the community who I invited to the first river launch event a while back. And that's the Friends of Frightened Rabbit band from upstream. It's alright, they're legit."

We swim towards the land. And, when we arrive, we're welcomed by a friendly crowd of well-wishers who help us out of the water. A familiar tune starts playing in the background: "And if I hadn't come now to the coast to disappear / I may have died in a landslide of rocks, and hopes, and fears." After all I've been through, the meaning of these words has changed for me, and I'm grateful to hear them as a welcome.

The four of us reach the rocky shoreline and walk ashore. As we do, I notice Daphne emerge from the water with the calm ease of a heroine who's slain the dragon she needed to slay. I catch myself for putting Daphne on a pedestal. Yes, she's a living legend, but so am I. So am I.

"Without further ado, here's our river-swimming hero, Freddy," says the lead singer whom I recognize from the initial launch party. He signals at me to come up onto the stage to talk to the crowd.

I swagger up to the stage a different man to the boy who started this journey. I am the Freddy I'm meant to be, the best version of me. I walk over to the microphone without feeling any nerves. There's no six-year-old here to cycle off the edge of the stage.

"Thanks," I say to the small crowd, "but I'm just a regular guy who lost hope and then found hope when I was saved by mother nature and the amazing people who helped me through this journey: Willard, Daphne and Alice."

The crowd applaud at just the right volume.

"However," I continue, "we do indeed have a hero to introduce to you today. This is someone who understands what it is to survive despite the pain, and then thrive through the pain."

I look down from the stage at Daphne. But she's visibly upset. Willard is shaking his head vigorously at me. OK, so it's clear she doesn't want attention drawn to her. She wants to remain a silent heroine. I'd expect nothing less.

"The hero I'm talking about is, in fact, more than one person, more than the four of us who swam the river to be here today. Look around. You guys are the real heroes and heroines of this adventure, because you believe. You believe life can and will be better in the future."

Maybe a little of Truin's rousing preaching style was somehow absorbed into me during our game of cat and mouse. I suspect that's a good thing. Unbeknownst to me when I first jumped into the river, I needed an injection of Truin's confidence, clarity and passion into my life.

"Thank you very much for your kind support. Being here with you at the North Sea is everything we hoped it would be."

Bigger Adventures

Our little adventure ended at the ocean that day, and our bigger adventure has continued since then.

As I look out of my new living room I can see the Tweed River gushing past. It's the best sound in the world. I moved into this homely cottage around two years ago, and it was one of the best decisions I've ever made. The cottage looks down upon the river like an old friend. And I'm only a short walk from Daphne and Willard's place, which is convenient, since we all spend so much time together these days. Like Daphne said in the river that day, we're now family.

Willard and Daphne are once again deeply in love—the way they were earlier in their relationship. They're perfectly in tune with one another, and are back to finishing each other's sentences. Being in their company is inspiring. And their big news is that they recently welcomed a baby girl into their lives, little Alecia. They couldn't be happier. I'm Alecia's godfather, and I'll always be there should she need me. I hope she does one day.

Daphne still refuses to even mention how she saved everyone's lives in the river that day, but she walks tall as the confident woman she is these days. With her quiet nurturing energy, she's one of the best listeners I've ever met, and I've met some great ones. Whenever any of us need to talk about something important, we go straight to Daph.

Willard knows he's once again married to the woman of his dreams. And he's become a father figure throughout the community, famous for helping all in need. I've never met anyone with such powerful paternal energy to share. He's so far removed from the stereotypical Scottish aristocrat, and, more than that, he's rewriting the playbook for what's possible for a man in his position. The other day he even popped in to see Donny, the Duke of Sutherland, on his estate. He asked Donny if he'd like to come fishing with him. Donny accepted the offer once the dancing vein on his forehead finally came to rest, and since then the two of them have almost become friends. More surprisingly, Donny has become noticeably kinder since Willard's friendliness towards him, and no longer causes havoc across the community.

Willard and Daphne have built their charity, the Little Georgie Trust, into a thriving support network for families dealing with grief after losing a child. Hundreds of families are living happy lives again as a result. When I think back to the day the seed of this idea was planted in their minds, it's amazing how far it has grown. It shows how powerful a positive mental attitude is, and provides a strong clue as to which salmon make it all the way upstream against the current.

Alice is still happily employed in their household. Her big news is that she has started dating the gardener, who enjoys karaoke almost as much as she does. The two of them sing while they're working around the estate, and take particular joy in singing the Alice song at the tops of their voices; the new version. Alice's smile has returned with interest. She's once again the center of the community, and is often organizing inspiring events with the locals, including stone-skimming events in which she actively competes as The Giver on the River.

And me. Well, I moved beyond surviving, and I'm now thriving. I chose life, and life has accepted me just like the river did. I emerged from the river the hero of my own life—not the type of hero they write books about, but the type of hero who helps keep the world spinning without making a song and dance about it. I'm proud to be my own brand of hero. I'm proud of me.

I'm not alone in seeing myself in a more positive light these days. After our river swim concluded, I was interviewed by a news channel about why I decided to swim all the way to the North Sea. Unbeknownst to me, the interview was being televised to millions of people around the world. And apparently it was remarkably popular for the simple reason I told my truth, mask off. As it turns out, there are many people out there who share aspects of my truth. I discovered that by freely giving my story to the world, it helped others to find their truth and, in turn, release it.

In the television interview, I remembered my career action plan and my promise to the little fish. So I mentioned my love of nature documentaries as well as my plan to become a documentary presenter. It's hard to believe, even now, but on the back of that little comment

I was invited to meet a documentary producer who concluded I have a great voice, backstory and character to present nature documentaries. He offered me a job on the spot. Since then, I've become an emerging voice of documentaries about the natural world. Who knows if I'm on track to become the next David Attenborough, but I've been told my passion for nature resonates through my voice, which in turn brings the stories to life. I love my job. Once I knew what I wanted, the river was listening. All I had to do was play my part, as there was no one else who could be me like me.

Whenever I present documentaries about salmon who are attempting the swim upstream, I insist upon presenting the salmon stories with empathy, and to delve deeper into what's happening in their world. I'm aware there's far more going on beneath the surface than what we can see from our limited perspective as humans. The natural world understands more than we do, so the best thing we can do is watch and learn.

I still listen avidly to Frightened Rabbit music, which not only helped define my river journey, but has also helped define my healing journey since then. Like Scott, I sing away my troubles whenever they attempt to reappear, and they do on occasion. It works like a charm every time. However, I still can't sing that one song, and I don't expect I'll ever be able to. There's no room in my life for those thoughts anymore.

We rarely talk of Truin and his people. We haven't heard a single word of their existence since we returned. Willard asked me the other day if I thought Truin ever really existed, or if it was the river playing a game with us to help us deal with whatever we needed to deal with. What a question! The one thing I know is that whenever I reminisce on our journey, Truin's face remains as real in my mind as anything I've ever encountered.

The four of us continue to embrace the river for a few days of river swimming each year. We're sometimes joined by a few friends who supported us on the first version of this adventure, but we limit the numbers to our inner circle. We're not ready, willing, or able to start a movement, or an annual pilgrimage, for the simple reason that we believe spirituality isn't a one-size-fits-all thing. It's an individual journey we must all undertake when we're ready. And the journey will take each of us where we need to go, as there's more than one river in the world.

And the little fish has stayed with me in his own way since leaving the river. He has become the voice inside my head which guides and advises me throughout life's ups and downs. He's become my greatest friend. I've even reached the point where I don't find his know-it-all attitude remotely annoying. The other day I was running a half marathon for charity, and, at the moment I was contemplating giving up, I heard the little fish's voice inside me saying, "You didn't come this far to only come this far. Obstacles are the price of greatness." I kept going.

Acknowledgments

I'd like to thank:

My friend Matt for all our magical, funny, almost hypothermic river adventures.

The River Tweed for being my guide and mentor.

My wife Jess and daughter Rosie for all your love and support.

My publisher Lou Aronica and The Story Plant team for being so supportive and believing in life-affirming fiction.

Heather Morris for your beautiful endorsement and encouragement after reading the novel.

Katie Zybdel for your compassionate editing services.

My friends Peter, Johnny, and Steve for your awesomeness.

My recently departed golden retriever Mia for her love and friendship.

The Duke with a rifle and a short temper who nearly shot us for swimming past his estate. I hope you've recovered from the shock of meeting two fishy humans. Word to the wise: rivers are for the whole world to enjoy.

About the author

SS Turner has been an avid reader, writer, and explorer of the natural world throughout his life which has been spent in England, Scotland, and Australia. Just like Freddy in *Secrets of a River Swimmer*, he worked in the global fund management sector for many years before making a career transition that better aligned with his values. In recent years, he's been focused on inspiring positive change through his writing, as well as trying not to laugh in unfortunate situations. He now lives in Australia with his wife, daughter, two cats, and ten chickens.